W9-AXJ-932

MINDING THE LIGHT

This Large Print Book carries the
Seal of Approval of N.A.V.H.

MINDING THE LIGHT

SUZANNE WOODS FISHER

THORNDIKE PRESS
A part of Gale, a Cengage Company

Farmington Hills, Mich • San Francisco • New York • Waterville, Maine
Meriden, Conn • Mason, Ohio • Chicago

LIBRARY OF CONGRESS CIP DATA ON FILE.
CATALOGUING IN PUBLICATION FOR THIS BOOK
IS AVAILABLE FROM THE LIBRARY OF CONGRESS.

ISBN-13: 978-1-4328-5151-4 (hardcover)

Published in 2018 by arrangement with Revell Books, a division of Baker Publishing Group

Printed in Mexico
1 2 3 4 5 6 7 22 21 20 19 18

To Peter Foulger (1617–1690),
grandfather to
Benjamin Franklin, spiritual mentor to
Mary Coffin Starbuck, and mayhap,
the first American Renaissance man.

CAST OF CHARACTERS

17th century

Mary Coffin Starbuck: daughter of one of the first proprietors of Nantucket Island, highly revered, likened to Deborah the Judge of the Old Testament

Tristram Coffin: proprietor of Nantucket Island, father of Mary, husband of Dionis

Nathaniel Starbuck: son of proprietor Edward Starbuck, husband to Mary

Catherine Starbuck: Nathaniel's mother, married to Edward Starbuck

Esther Starbuck: Nathaniel's younger sister

Jethro Starbuck: Nathaniel's younger brother

Peter Foulger: surveyor, missionary to the Wampanoag Indians of Nantucket Island, joined the proprietors

19th century

Daphne Coffin: great-great-great-granddaughter of Mary Coffin Starbuck

Reynolds "Ren" Macy: whaling captain on the *Endeavour,* father of Hitty and Henry, husband of Jane

Jane Coffin Macy: wife to Ren, sister to Daphne

Lillian Swain Coffin: mother of Jane and Daphne

Tristram Macy: cousin of Ren

Jeremiah Macy: father of Reynolds

Hitty and Henry Macy: twin children of Ren and Jane Macy, age six

Abraham: black officer on Ren's ship, the *Endeavour*

Patience: Wampanoag maidservant to Jane Coffin Macy

GLOSSARY
LANGUAGE OF 19TH-CENTURY NANTUCKET

Many of these nautical expressions have found their way into our modern vernacular, such as "feeling blue" (when a ship lost its captain during a voyage and would fly blue flags) or "crew cut" (a short haircut given to the entire ship's crew).

ambergris: a waxy, grayish substance found in the stomachs of sperm whales and once used in perfume to make the scent last longer

baleen: the comblike plates of cartilage in a whale's mouth to strain plankton and other food from the water; very valuable for its strength and flexibility

boatsteerer/harpooner: crew at the bow of the whaling boat whose job is to spear the whale

broken voyage: a whaling ship that returns home with less than a full load of oil

cooper: barrel maker

cooperage: workplace of the cooper

cranky: an unstable sailing vessel, from the Dutch

crew cut: a short haircut given to the whole crew

cut and run: an act of cutting the anchor line in an effort to make a quick getaway

deep six: a fathom, the unit of measurement for the depth of the sea, is six feet; sailors used the term to refer to throwing something overboard

disowned: under church discipline

elders: historically, those appointed to foster the ministry of the Quaker meetinghouse and the spiritual condition of its members

facing benches: the benches or seats in the front of the meeting room, facing the body of the meeting, on which Friends' ministers and elders generally sat

feeling blue: a custom when a ship lost its captain during a voyage — the ship would fly blue flags and have a blue band painted along her hull when she returned to port

fin up: dead

First Day: Sunday (Quakers did not use names for days of the week, nor for the months, as they had originated from pagan names)

First Month: January

flensing: butchering of the whale

forging ahead: a naval term for pressing on

Friends and Society of Friends: Quaker church members

from stem to stern: all-inclusive, very thorough

gam: to visit or talk with the crew of another whaling ship while at sea

gangplank: a movable bridge used to board or leave a ship

greenhand or greenie: an inexperienced sailor making his first whaling voyage

hold in the Light: to ask for God's presence to illuminate a situation or problem or person

hulk: an old sailing vessel that is no longer seaworthy

idler: a crewman whose tasks required daylight hours (cook, cooper, cabin boy)

lay: the percentage of a ship's profit that each crew member receives; a sailor's lay usually depends upon his experience and rank

lookout: the sailor stationed in the crosstree to watch for whales

Meeting: Quaker term for church

minding the Light: an expression used to remind Quakers that there is an Inward Light in each of them that can reveal God's will, if its direction is listened to and followed

mortgage button: a Nantucket tradition of drilling a hole in the newel post of a household's banister, filling it with the ashes of the paid-off mortgage, and capping the hole with a button made of scrimshaw; in the south, it's called a brag button

moved to speak: an experience, in the quietness of the meeting, of feeling led by God to speak

mutiny: an uprising or rebellion of a ship's crew against the captain

Nantucket sleigh ride: a term used to describe the pulling of a whaleboat by a whale that has been harpooned and is "running"

on deck: a phrase used to ask if someone is present or available

Quaker: the unofficial name of a member of the Religious Society of Friends; originally the use was pejorative, but the word was claimed by Friends in recognition of the physical sensation that many feel when being moved by the Spirit

quarterboard: a wooden sign with carved name displayed on each ship

rigging: the ropes and chain used to control a ship's sails

saltbox: traditional New England–style wooden-frame house with a long, pitched roof that slopes down to the back; a saltbox has just one story in the back and two stories in the front

scrimshaw: whalebone adorned with carvings

seasoning: a process to ensure that decisions are truly grounded in God's will

seize: to tie up a sailor in the rigging as a form of punishment

slops: sailors' clothing (a ship's captain will charge his crew for any clothes he supplies)

syndicate: a group of businessmen who own a whaling ship or ships

Weighty Friend: a Friend who is informally recognized as having special experience and wisdom

worldly: having to do with secular values

1

As Daphne Coffin made her way onto the wooden planks of Straight Wharf, she heard someone call her name and whirled to see her sister Jane hurrying to catch up with her. Holding Jane's hands were two tow-headed children, a boy on one side and a girl on the other.

"Has thee heard the bells?" Jane said, her face bright with happiness. "Ren's ship is in!"

"The *Endeavour*?" Daphne's eyes widened in disbelief while her mind took hold of this stunning surprise. Ren was home? At long last! "I heard the bells but didn't realize they rang for Ren's ship."

"Imagine, Daphne. Ren has not even met his own children yet."

Her sister looked exceptionally pretty, though her face was flushed with heat from the warmth of this sun-stippled day. Jane Coffin Macy was one of the loveliest girls on Nantucket Island. She had high, wide cheekbones and a dainty, pointed chin that gave her face a charming sweetheart shape. Brown eyes, blonde hair, a peaches-and-cream complexion, with lips that were always red, as if she'd been eating berries. "I'm so glad thee is here this morning, Daphne." She straightened the organza fichu that draped her shoulders and smoothed her skirt. "Thy presence will help me stay calm."

Daphne looked a little closer at her older sister. There was a trembling air about her, a vulnerability that was nearly palpable. "Thee must be beside thyself with excitement. Here, let me take Hitty." As she reached out to take her niece's hand, Jane suddenly swayed, as if she were on the verge of fainting.

"M-Mama!" Jane's son, Henry, clutched her arm.

Daphne grabbed her sister's shoulders to steady her. "Jane, is thee not well?"

Jane dipped her chin so that her black bonnet shielded her face from the sun. "I'm fashed, 'tis all. A bit dizzy. I'm sure 'tis from anticipation."

Daphne spun around as she heard the rhythmic slap of oars on water. The lighters were coming in now, slipping through the calm waters of Nantucket Bay, bringing the crew off the ship *Endeavour.* As captain, Ren would be the last one off, that much she knew. It would be a long wait this morning, but they would not budge from their post on the wharf. The wharves were no place for maids, so unless a ship was arriving into port, she did not go near them. But how she loved being down by the harbor! So many strange accents, unusual skin colors, piercings, tattoos.

The *Endeavour* stood black-limned behind the bar that lined Nantucket Harbor. Lighter after lighter sailed up to release crew to pour onto the wharf and hustle down to greet their loved ones or make their way to the taverns to celebrate their return.

Jane's eyes were fixed on each lighter as it docked, gazing over the sailors, nodding to each one as they hurried past them, sea chests hoisted on their shoulders. Overhead, seabirds circled with shrieks and cries. "Over six *years,* Daphne," Jane said in a low voice. "He's been gone six *years.* Nearly seven."

Daphne grinned. "I wonder if Ren might be covered in tattoos. Or wearing a thick tangle of whiskers that hides his chin." She wrinkled her nose as some rank seamen went past. "Hopefully he will not smell like a beached whale." When she caught the solemn look on her sister's face, she quickly added, "Jane, 'tis a jest. Hand over heart, I was only jesting. Ren will return back as the same man."

"How do I know what he's like after six years at sea? We were married less than a month when he set sail."

Daphne's smile faded. "I suppose that is the plight of a captain's wife. More good-byes than hellos."

"Still, I did not expect an absence of six long years."

"He's missed quite a bit."

"He's missed everything. The birth of his children, the death of Father, and everything in between."

Daphne glanced at Jane and noticed a drip of perspiration trickling down the side of her cheek. "He is home now, Sister. Safe and sound."

"But for how long?"

"Today is not the day to concern thyself with the next voyage."

Jane paused a moment, as if she'd become lost in thoughts, or memories. "Thee is right." She pushed the words out on a sharp expulsion of breath, then flashed a rueful smile. "Not today."

She was a fine captain's wife, Jane was.

Reynolds Macy chose well, Daphne thought. She'd never heard her sister complain of loneliness, not once, not even after Hitty and Henry were born. Not until this moment.

Jane's eyes were fixed on the ship. "I have changed much in these six years."

"Not so much."

"But I have. Starting the Cent School, for one. Who knows what Ren will think of that venture?"

"It provides a great deal of help for island women, Jane, whose husbands are at sea. I'm certain he will understand."

"I'm not at all certain. And while thee might jest, no doubt Ren has changed too. What if we don't feel the same way about each other?"

Daphne put an arm around her sister's small shoulders, a vivid reminder of how opposite they were. Jane was delicate and fine-boned where Daphne was sturdy and curvy. Jane was reserved, graceful, as even-keeled as a ship, instinctively knowing how to react in any situation, while Daphne could be clumsy, blunt, at times socially awkward. In Daphne's eyes, her older sister was as close to perfection as a Quaker woman could be, one whose Inward Light reflected such a strong and steady beam.

Despite being reprimanded by the Friends for marrying out of unity, Jane's faith never wavered.

They heard a shout and pounding feet coming up hard on them. "Any sign of him yet?" Tristram Macy, cousin and business partner to Ren, flew past them, turning his head for an answer.

"Nay, not yet," Jane called back, smiling. It was hard not to smile when Tristram was around.

Daphne lifted her hand in a wave to Tristram, whom she had seen only yesterday. He gave her no greeting, she noted.

Jane noticed as well. "He's distracted, that's all."

"Of course." Of course he was. And yet, and yet . . . there was always something off between them.

"Mayhap, with Ren safely returned, Tristram's thoughts will turn to the future. Thee knows how worried he's been about the business. Soon, I think, he will propose marriage." Jane squeezed Daphne's hand. "Everyone hopes so."

All the world, or at least all of Nantucket, considered Tristram Macy to be Daphne's intended. The man she would marry, although he hadn't gotten round to asking her yet. How many times had Daphne thought Trist was going to propose marriage? Just the other day, they were walking along the beach at sunset — a perfect Nantucket evening. He had taken her hand and covered it with his own, and she thought, *Tonight. Surely, tonight he will ask.* But he didn't. Instead, he spoke with ardor about his new ship.

So how did Daphne feel about him? She and Tristram had known each other all their lives. She knew him when his stutter made him the target of school yard mocking. He knew her when she was round as a barrel, much like Hitty is now, before she started to grow and grow and grow, and her body rearranged itself.

She had watched as Trist evolved into a very handsome man, dashing and decadent, whose charming personality had a dazzling effect on women — including her own mother. Daphne did not feel dazzled by Tristram Macy, which might be why he favored her. Her feelings for him were akin to sitting by the hearth on a rainy day with a well-loved book to read and reread, warm and cozy.

Daphne saw Trist make his way toward the far end of the wharf, picking his way between clusters of townspeople, clapping hands with the crew as they emerged from lighters. By the pleased looks on their sun-weathered faces, added to the fact that the *Endeavour* sat low in the brine, it seemed the rumors were true — it had been a greasy voyage. Mayhap Jane was right. Now Tristram would believe the business he and Ren had started was on solid footing and he would make plans for the future.

The two cousins had a business arrangement that suited them well. Reynolds captained the ship, Tristram found and managed investors. Or, as Trist liked to describe it in his cheeky way, "Ren makes the money. I spend it."

Before long, Straight Wharf nearly emptied of sailors but for stevedores who unloaded the heavy wooden casks of whale oil off the lighters, rolling them down a wooden gangplank with a loud rumble — precious cargo ready to head to the warehouse. The same four remained in a tight clump: Jane and Daphne, Henry and Hitty. And Tristram, of course, though he was engaged in a deep conversation with the *Endeavour*'s first mate at the wharf's edge.

Jane's eyes snapped to a lighter approaching the dock. "There he is," she said. "I'm sure of it." Her fingers tightened on both of her children's hands. "Come. It's time to meet your father." She started down the wharf to meet the lighter as it docked.

Ren stood at the bow with legs straddled, hands on his hips, elegant and graceful on the swiftly moving lighter. When he spotted his wife, he lifted both arms in greeting and she waved back, laughing.

Daphne was so pleased to see her brother-in-law return hale and hearty, she nearly lifted her skirts and ran down the deck, shouting his name. Five years ago she might have — nay, *would* have — done such a thing, but it would hardly be proper now. Then, she was still a girl, only fifteen. Today, she was a woman, trying to be proper, but it made her feel so stiff, like the whale-boned spikes that squeezed her middle so tight she could hardly breathe. How she missed the freedoms of girlhood! She squelched the desire to tumble straight into the family's sweet reunion and watched demurely from a distance.

She'd forgotten how alike in looks Tristram and Ren were. Both with those broad Macy faces and deep-set eyes, dark hair. Ren's hair was sun streaked but cropped close, Tristram's was held back in a queue. Both with striking figures: trim, upright, confident. Standing behind Ren was a dark-skinned sailor she did not recognize. And then a familiar and weathered face, Jeremiah

Macy, Ren's father, who coopered on the *Endeavour.* She hardly knew Jeremiah but by reputation — his older brother, Matthew, had married Phoebe Starbuck, great-grandmother to Daphne and Jane. Like most Nantucketers, they were all distantly related.

When the lighter drew within a rod's length, Ren leapt onto the deck, not even waiting until the mooring lines had been tied to the cleats. As soon as his boots — cracked white with salt — touched the solid planks of the wharf, he strode toward his wife and lifted her up in an embrace, swinging around in a circle. He gently set Jane down and bracketed her face with his two hands, holding it as if it were a precious treasure, gazing down into her eyes as if memorizing every feature.

Jane was the one who broke the intimate moment as she remembered the boy and girl who peered up uncertainly at the stranger. "Ren. Oh Ren. There will be time for us later. But now . . . come meet thy children."

Daphne watched a sudden transformation come over Ren. He blanched, losing that ever-imposing captain's countenance, and drew in a deep breath, as if having to recover from having the wind knocked out of him. As he turned his attention to his children, he seemed . . . ill at ease, unsure of what to do next, so he did nothing. Nothing but peer back at them. Prompted by Jane's elbow, Henry extended his hand for a shake.

Ren bent over to shake his son's small hand. "Um, lad, hello."

Henry kept a quizzical expression on him. The boy was so like Jane, reserved and formal. He poked his eyeglasses up on the bridge of his nose, staring at his father, until he received another elbow jab from his mother. "Hello, Captain, sir. I am Henry Jeremiah Macy."

Jane gently pushed Hitty forward. "And here is Mehitabel."

Ren turned to the girl. He crouched down to her eye level. "Mehitabel. Hello, lass. I am pleased to make your acquaintance."

"Everyone calls me Hitty," she replied and curtsied very low, as if she were a lady.

"Then, Hitty it will be."

"Did thee bring us presents?"

Again, Ren seemed baffled. "I'm certain," he said at last, "that I have a few treasures in my chest." With that, Hitty threw her arms around his neck. Daphne saw Ren's eyelids slide closed for a moment as his daughter's small arms clung to him.

Jane glanced up to see Daphne and raised an arm to her to bring her into the circle. "Ren, thee remembers my sister, Daphne."

Ren lifted his chin over the top of Hitty's head. His dark eyes moved back and forth over her face, wide with surprise. "Daphne? Why, you was just an awkward foal of a girl when I saw you last."

Daphne took a few steps forward to join them. "When I last saw thee, Reynolds Macy, thy hair was in a queue —"

He brushed a hand over his head. "Crew cut. The entire ship. A lice outbreak."

"— and thee was wooing my favorite sister and stealing her away from our childhood home."

Ren laughed, as did Daphne. She turned, expecting to see Jane smiling too, and was startled to see the color drain from her sister's face as if a stopper was pulled from a sink. Her eyes rolled back in a most unholy manner, and she wilted onto the deck.

Jane lay under the canopy of her four-poster bed at home, drifting in and out of consciousness, speaking a few garbled sounds now and then. Daphne sat in the chair next to her, watching for any significant changes, waiting for Ren and Jeremiah to return with

26

Dr. Mitchell. Jane's breathing was what concerned her most. It went from shallow breaths, slowing to nothing, then a shuddering gasp to get enough air. Her eyes opened now and then, looked around the room without any apparent recognition, before closing as if her eyelids weighed a hundred pounds.

Daphne felt tears welling, and struggled to keep them under control. *Stay calm,* she told herself. *This is nothing more than a fainting spell, brought on by the anticipation of Ren's return.* "It's all right," Daphne said to herself. Surely, this spell was nothing more than overexcitement. "Everything's all right."

But it didn't *feel* all right.

In her heart, Daphne knew something was seriously wrong. This was no mere summer cold. Jane hadn't seemed hardy this last year, prone to colds that led quickly to grippe or influenza, once even to a bout of pneumonia.

The door to Jane's chamber opened quietly, and Patience, the Indian maidservant, came in carrying a glass of sugared water. She lifted her dark eyebrows to give Daphne a questioning look.

"There is no change."

Patience handed Daphne the glass. Yet her

hands shook so much as she dipped the spoon into the water that Patience took it away from her. Instead, she fed Jane tiny sips, rubbing her throat to make her swallow. Patience radiated a calm authority, soothing, serene, silent. Not knowing how to help, Daphne stood and backed away, letting the maidservant sit in the chair next to the bed and take over. Patience had been with Jane and Daphne their entire lives, and the lines of servant/employer blurred together more times than not.

"The little ones are in the kitchen," Patience said. "You should go to them, reassure them that their mother is well."

How could she possibly tell Henry and Hitty that their mother was well when, clearly, she wasn't? "Captain Macy should be here soon with the doctor. I don't want to leave Jane's side until he returns."

Patience set the glass on the nightstand and turned to Daphne. "She takes no more. Try again later."

After Patience left, the room seemed eerily quiet but for Jane's labored breathing. Daphne noticed a trickle of sugar water had slipped down Jane's neck. She opened a drawer in the nightstand to look for some kind of cloth or handkerchief to wipe it. Instead of a cloth, she found an old sheepskin book, wound tight with a leather string. She lifted it from the drawer and untied the string. She opened it to the first page, ever so carefully, for it was very old, and a slip of paper fell out. A pang pricked Daphne's heart as she recognized the handwriting, the familiar script of her father.

To my dearest daughter, Jane, on the occasion of her wedding.

This journal belonged to Great Mary, a woman renowned for her wisdom. It has been a Starbuck family tradition for the one who receives the journal to quietly and carefully choose whom to pass it along to. My grandmother Phoebe bestowed it to my mother, and she gave it to me, so I am now giving it to thee. May it bring thee some of Great Mary's wisdom.

With love from thy adoring Papa

Daphne picked up the sheepskin book, felt the weight of it in her hands. She had grown up hearing stories of Great Mary, everyone born on the island had, and if they were off-islanders, they didn't deserve to know of her. Mary Coffin Starbuck, one of the first proprietors who settled the island, was referred to as the Deborah of Nantucket, a nod to the only female judge in the Old Testament. She was considered the wisest woman on the island. Settlers and Indians alike had sought out her opinions and judgments.

Daphne smoothed her hands over the leather. What would *that* be like? To be so highly respected and admired? It was an interesting notion. She knew without doubt that among Friends, her family was more a focus of gossip and rumor than admiration and respect. Daphne's mother, Lillian Swain Coffin, spent most of her time trying to cover scandal quickly before others learned of it. Sadly, scandal kept arriving at Lillian's doorstep, unbidden and unwanted.

Gently, Daphne opened the journal to a random page and squinted. The ink was faded, difficult to make out in places. And yet here were the thoughts, written for posterity, of her ancestor Great Mary.

Daphne wanted to ask Jane about this journal, to ask if she'd read it through, of what she'd learned of Great Mary. She closed the journal and tied the leather string around it, leaving it just as she'd found it. As she tucked the journal back into the drawer, she wished Jane had not kept its existence hidden from her. She thought they had no secrets between them, but apparently, like so many things of late, she was wrong.

MARY COFFIN STARBUCK

23 April 1662

'Tis not an easy thing to meld into another's family. Today, Nathaniel and I have been married for one month. For the most part, I have found married life to be quite pleasant, quite agreeable. My father-in-law Edward has been thoroughly welcoming, though he is frequently absent with his work with the Wampanoags on the other side of the island. Jethro, only eleven, is a darling boy, sweet and thoughtful, much like my Nathaniel. But Catherine, my mother-in-law, and twelve-year-old Esther display a shortage of patience with me. I don't seem to do anything in the "Starbuck Way."

For good reason!

There were seldom, if any, occasions when I had been invited to Nathaniel's home prior to our marriage, and now I understand why Catherine was reluctant to open her home. Her housekeeping is shockingly chaotic. There does not seem to be an order to household work. After one month, I have yet to discern any rhythm in the household. Which day is wash day, or bake day, or garden day? They all blur together, depending on what need is most critical.

I try to be helpful, as I was yesterday afternoon when I cleaned the kitchen while Catherine and Esther were visiting Jane Swain. I scrubbed every inch of the dark and dank kitchen, and made a place for everything on the sideboard so that I could put the crockery in its rightful spot. Muddled housekeeping leads to muddled thinking, my dear grandmother Coffin always said.

When Catherine and Esther returned, they gasped at my work — a gasp of delight, I first assumed. But no! Catherine was furious — in a cold, unexpressed way that I have become all too familiar with. Esther glared at me. They spent the evening undoing all I had done. And they said not a word of appreciation to me about my scrubbing and sweeping.

I was just trying to be useful!

And another "opportunity" to increase my tolerance arrived last evening, during the meal. Catherine criticized me for speaking my mind. She shushed me at dinner last night. Shushed me! I have never once been shushed in my family home. I noticed a smirk on Esther's face. Nathaniel kept his eyes fixed firmly on his plate. Edward was not at home. He alone seems to have influence over the women in his household.

And yet, I must not be unkind. Mother warned me to be mindful of my tendency toward forthrightness. Soon, she assures me, they will come to know me, and will love me as a daughter and sister.

No doubt she is right. Adjustments take time. Still, it is hard to feel settled in a place that itself is so unsettled. I wonder of the other Starbuck siblings who live off island but are considering their mother's request to move here, if they are all so difficult to befriend.

And as I went to bed last night, I said an extra prayer of thanks for how greatly Nathaniel takes after his father.

2

Children. I have children. Two of them. I am a father. Reynolds Macy kept turning those words over and over in his mind and they still didn't make sense to him. Never had he felt so keeled over, so shocked, never in all his life, as that moment on the wharf when Jane said, "Come meet thy children" and introduced two little people to him.

He was a father. A father!

It was a staggering reality, one that he could barely get his head around . . . when suddenly Jane collapsed. He scooped her up, his father Jeremiah retrieved a horse and cart, they took Jane home to Orange Street to rest in her bedchamber, then he and his father hurried the poor horse back to town to find the doctor. That was a hunt in itself, for the doctor was on a call and reluctant to leave his patient, especially when he learned that Jane had merely fainted. "Revive her with a wisp of ammonia on a piece of cloth,"

Dr. Mitchell instructed Ren. "I'll get to the house as soon as I can."

But Ren would not be placated as easily as that. Whatever had caused Jane to faint was no small thing; something about it troubled him greatly, and he was a man accustomed to giving orders, not taking them. It took a promise that the doctor need only check briefly on Jane's condition, then he could return to his patient's side — a laboring young woman — and finally the doctor relented.

It was in that drive back to Orange Street, doctor safely stowed in the cart, while Jeremiah and the doctor exchanged a bit of Nantucket news, that Ren was allowed a moment of quiet. His mind left the urgency of Jane's predicament and turned to ponder those two blond-headed children who belonged to him. How could word not have trickled to him that he had become a father? Of twins! He had received two letters from Jane, but children were not mentioned.

Wait. Hold on. Maybe they were. Those names, Henry and Hitty. He vaguely recalled she had mentioned those names in one of her two letters that *had* reached him, a miracle in itself, through mail delivered from one Nantucket ship to another to another. The names were without explanation. He had assumed they were Jane's neighbors, or some cousins. Certainly not their own children! She must have thought he'd received her other letters, one in which she told him their family had begun, with two babies named Henry and Hitty.

And they were already six years old. He'd missed their entire babyhood, their first of everything. Crawling, walking, talking. They were strangers to him, and he to them. The little girl seemed to have an openness to accept him, but the boy . . . none at all. Henry had a natural suspicion that Ren recognized, as he shared the characteristic. Until someone proved himself, Ren remained guarded toward others.

He snapped the reins to hurry the horse along the narrow streets. Even in his preoccupation with Jane, with the children, he could not help but be mindful of how Nantucket had changed during his absence. The harbor was twice as busy, littered with fishing dories. Beyond the bar, anchored ships bobbed on open water. The streets were crowded, new houses were tucked into what he'd remembered as empty lots, brick business buildings framed an expansive and still-uncobbled Main Street.

As long as he could remember, there'd been talk of rock paving Main Street, though he saw no signs of it. He recalled the debate rested on the fact that no one knew where to find the cobbles on a sandy island. Apparently, they still had no answer.

On every street were Quakers, women in big black bonnets, men in flat low-brimmed hats, all dressed in solemn clothing. When they saw him, they waved, welcoming him home, and now and then Jeremiah elbowed him to notice and respond, so he would lift a hand in greeting. His heart wasn't in it, though. It was at Orange Street.

A rumbling of horse and cart outside the window of Jane's bedchamber signaled the arrival of Dr. Mitchell. Daphne flew to the sill to peer out. "He's here. Thank God! All will be well." She hurried to open the door to Jane's chamber, and there, standing in the doorway, stood Henry and Hitty, with worried looks on their small round faces.

Daphne crouched down to gather the children against her, to keep them from seeing their mother in such a weakened condition. Dr. Mitchell marched up the stairs and straight into Jane's bedchamber, closing the door behind him. He'd been to 15 Orange Street many times after the twins were born. Ren followed behind the doctor, only to stop halfway on the stairs, as if he didn't know where his place was. With his wife? With his children?

Poor Ren. Not an hour ago, he was experiencing the happiest moment of a whalemaster's life. A joyous homecoming. Suddenly, it had been snatched from him. "Ren, go inside and stay by Jane's side. Thy presence will bring her comfort. I'll stay with Henry and Hitty."

His gaze shifted to Daphne, and he nodded, almost bewildered, grateful for the direction. Any direction. He walked slowly up the rest of the stairs to the landing, held his hand on the doorknob to Jane's bedchamber for a moment, as if gathering his strength, then went inside.

Henry's eyes followed his father. When the door shut behind him, he tugged on her sleeve. "What's wrong with Mama?"

"I'm not sure, Henry. Dr. Mitchell will have to examine her." She made her voice sound as calm and confident as she could muster. "Let's go downstairs and get something to eat while we're waiting. Patience was cooking something special for thy father's homecoming, was she not?"

Hand in hand, they went down to the kitchen, tucked at the back of the house, on the street where most Nantucket captains lived. A typical weather-shingled Nantucket house, modest and practical — at least for Orange Street. Two-sided with a central chimney, a parlor and a dining room on either side of a measured staircase. And blue shutters, a color unique to captains, to frame each sixteen-over-sixteen double-hung window.

Patience was in the kitchen, kneeling by the hearth, her dark head bowed in prayer. Daphne stilled, not wanting to interrupt her, shamed that she had not thought to pray for her sister's welfare. She'd only thought to worry about it. She squeezed her eyes shut and silently breathed a prayer in and out. *Let her be well, O mighty Lord. Let Jane be fine. Let this be nothing more than a story we will tell one day and laugh over.*

A sneeze burst out of Hitty, startling Patience. She jumped up and whirled around. "Mistress, be there news?"

"Nay, not yet. It might be a long wait. I thought there might be something for the children to eat. Ren, too. He is no doubt famished. And his father will be joining us."

Patience sent the children to the table with a sweep of her arm. Words were few with Patience, but the children understood her every gesture. She had helped Jane raise them from the moment they were born, was nearly a second mother to them, even more

40

so than Daphne, which at times evoked a tinge of envy in her. That wasn't fair, Daphne knew. Patience was the one who helped Jane during long nights, wiped their brows when they were fevered, changed their nappies, tucked them into bed.

As Patience bustled around, filling bowls with fresh berries and plates with slices of buttered bread, Daphne watched her, admiring her quiet confidence during this family crisis. She had a certain beauty, Patience did. Skin the color of molasses, bold cheekbones, high forehead, long black hair. A Wampanoag princess, Jane once called her. A princess without anyone to reign over, for there were not many Wampanoags left, not after the Year of the Extraordinary Illness in 1763, a year that swept in and swept out, taking so many native islanders.

Daphne heard a rap on the back door and looked up to see Tristram peering down through the diamond-cut glass. Patience opened the door with her chin dipped, and Tristram brushed past her to reach Daphne, eager for news. "Is Jane revived?"

"Dr. Mitchell is here now. Ren is with them."

"Ah, good." Tristram dropped to a chair at the table, heaving an enormous sigh. He slanted a look at Daphne. "Was it her corset, tied too tight again?"

She frowned at him and tipped her head in the children's direction.

"Is there anything I can do? I want to do something. I'm not good when Jane comes undone. 'Tis all I can do to keep investors from histrionics."

"Tristram," Daphne hissed. She glanced at the children, but they were wholly occupied with bread slathered with jam, dripping off its edges, and hadn't paid attention to Tristram's blunt remarks.

He sprang to his feet and began pacing around the kitchen, back and forth, nervous and anxious, as if his energy were so great it could not be controlled. Patience scurried out of his way. "There must be something I can do. This isn't at all like Jane, to collapse under pressure."

Daphne needed to get Tristram out of the house. His presence was only amplifying anxiety. "I think . . . indeed, I think there is something. Would thee mind fetching Mother? She should be here." While that was true, Daphne knew Lillian Coffin wasn't going to be much help. After all, Lillian wasn't even down at the wharf to welcome her son-in-law into port after a six-year voyage. Nearly all of Nantucket had come to see the *Endeavour*! But to not inform her mother of Jane's collapse would offend her deeply, and that would bring serious ramifications. Tristram would be just the one to break the news to Lillian. He could do no wrong in her eyes.

"I'll go," he said, looking pleased to be given something to do. "I'll go now to fetch her."

He made for the door until Daphne called to him to wait. She hurried and whispered, "Tristram, please don't tell Mother anything more than the truth. Jane fainted, that's all. Dr. Mitchell will let us know more after he's examined Jane."

He nodded solemnly. "But that *is* the truth. She's merely overcome."

As Patience closed the door behind him, Hitty asked between bites of bread and jam, "Will thee marry Uncle Trist?"

Bright red raspberry jam dripped down her chin. Henry had carefully licked all the oozing raspberry jam off the sides of his bread before he ate it. There were times when Daphne could hardly believe they were related, much less twins. While their coloring was similar, their personalities could not be more different.

Daphne took the corner of a napkin and wiped Hitty's chin with a smile. "Never thee mind." Before she could say anything more, she heard the voices of Ren and Dr. Mitchell float down the stairs.

"Patience, stay with the children. I'll be right back." Daphne hurried to the foyer but remained at the bottom of the stairs, watching the two men on the landing outside of Jane's chamber door. They stood facing each other. Ren, though average height, towered over the plump little doctor. Dr. Mitchell's round face had always reminded Daphne of a soft hot-cross bun, with two black raisins for eyes.

"Thy wife, I'm sorry to say, is in respiratory distress."

"I can see that for myself," Ren said, his voice growing louder with every word. "She's huffing worse than a beached whale. The question is why? And what can be done to help her recover?"

"To tell the truth, I am not sure."

"You're not sure?" Ren rocked back on his heels.

"I don't know what has caused her to go into respiratory distress." Dr. Mitchell looked down the stairs and noticed Daphne. "Has Jane spoken to thee of any ailments?"

Daphne shook her head. "She's been . . . as she's always been."

"And today?" the doctor said. "Today she

44

was not unwell?"

"She was fine, earlier today. Somewhat fine. Shaky. Nervous. Trembling a little, I noticed. But she was excited to see Ren."

The doctor scratched his forehead, still focused on Daphne. "Has thee noticed any signs of heart trouble?"

"Heart trouble?" Ren roared. "Are you daft?" The doctor's head jerked up at the sharp tone in Ren's voice. "I can tell you why my wife collapsed like a rag doll. I've seen it before." He jabbed a finger at the doctor's chest. "Laudanum. Poppy sauce. Did you give her any?"

The doctor blinked, then sputtered, "Mayhap once or twice."

"Once or twice? She's overdosed on it. I saw the pupils of her eyes before she collapsed on the wharf. Like pinpoints."

"But . . . but . . . that's preposterous! 'Tis but a sunny day. Her pupils were contracted."

"I know what a laudanum addict looks like."

"Addict? Impossible! No one can be addicted to laudanum."

"Indeed they can. It's rampant among sailors."

"Why, it's been around for more than two centuries. The drug is wonderfully benefi-

45

cial. 'Tis called 'Mother's Friend' for quieting colicky infants. I take it myself, every morning. A grain, at most two." Dr. Mitchell glanced down the stairs. "Some — many — of our own Brothers and Sisters indulge. 'Tis perfectly harmless. Tell him, Daphne. Tell him how common it is."

"I . . . I . . ." *I don't know what to say, what to think.*

The doctor turned back to Ren. "If Jane Macy overindulged, she took more than I ever prescribed."

"But why? Why did you prescribe it for my wife in the first place?"

"Same reason as most women on Nantucket require it. For female hysteria. Laudanum gave her spirits a lift."

Ren pulled a silver flask out of his pocket. "So this is it? I found it in her chamber. It has an *M* engraved on it. 'Tis not yours?"

"I . . . I don't know that it is. I don't know that it isn't."

Ren opened it and sniffed. "I can smell the bitter scent of laudanum in this flask."

"I only give my patients powdered opium. The price has grown so dear in Boston that it's easier to transport. I suggest they mix it with wine to mask the taste." Dr. Mitchell took the flask from Ren and took a whiff. "That is not wine in the elixir." He screwed the lid back on. "It's some kind of tainted tincture."

"Tainted?" Ren frowned. "As in, poison?"

"Ethanol, most likely. Not a poison, unless the amount mixed in was of a lethal dose."

"Lethal?" Ren nearly choked on the word.

Daphne felt her heart start to race. *Lethal?* How could this be? Her mind started spinning, her legs felt wobbly, and she grabbed on to the newel post for support. Lethal? How could this be happening to her sister?

"The next few days will be critical," Dr. Mitchell said, all business. "Jane is young. She has much to live for. Mayhap she will have a chance to survive this crisis."

"Survive?" Ren's face blanched. "Has a *chance?* Do you mean to say she might die? She is but a lass of six-and-twenty!"

Dr. Mitchell started down the narrow stairwell. "Continue to feed her the sugared water. I'll return later in the day to check on her. Laura Swain is having her baby. A breech. I must return to her at once. Thee can reach me at the Swains' if anything changes."

"Is there not . . . ?" Ren put a hand to his head. "There must be something you can do for her! Some medicine that can counteract the effects of this . . . tainted tincture?"

Dr. Mitchell stopped on a stair and turned to answer Ren, his voice surprisingly tender. "Her age will be to her benefit in this struggle. But if there is sign of intestinal bleeding . . . 'twill be too late. The end will be near."

Ren swallowed, his face blanched, his hand stopped halfway down his shortly clipped hair.

"I'll see myself out."

As the doctor passed by Daphne, he patted her shoulder in a sympathetic way that caused her eyes to blur with a wash of tears. She was gripped by a sick feeling of dread. *Dear God,* she thought. *Dear God, how can this be?* More tears crowded her eyes.

An ominous silence filled the stairwell as the heavy front door shut behind the doctor. It felt as if hope had left with him.

Ren stared at Daphne, a haunted look on his face. "Daphne, did you know of this . . . this . . . laudanum that Jane took?"

She averted her eyes from Ren, wiping them as she looked down at the toes of her kid slippers peeking out from under her silk dress. "I knew of the powdered medicine that Dr. Mitchell prescribed, and she took it but rarely."

"Only rarely?" He walked down the stairwell, stopping halfway. "Why at all? What

48

has been going on in my absence?"

She lifted her head. "What does thee mean?"

"For Jane to indulge in poppy sauce . . . while caring for two small children . . . that doesn't sound like the woman I married. Jane is a woman of strength. Of substance. Of independent means. I would never have expected Jane to become a Nantucket hen . . ."

A Nantucket hen? That was an insulting name given to sailors' wives who were considered dotty after spending so much of life alone. Daphne glared at him, anger replacing anguish. "How dare thee sound so roiled!" She could hear the rising hysteria in her voice, but she couldn't seem to stop it. "And what gives thee the right to sound off like an indignant husband? After thee's been away six long years!"

He peered into her face. "Jane knew what it meant to be a whalemaster's wife. Other women endure their lot. So tell me why is . . ." he lifted a hand toward the bedroom door. "Why is she this way? Who is to blame?"

To blame? How dare he! "I don't know! She's been under stress . . ."

"Tell me why! What has caused such stress?"

Daphne took such a deep breath that the points of her whalebone stays poked into her sides. How she hated corsets! "Why? Why? Oh, what men do not know about women!" He winced at her bluntness but she was too intent to notice; her hands curled with annoyance, her voice rose in frustration. "She bore thee twin babies, one of whom was pindling. She has been raising them alone. And then there is her financial situation."

Ren's eyes widened in shock. "What do you mean? What financial situation?"

Daphne came back to herself with a start. "Thee should speak to Tristram."

"What are you not telling me? What should I know?"

"Thee should know that thy wife did all she could to manage and keep this house, to provide for thy children, while thee . . . thee was traipsing around the world with nary a care!"

"Nary a care!" Ren clapped his palms against his temples. "Nary a care! I was trying to fill the hold as quickly as possible and return to my wife."

"Ren," she said, her voice cracking, "when Tristram returns to the house, go to him with thy questions."

He glared at her. "I will. I will do just that.

I will get to the bottom of this. I will find out who is to blame for the condition my wife is in."

"Son." A calm deep voice filled the stairwell. Daphne turned to see Jeremiah Macy by the front door. Had he been there this whole time? She hadn't even noticed. "Son, go sit by your wife and say a prayer for her."

Ren dropped his chin to his chest and went into Jane's chamber, quietly closing the door behind him.

Daphne brushed the tears from her face and put out her hand to welcome Jane's father-in-law. "Jeremiah, this is not the homecoming Jane had planned for thee and Ren." She sighed. "Please stay. I can get thee refreshments. Thee must be famished."

He shook his head. "I'm not much good at waiting around," he said. "I'll be down at the Seven Seas Tavern if you need me. Assuming it's still there?"

"It is."

He appraised her for a long moment. "Land sakes, Daphne Coffin. You've gone and gotten tall."

It perplexed her that so many felt the need to point that fact out to her.

He gave her a pat on her shoulder. "All in all, you've grown into a right fetching young woman. I would not have predicted such a thing, back in '15 when the *Endeavour* sailed off."

There was a compliment in there somewhere, though Daphne was too preoccupied with concern for Jane to put much thought to Jeremiah, other than annoyance. As she closed the door behind him, she pondered why men felt the need to talk or move restlessly during a crisis, both of which were not at all helpful.

As Daphne swung open the kitchen door and entered the room, she had to blink once, then twice. There at the kitchen table sat a Negro man, being served a cup of tea by Patience.

Patience took Hitty and Henry outside so that Daphne could speak to the man in the kitchen. She studied the man's skin: he wasn't as dark as most African sailors she'd seen. She wondered if he was Azorean. Or Ethiopian? He reminded her of a cup of coffee, stirred with rich cream.

The sailor had jumped to his feet as she entered the room, and now was studying her too. Perhaps he had not seen many Quaker women before. He had round and clear dark eyes and held her gaze with confidence, so unlike the former slaves living in a corner of the island called New

Guinea, who ducked their chins in deference when they crossed paths with Nantucket whites.

He eyed her as a curiosity, as surprised by her appearance as she was of his. It reminded Daphne of the way her own mother would gaze at her when she didn't think she knew she was being observed. Her mother often seemed completely baffled by Daphne's height and looks, as if she wondered where she'd come from.

"Ma'am, I am here to speak to Captain Macy. He asked me to supervise the unloading of the *Endeavour.*"

The sailor's voice was gentle and well-spoken, with crisp enunciation of consonants. She did not detect an accent, though she assumed he had been born in the south. A former slave, perhaps? Now a freeman?

"Captain Macy asked me to bring him a report," he prompted.

"I see." And yet she didn't. She did not believe him. It was unlikely he could read or write; surely Ren would not have a low-ranking seaman supervise such precious cargo. Yet why would the Negro lie? There was no reason to doubt him, aside from the color of his skin. A tinge of shame for her suspicion rippled through her.

"Captain Macy is upstairs with his wife.

May I take him a message for thee?"

"Thank you, ma'am, no. I must deliver this message myself."

"Could thee return tomorrow?"

"No, ma'am. I will wait. I will wait outside until the captain is available to me." He nodded to her and went out the back door.

She had a feeling this curious black sailor would wait for Captain Reynolds Macy as long as it would take.

When an hour had passed and Ren had not come down, Daphne went upstairs to check on her sister. The chamber door was slightly ajar. Jane lay in utter stillness. If it weren't for a sudden shuddering breath, Daphne would have thought her dead. A sigh of relief escaped her throat and Ren glanced up at the sound.

He shook his head to her questioning look. "There is no change."

She crossed the room to give a cup of hot tea to Ren. He sat in a chair next to Jane's bed and held the delicate porcelain teacup in his large rough hands, such an odd combination that it almost elicited a smile from Daphne. Almost. She was still angry with him for how brusquely he had spoken to Dr. Mitchell, and then to her. Yet she also had empathy for the poor man. How much had changed in a few short hours.

She studied his face as he blew on the steaming tea. Ren's was a handsome face, with its sharp, shapely nose and high cheekbones, the wide mouth that held a certain wild charm. He was a lithe man of medium height, sun-tinted skin, and dark eyebrows that framed his piercing brown eyes. Eyes that now had sun creases fanning at their edge. Her eyes followed the trimmed beard that framed his strong jaw. He looked older than she remembered him — how old was he now? Twenty-nine? Nay, thirty-one.

When he looked up, the face he turned to her was empty but for sorrow that darkened his eyes. "I must ask your forgiveness. I had no call to speak to you the way I did."

"There is no need to apologize."

"Ah, but there is. Jane is your sister. You are as distraught as I."

She swallowed around an ache in her throat that felt strangely like a lump of tears. "Apology accepted." She sat in the chair on the other side of Jane's bed. "I can ask Patience to bring thee something to eat."

He looked up at her over the brim of the teacup. "Patience?"

"Jane's maidservant. A Wampanoag." She paused. He *should* remember her. She'd been at her mother's house for as long as

55

Daphne could recall. "Patience is a fine servant for Jane. A wonderful help with the children."

Ren set the teacup down on the nightstand. "I don't doubt it. I'm just . . . bewildered by all the changes." He leaned back in the chair. "I did not know I had become a father."

She had been stroking Jane's arm, but stopped at this news. "Surely thee jests."

"Nay. I had no idea."

"But thee must have received Jane's letters."

"I received two, but neither mentioned that she had given birth to twin children."

"I know she wrote to thee regularly. Whenever a ship left port, she would send a letter to thee. Each time!" She kept on talking, as if by saying enough, the letters would suddenly appear.

But Daphne knew better. There were all kinds of reasons why letters failed to reach their destination; it was more of a miracle when one reached its intended. Even then, tidings would be stale by a year, often longer. It was more reliable for ships gammed on the open sea to send letters to Nantucket, as the port was everyone's final destination. Receiving mail from Nantucket, intended for the crew of a particular ship, was a game of chance with poor odds.

"We didn't come across a Nantucket vessel for well over two years. I wasn't entirely sure I'd have a wife waiting for me on the docks this morning as the *Endeavour* sailed into port. But there she was, looking just like the sweet lass I'd said goodbye to so soon after we'd wed." He turned to look at Jane, lying so still on the bed. "And then . . . this happened." He sipped on his tea, and she knew it was to hide the tears that glistened in his eyes. "Which one was pindling?"

"The twins? Henry. He was born small, quite a bit tinier than Hitty. Jane nursed him 'round the clock those first few months. Even as a toddler, everything came slower for Henry than it did for Hitty. Everything but illness. If Hitty caught a cold, Henry would catch pneumonia. 'Tis better now. They are more on an even keel."

He nodded, interested, still sipping his tea. He set the cup on the nightstand. "Do you think Jane can hear us?"

"I don't know. 'Tis a question for Dr. Mitchell." She hoped so, though. She wanted Jane to know she was surrounded by those who loved her. How hopeful they were to have her return to them. "There's a sailor downstairs who's been patiently waiting to speak to thee. He says thee wanted him to report on the unloading of cargo for the *Endeavour.*" She leaned forward and whispered, "He is a Negro."

"Aye. Abraham. My second mate."

Daphne's mouth opened. "He is thy second mate?"

"Indeed. Abraham is the most praiseworthy man I know. Best hand I ever hired. I picked him up in the Barbados. I lost three hands while there — three Swain cousins. I had to scupper them. They are meant to be landlubbers."

Daphne knew those Swain boys to be a lazy lot. They would never work again on a whaling ship. There was no worse insult to bestow on a man than to dismiss him as a landlubber. "Then, this Abraham, he can read? And keep accounts?"

"Not only can he read and do sums, he has a knack for navigation. He can captain a ship as well as me. I have a thought to make him my first mate on the next voyage."

A dark-skinned man . . . first mate? Daphne had never heard of such a thing. She wondered if Ren might have trouble finding crew to sign on. They were not accustomed to taking orders from a dark-skinned man.

As if he read her mind, he murmured, "On a ship, the crew is color-blind if the captain says so."

She wondered.

"I'd ask you not to mention my plans to promote Abraham to Tristram." He rose to his feet. "If you'll stay with Jane, I'll go down to speak to Abraham."

"Of course. And I won't speak a word of thy plans, not to Tristram nor to anyone else. Tristram is fetching Mother."

Ren nodded. "Lillian. How does she fare?"

"She is the same as she has always been."

"And thy father? He is well?"

Ren did not know? But of course he didn't. How could he? "Father passed away. Four years ago now."

Ren dropped his chin to his chest. "I am sorry to hear that. I know how Jane adored him." He glanced at Jane. "She had to endure so much, all alone."

"Yes, and yet, she wasn't alone. Nantucket women, they rally together. Jane is much beloved. Especially so after she started the Cent School for some local children."

"A Cent School? What is that?"

" 'Tis a day school for little ones. It costs but a penny a day to attend."

A confused look filled his eyes. "Why in the world would she do such a thing?"

Daphne hesitated. There was so much Ren did not understand. "So mothers can work and know their children are well cared for. The women whose husbands are at sea." Which was most everyone, for all industries on Nantucket involved the sea.

A commotion downstairs meant the arrival of Lillian Coffin. Ren flinched at the sound of his mother-in-law's voice, floating up the stairwell. Daphne noticed.

"I'll greet Lillian, then see to Abraham." Before Ren left Jane's bedside, he touched the corner of her mouth with his lips. He glanced up at Daphne with a startled look. "They are so cold, her lips. Like ice."

Daphne sat in the chair next to Jane's bed. She picked up Jane's hand — so cold, and her fingernails, they seemed to have a tinge of blue. She rubbed her sister's hands, hoping to warm them up, and then tucked them under the covers. She wished there was something she could do, other than sit here. Her eyes slid to the bedside table, and she opened the drawer to take out Great Mary's journal.

Mary Coffin Starbuck

12 May 1662

Eleven-year-old Jethro has been a friend to me. This morning, I went out to fill the water bucket in the well and discovered he had already done it for me. I thanked him and he blushed. He is a dear boy. I met Nathaniel in Salisbury when he was a grown man, nearly twenty, and could not have imagined him as a boy. He was so tall, distant and mature to me, and I was but a child still, only ten years old.

But when I am with Jethro, I feel as if I am peeking through a window into the past, to get an idea of my husband as a boy. Shy, sweet, thoughtful. And like Nathaniel, Jethro cannot read. He simply cannot. I have tried to teach both of them, and it is a futile endeavour.

It is not a lack of intelligence, as both of them are quite capable and insightful and overly blessed with common sense — which might be the most valuable form of intelligence any one could have. I think their inability to grasp the written word has something to do with the way their mind is shaped. They do not seem to be able to remember letters. When they do try to write, letters come out backward or upside down. I have come to believe that is why the X is the preferred signature for those who are illiterate. Backwards or forwards or upside down, it is the same.

How difficult it must be to not have the ability to read or write. I take such comfort and solace in words. I would feel quite excluded from the world if I could not partake in language.

I said as much to Esther and she suggested that I might try it sometime.

13 May 1662

Nathaniel believes that Esther dislikes me so intensely because Jethro is equally devoted to me. "You've taken the spot in his life," he said, "that Esther wants to have."

Mayhap he is right, as he often is. Still, I think there might be more to Esther's unreasonable hostility. Though I accept it as a silly thought, I have wondered if Esther has been so cold to me because she is envious of my role at the store. 'Tis not common for a woman on this island to work outside the home, especially to interact with so many different kinds of people. Wampanoags come in to trade plowing for food, fishermen stop by from the Cape to pick up supplies. I listen, I ask questions, and I learn. There are so many interesting people in this world, each one with a story to tell.

As often as I am overcome with awe by a colorful sunrise or sunset, or when I listen to the eternal sound of waves cresting onto the shore, I think I am most filled with wonder of God when I observe the variety of people on this earth. It brings to mind a Bible proverb: "The rich and poor meet together; the Lord is the maker of them all."

18 May 1662

I had what I thought was a wonderful idea, a test of my theory. I asked Esther if she might like to help out in the store with me, now and then, during times when her mother didn't need her at home.

She gave me a flat no.

3

Captain Reynolds Macy gathered every ounce of stoic courage he could muster as he prepared to meet his wife's mother. Fortifying thoughts ran through his mind: *I have stood in the face of gales that threatened to topple m' ship. I have speared mighty leviathans. Surely, I can face Lillian Swain Coffin.*

But as he closed the door to Jane's chamber, his courage faltered. His mother-in-law, although she had a striking elegance even he could not deny admiring, was a force unlike anything in nature. Her skin was markedly white, her eyes nearly black, her hair a flaxen blonde. She carried herself with an unmistakable patrician manner, amiable to those she considered peers, haughty toward inferiors. While it was true that many folk in Nantucket had long memories, unforgiving natures, and a deep suspicion of newcomers, Lillian nursed grudges like no one else. She was the reason he had bought the house on Orange Street for Jane, though he could scarcely afford it. Besides security, he thought it would provide well-deserved status for Jane as a whalemaster's wife, and hoped it would appease Lillian.

He had not realized Jane would have had to face so much alone, though. To bear his children, all alone. To face her beloved father's death, alone. He shook inside with fear and shame, and a wonder at himself. *How could I have expected so much of my bride? How could I have given her so little in return?*

He squared his shoulders, for he knew Lillian would find any apparent weak spot and drive a wedge into it. At the top of the stairs, he saw his cousin Tristram in the foyer, standing beside Lillian in her starched gray dress, white lace–caped shoulders, and stiff black bonnet. Closing the front door behind them was the native maidservant, a woman he vaguely recalled — what had Daphne called her? Patience. Ahhh . . . A timely reminder.

"Where is she? Where is Jane?"

A shiver went down his spine. Lillian's voice was not shrill, but even still, it had always had that effect on him, like biting down on a piece of tin.

When Patience didn't answer, Lillian looked up the stairwell and spotted Ren. She lifted a hand and pointed a finger at him, a confirmation to Ren that this would be a difficult reunion. There was no tie of blood or love to bind them, only a connection to Jane. "Thee! Thee brought this on! I told Jane, she never should have married thee! It would ruin her. I *told* her. Thee convinced her to elope and then thee ran off to sea! Thee has broken her spirit."

Blame. Accusation. Condemnation. Woven together like three strands of rope. He expected as much from her, but guilt sent color rushing hot to his face. He cleared his throat and tried for a smile as he went down the stairs. "Hello, Lillian. If you can compose yourself to be calm and quiet, you may be escorted up to see Jane."

"Escorted! To see my own daughter? I will not be told what to do." She held up her skirts so she wouldn't trip and started to climb the stairs.

Ren blocked her path. "I realize this is upsetting news. But Jane does not need to be distressed. She needs rest to recuperate." As soon as the words left his mouth, he realized he had made an error in revealing too much.

Lillian froze. "Rest to recuperate?" She looked down at Tristram. "Thee said her corset was too tight and she had fainted!"

Tristram's mouth tightened a little at the corners. "Apparently, I did not have all the facts."

"*What* has happened to Jane?"

Ren hesitated. "She's had a . . . nervous collapse."

A gasp escaped Lillian's lips and she swayed. Ren caught her before she toppled down the stairs. "William. He . . . he died of such a collapse."

"This is nothing like William's circumstances, Lillian," Tristram said. To Ren, he mouthed, "He died in the arms of another woman."

Ren stared at his cousin. Tristram lifted his eyebrows in such a way that spoke the truth.

Ren was shocked that Jane's father was no longer, but not by those details. It was a poorly kept secret on Nantucket Island, that of William Starbuck Coffin's transgressions. While Friends did not approve, most everyone pitied the man for his unfortunate choice of a wife.

Lillian had always confronted rumors of her husband's mistress by refusing to acknowledge them. It was the second reason she objected to Jane's marriage to Ren. She was convinced that all seamen had the same philandering tendencies. Certainly there were powerful temptations for seamen in exotic ports-o-call, where a man could find a woman and never worry he would see her again. But Ren fought those temptations and did not leave the ship when in port, for he loved his wife and had made a promise to her, to forsake all others.

But Lillian's primary objection to Reynolds Macy was that he was not a member of the Society of Friends held in good standing. Nor did he care to be.

Lillian's hands still gripped the banister. She looked up to find Ren watching her, and she lifted a hand to her forehead. "I fear a spell is on its way. I must return home at once." She recovered herself, smoothing out her skirts, and darted back down the stairs. "Tristram, let us be off."

Lillian's words so shocked Ren that for a moment he couldn't speak. Could the woman not put aside her own self-interests for a single moment, even when her own daughter may be at death's door? "But what of Jane?"

"Thee said she needs her rest. I will return another time." She swept straight to the door like a ship under full sail.

Tristram looked up at Ren, baffled. "What would thee have me do?"

"Take her home." Unfortunate, but illuminating. Lillian would be of no help during this time of need. "Tristram, after you get Lillian settled in, please return here. We have things to discuss."

As the door closed, he squeezed his eyes shut. Was this God's way of testing him, of reminding him that he was not in control of his life? It was a lesson he had been schooled in many times at sea, and now on land. When he opened his eyes again, the servant girl stood at the base of the stairs, her chin tucked down, her eyes peeping up at him.

"Patience, is it? I do recall meeting you at Lillian's house, long ago. I am Reynolds Macy."

She dipped in a small curtsy. "Yes, Captain, I know. There is a man in the kitchen who says he needs to see you."

Abraham! "Thank you. I'd forgotten." It was a gift to return to a normal task, to oversee the unloading of the *Endeavour.* Another reminder from God, he pondered, as he walked to the kitchen at the back of the house. Life must keep going.

Abraham jumped up from the kitchen table when Ren entered the room, as if he'd been caught sleeping on watch. Hardly the case. Ren smiled at Abraham, or tried to, anyway. "You bring good tidings, Abraham?"

The sailor bowed his head a little. Humble, Ren thought. So unusual for a whaler. Any whaler, low ranking or otherwise. Seamen were a proud bunch, especially on land.

"I am bringing word from the counting-house. As you asked of me, Captain."

"Yes, yes. Sit down, Abraham. Tell m' what they have said. Did the barrels match with our accounting?"

Abraham did not sit, but Ren did not expect him to. He refused to sit in Ren's presence — the only order he did not obey.

Ren glanced at Patience. "Would thee take a turn at m' wife's side?"

Patience gave a brief nod, filled a teacup for Ren, served it to him, and quietly slipped through the door. Abraham's eyes remained fixed on the maid. Ren noticed.

Interesting. It would please Ren if Abraham found himself a lass from Nantucket. That would keep him island bound.

Abraham was the finest crewman Ren had ever captained — smart, quick, a cool head under pressure. He'd found him last year in the Barbados and took him on as boat-steerer, a position of skill, intelligence, and keen importance. Abraham was the first

70

Negro employed as crew on the *Endeavour.* Ren had known of Abraham's capabilities, though under another captain's flag. He had little regard for that captain, a cruel and selfish man. That first day, Ren observed the excellent skills of Abraham during a whale hunt. Not only had he made the killing lance, but he had saved the life of another sailor, a foolish lad whose foot had gotten tangled in the rope. After the whale had been caught and butchered, and the oil rendered — a lengthy process — Ren learned that the crew had refused to allow the Negro a bunk or hammock in the forecastle. Abraham had slept his first few nights on the open deck of the *Endeavour,* its boards still slimy, reeking of whale blood and oil.

When Ren rose unusually early one morning and found Abraham asleep, tucked under the bow, he quickly surmised what had gone on and was outraged with his crew. He called all hands to the upper deck to commend Abraham for his fine work, then promote him to second mate. Ren remembered the silence that fell over the upper deck as shock registered on the faces of the crew. The only sounds were the slapping of the sails above them and the waves below. No man of color had ever advanced further than boatsteerer on a whaling ship.

It was a critical moment for a sea captain. If Ren's crew walked off, he would be in a dire situation. No doubt they knew it. They would put off in the Azores and find work at the next whaling ship that came through, of which there were plenty. But they'd be losing out on their share of profits as well, a substantial lay. The ship's hold was nearly full. Nearly, but not quite. He needed each one to remain and bring the ship back to Nantucket Island.

It was his father, cooper Jeremiah Macy, who stepped into the void. "I'll help thee move thy things to the officers' cabin, Mr. Abraham."

And with that one show of respect by Jeremiah, Abraham was accepted by the other crew, even if grudgingly, as an officer. His keen eye and superior skills with the harpoon brought in two sperm whales without incident, one right after the other — the most prized whale of all for the waxy spermaceti oil in its large head. Spermaceti oil candles burned brighter and were odorless. Sperm whales were difficult to hunt, able to dive deep and hold their breath for long periods. Afterward, Abraham had told Ren he'd counted ninety minutes between blowhole spotting of a particular sperm whale he'd been tracking.

The voyage was finished at last as the hold was finally full — no captain worth his pay returned to the home port without a chocked-off hold, regardless of how long a journey took — the tryworks was broken apart, its bricks thrown joyfully into the ocean, and Abraham had secured his place in the crew's eyes. That, and a greasy voyage, a full hold, and not a single injury or death of a crewman the entire time. They were on their way home. Home to Nantucket, home to Ren's darling Jane.

Ren drew himself back to the present with a squaring of his shoulders. He turned to his second mate, mustering up a tired smile. "What did the countinghouse have to say?"

"They are saying they want to talk to you, Captain, before the lays are distributed."

"There is a problem?"

"They will not talk to me."

Ren nodded. That did not surprise him. Free men of every color lived and conducted business in close proximity to their Quaker neighbors on Nantucket, yet there were invisible lines that were not crossed. Just like the one on the *Endeavour*. "Tristram can manage, can he not?"

"They say they want to talk only to you, Captain."

Odd. Tristram had been the one to deal with the business end of the *Endeavour* for the past six years. "I'll try to get over there this afternoon."

"The day is spent, sir."

Ren ran a hand through his hair. How late was it? He'd lost track of time. It was a strange feeling for a man who was so conscious of time that he was aware of the earth's fifteen degrees of rotation throughout each hour. He had an innate awareness of such precise details in order to calculate the ship's position. Time was something he knew intimately. He felt disoriented, as if he'd walked off the ship into another universe, one that careened him off-kilter.

A rapping on the front door startled Daphne. She heard the door open, the murmuring of voices, then heavy footsteps starting up the stairs. Tristram had come. She knew it was he bolting up the stairs because he ran everywhere. He was always in a hurry, always eager to move on to whatever was next.

She closed the journal and tucked it back in the nightstand drawer. She would like to know more of Mary Coffin Starbuck. She wasn't sure what she had expected to learn of her, but so far she was thoroughly surprised by Mary's revelations. How genuine she was, Daphne supposed, how authentic.

Tristram's face poked through the doorway. "Is Jane awake?"

"Nay, not yet." Daphne put a finger to her lips. "Hush. Thee makes more noise coming up the stairs than Hitty and Henry at full gallop."

He made his face go all soft and wounded-looking. "I just had to escort thy dear sweet mother here and then back again . . . and this is how I'm greeted? Why, thee has had no idea of the torment I've endured —" He stopped abruptly when he caught sight of Jane's face, heard her labored breathing. He came into the room and went to Jane's bedside, taking one of her hands in his. A stricken look overcame him. "So what did the doctor declare to be the cause of Jane's ailment?"

Daphne glanced at her sister. Jane was both sweating and shivering. "He will return later, he said, for a more thorough examination."

Tristram gazed at her. " 'Tis more serious than first thought?"

She nodded, then looked at her sister, whose breaths came in slow, shallow intakes of air.

He lifted Jane's hand and turned it over,

kissing her palm tenderly. "Jane, dearest Jane, come back to us."

Oh do, Jane. Please come back. Daphne added one more plea. *Don't leave me. I'm not sure I can do life without thee.*

MARY COFFIN STARBUCK

21 June 1662

I have learned something about myself in this season of adjustment. I find limitations trying and I crave variety. Growing up in Salisbury, I had been accustomed to the mingling of foreigners, with the coming and going of ships. There was always something different to see, new faces and strange accents to ponder.

I think that's what I enjoy about keeping a store and why I spend most of my time over at the shop Father built for me near Capaum Harbor. While weather obliges this summer, schooners sail in from the Cape or from Boston. Some bring supplies, some bring curious onlookers who are making preliminary visits with the purpose of moving here. When they come into the store, I study their clothing and listen to their talk about politics or the weather or the condition of their crops, or what the foolish governor of Massachusetts has done now.

These interactions make my mind spin with new ideas. I feel so vital. Dare I write it here? I feel valued. Important. Rather than the unwanted extra, as I do so often in the Starbuck household.

My shop does a brisk business when a ship arrives. I am quite pleased, and have started to draw up plans for Nathaniel to enlarge the shed at his earliest convenience.

I have not yet mentioned these plans to him. Timing is everything and today is not the day to bring up such a request. 'Tis summer solstice and Nathaniel's heart is downcast. Winter will soon be upon us, he said in a doleful tone. I laughed and laughed at his gloomy forecast — he's troubled about something that he cannot control, and it is six months away! — but he did not appreciate my amusement at his expense.

28 June 1662

It is unfortunate that Esther and I did not get off to a good start. I hear her whispering to Catherine about me when they are working together in the small kitchen. Catherine does not defend me. Just the opposite. Catherine agrees with Esther's assessments! She does not approve of me sharing opinions on politics with Edward, nor that I speak in such a straightforward way to Nathaniel.

I am baffled by Catherine's complaints.

If my candor does not bother Edward or Nathaniel, why should it bother her?

1 July 1662

Last night Nathaniel asked me if I could set aside time each week to help his mother, and not go to the store quite so often. I explained that my time is much better spent in the store, that it is a bustling place, and how I long for bustle! For lively conversation, for friendly faces. (I didn't add that part.) He said that he felt some effort toward preparing for winter in the Starbuck household would go a long way in his mother's eyes.

Preparing for winter? 'Tis barely July!

I reminded him that when I did try to help his mother, that first month after we were married, it did not go well. "Mary, m' love," he started and gave me his tenderest smile that instantly swept my upset away, and suddenly I agreed to set aside two afternoons a week to help Catherine winterize.

This morning dawned particularly hot and humid, the air still and heavy, with hardly a sea breeze. Catherine has set me to task on mending moth holes in quilts to "keep everyone warm and snug as a bug in a rug on a cold night," and all I can think is that 'tis only July!

4

The next day was more of the same. Sitting beside Jane's canopied bed, watching her struggle to breathe. After the doctor dropped by to check on her, Ren wanted to press him: What now? What next? Surely this couldn't go on indefinitely. Surely Jane would turn a corner soon and revive, get well. Yet he wasn't sure he wanted to hear the doctor's answer.

Tonight, he watched the Indian maidservant slip sugar water through Jane's lips, massage her throat to get her to swallow, wipe the drips that rolled down her cheeks. She cared for Jane as if she were but a babe and not a grown woman, uncommonly devoted to her. She was a blessing to them, that woman, so quiet, so calm. Patience was her name, and patience was her gift.

There were other gifts, as well. Jane's sister, Daphne, hadn't left Orange Street. She stayed close to Jane's bedside and slept in the spare bedroom to be available for the children.

Children.

Ren still couldn't grasp the notion that he was a father. While what he had said to Daphne was true — that the oceans were large and ships were few — still, how could his letters have made their way to Jane, and so few of hers to him?

It wasn't that fatherhood was out of his scope. He had a hope that raising a family was ahead for them.

Yet to be presented with two six-year-old children and told they belonged to him? That thought alone made him flounder. And in the very next moment his Jane, his darling Jane, collapsed like a rag doll onto that filthy dock. If he thought he had floundered by the news of fatherhood, his keel had run aground by Jane's collapse.

Jane's chest lifted as if she were suddenly drawing back in all the breath she had lost.

Breath.

He could see how she struggled to get the oxygen she needed into her lungs. It reminded him of the time he had nearly drowned when he'd fallen overboard, how his lungs had burned like fire within him, had felt close to exploding. *Is that what Jane is feeling now?*

Her lips had an increasingly husky blueish tinge to them, as did her fingernails. He reached out to take her hand in his, entwining his fingers through hers like the strands of a rope. She was always a tiny thing, his sweet Jane, yet she had such vitality, such determination. He remembered how her eyes would sparkle like diamonds when she had something to tell him.

He released her hand and sat back in the chair to stretch his legs. How well had they really known each other when they married? Hardly at all. Though born in Nantucket, Ren had signed on as cabin boy to a ship to accompany his father, a cooper, and never looked back. At that point, his mother, Angelica Foulger Macy, finally decided to return to the Bahamas to live with her elderly mother and her brother, as she had never felt she truly belonged to Nantucket and doubted she ever would, especially without a husband and child on land. She concluded she might see more of her husband and son passing through the Bahamas than she ever would in Nantucket.

For many years, Angelica had guessed correctly. Jeremiah purchased an old whaling schooner, the *Endeavour,* and appointed himself captain, with his able son serving as first mate. They made frequent passes through the Bahamas, as the whales they chased were minke whales, plentiful in the Atlantic. And then an epidemic swept through the islands of the Bahamas, brought in from the ships, one that was particularly vicious for the vulnerable natives. Angelica was half native.

After burying his wife, Jeremiah Macy felt that perhaps he'd had enough of the seagoing life, that it had taken too much from him. He said he was returning to Nantucket to pick up where he'd left off, as cooper. Ren, he announced, was ready to captain the *Endeavour* on his own. "After all, you've been more of a captain for this old hulk than I've been."

It was a rare word of encouragement from his father but for one thing: Ren did not have the kind of capital needed to outfit a ship for a whaling voyage. Nor did Jeremiah, for the *Endeavour* had cost him most of his life savings, and Angelica's extravagant taste for fine living had taken the rest. Guilt ridden that he had loved the sea even more than he had loved his wife, Jeremiah had never begrudged her a cent.

And that was where the partnership with Tristram began. As third cousins once removed, both only children, the two boys had shared a special kinship over the years.

Once or twice, Tristram had signed on as crew for the *Endeavour,* and proved his seaworthiness to Ren and Jeremiah. Trist had a persuasive way with people, and Ren knew he could muster investors to back the ship. Jeremiah was skeptical; he thought Tristram had a tendency to sail too close to the wind, defying rules and pushing limits. Ren felt his father had a bias against all shipping agents and considered them to be rabid extortionists. But Tristram had already built a reputation as a shipping agent, connecting investors to syndicates — owners of ships. So he went forward and proposed the idea of a business partnership. It took no longer than a half second for Tristram to agree and thrust out his hand. "Consider it done, cousin!"

Ren had wanted to seek out an experienced captain for this first voyage, despite his father's intent to pass it into his hands, for he had not the confidence that the investors would overlook his casual religiosity. He understood the thought process of Friends, and suspected they would only provide funds to outfit a ship if a devout Quaker was at the helm. But Tristram was the one who nixed that notion. "Thee is more able than any Nantucket captain, cousin. Watch and see. The investors will be the judge. They care only about the safe and generous return on their investment." He patted Ren on the back. "Watch and see."

Tristram called that one correctly. Investors heartily backed the *Endeavour* with Ren serving as captain. Such assurance gave Ren the confidence he needed, for it was no small thing to captain a ship for the first time. He was only twenty-six years old when he assumed command.

And then Tristram happened to point out a stunning young Quaker woman named Jane Coffin to Ren, a woman with the kind of beauty that made men stop to stare at her. Trist was an earnest and devout Quaker; Ren, if generously assessed, would be considered a lapsed Quaker. His father, Jeremiah, had become spectacularly unconcerned about conforming to Friends' expectations after seeing how his wife, because of her Bahamian blood, had been excluded from Nantucket society. He raised Ren with a heightened sensitivity to Quaker hypocrisy, and they saw plenty of it among sailors on the sea.

Yet Ren had something of his mother in him too, apart from olive skin, dark hair and eyes. Angelica's spirituality ran deep, an unwavering belief that God had a purpose for each life, and she had been influenced by the Friends to seek the Light within each individual. His parents' separate outlooks shaped Ren's personality. He was tolerant and accepting of others, but only after they proved themselves to him.

Jane's legs twitched, startling him out of his musings, and he sat up in the chair.

Darling Jane.

When he'd first laid eyes on her, he remembered feeling as if the axis of his world tilted a few degrees. He'd always heard of the beauty of Nantucket lasses, but she was like a delicate orchid among common daisies. He was a changed man, everything looked different. She was the one for him, the woman he'd been waiting to meet. As soon as possible, he insisted Tristram introduce them. From that day on, he pursued Jane the way he pursued whales — singlemindedly. He spent every possible moment with her when he wasn't at work preparing the *Endeavour* to make voyage. As the day of departure loomed large, he knew he could not leave this island without knowing Jane would be waiting for him when he returned. He asked Jane to marry him, to be his wife, she said yes without any hesitation. But there was a serious glitch. Lillian Coffin, Jane's mother. She would not allow the marriage, not with Ren's poor standing, and threatened to disown her daughter. Despite her mother's firm resolution, Ren convinced Jane to sail to Boston to elope.

When they returned to Nantucket, Jane's belongings were packed and deposited at Tristram's loft. By day's end, she'd been read out of Meeting for marrying a lapsed Quaker. It was all her mother's doing.

He would never forget the hurt in Jane's eyes; it was palpable. It made him realize what he had taken from Jane when he persuaded her to elope with him. Her life had been ordered and without surprise, and he had thoroughly disrupted her. He had swept her off her feet, thereby causing a wedge between her and her mother, and her church.

So Ren scraped together everything he could to purchase the Orange Street house for her to live in, a substantial cost, as her mother refused to allow her to return to her childhood home. He had a hope that Jane's father, a reasonable and sympathetic man, would have influence to soften the Friends' stance, if not Lillian's.

He squeezed his eyes shut. He had assumed incorrectly. Her father, with his great flaw of adultery, had no such influence among the pious Friends.

The whistle of a teakettle pierced the silence. Ah, a cup of tea was just the thing he needed right now. He tucked a lock of hair behind Jane's ear and left her for a brief moment.

When he came into the kitchen, he saw Henry was at the table, sitting with Daphne. "Why is the boy still up?"

"He had a nightmare, so I thought a cup of warm milk might help."

"He should be asleep."

Daphne stiffened. "And he will. But first he is having some warm milk." She frowned at him. "He is worried about his mother. He needed some reassurance."

"He needs sleep." He tipped his head toward Henry like a schoolteacher. "Off with you, then, lad."

Henry jumped out of his chair and bolted through the kitchen door.

"Too harsh, Ren. Thy voice — it can sound too harsh."

Ren glanced at her, then watched the boy go. He set his elbows on the tabletop and rubbed his temples. He dropped his hands. "I . . . I will be more mindful of the tone of my voice." The frown left her face, which relieved him. "I just came down to get a cup of tea. I'll head back up to stay with Jane."

"I will take a turn. Get some rest. Thee must be exhausted."

"And you? You must be just as tired." Just as frightened, just as uncertain of what the future held. "I don't know how long this will go on. Dr. Mitchell had no answers for me." *He's a quack,* Ren thought. *A charlatan.* He was convinced the doctor had provided the tincture for Jane, despite his protests.

"Tomorrow, I plan to take the children out for the morning. They don't need to be waiting vigil."

He looked up in alarm. Already, he'd grown dependent on Daphne's presence. "What about Jane? I must be off to the countinghouse in the morn, as soon as it opens."

"Patience will be here. And Jane has many friends. They have been stopping by all day, offering to help."

"Is there any way to convince your mother to come and stay by Jane's side for a spell?"

"I'll send word. I don't think she understands that Jane is . . ." Her voice trailed off.

Ren finished her thought. "That the situation is as grave as it is."

She nodded. "Jane was always far more accommodating to Mother than I. She carefully avoided aggravating Mother."

"Until I came along."

"I suppose Jane felt thee was worth the aggravation." Daphne smiled. "Tomorrow is covered. Jane will be attended to."

"Assuming there is a tomorrow for Jane." As soon as Ren said the words, he wished them back. Daphne's eyes took on a glassy sheen, and he was sorry he voiced aloud the fear they both kept right under the surface.

"There is milk warmed by the fire. I will be in Jane's chamber if thee needs me." At the doorjamb, she turned. "Get some sleep, Ren. Jane needs thee to be rested for when she returns to us."

He gave her a weak smile, and nodded. "Thank you, Daphne." Though by the time he said it, she had gone.

The following morning, a dank fog settled over Nantucket. Normally, the changeable island weather didn't affect Daphne's mood, not the way it did with her mother. This morning, it added to her unsettled mind.

It didn't feel quite right to leave the house with Jane so ill. Yet it didn't feel right to stay at Orange Street either and postpone yet another morning of the Cent School. Nantucket mothers counted on them, and Daphne knew Jane would be upset, after she recovered, to hear that so many lives were disrupted because of her illness.

Patience assured her that she would not leave Jane's side, that she would send word if there was any change, any at all. Daphne had complete confidence in Patience, but as she walked away from Orange Street with Henry and Hitty, hurrying toward Centre Street, she couldn't shake a sense of dread. But this school of Jane's, it was her mission, and thus Daphne would forge on.

In spite of the damp, gray day, Reynolds Macy threw his cloak over his shoulders, relishing that his clothes were dry and clean after six years of being splattered by ceaseless waves.

As he strode toward the countinghouse at the foot of Main Street, the sound of his boots on the streets magnified like a beating drum. Almost at each half beat came the sound of Abraham's boots, following behind Ren.

Nantucket town had changed much throughout Ren's thirty-one years. When he was a boy, it had been little more than a cluster of shops and houses, its few streets wide and laid out in a grid oriented from the harbor.

The shops were now mostly on Main Street, and the variety dazzled him, with several groceries, two butchers, a cobbler, a barber, a dentist, a milliner, and even a bookstore. The street looked somewhat improved — wider and less rutted, though planks had been laid in front of the shop for pedestrians, so he assumed the street was still prone to mud when it rained. When, he wondered again, would it ever get cobbled?

There was also more traffic: horse-led buggies and wagons heading their way, or passing them in the opposite direction to head toward the tiny village of Siasconset. Ren maintained a strained smile as he passed by Friends, women peering at him from under their bonnet rims, men from their black broad-brimmed hats. Vaguely, he remembered them. He tried to mask what he was thinking: *Save your false smiles and welcomes and tell me instead, did you treat m' Jane as you treated m' own mother? Did you turn away from her because she made a choice that didn't line up with the Friends' rigid rules?*

When Ren's hand touched the door latch of the brick countinghouse, Abraham stopped. "I will be waiting here, Captain."

Ren nodded.

Inside, the place swarmed with activity as it always did after a whaler sailed into harbor. Ren exchanged greetings with clerks as he made his way to the office of William Rotch, who oversaw the entire counting-house. Rotch was a jovial, mutton-chopped man, but Ren never fully trusted his good humor. Lurking just under the laugh lay a shrewd businessman.

When Ren appeared at his doorjamb, Rotch hurried forward with hand extended. "How good to see thee again, Reynolds. Come in, come in. Sit . . . over there." He motioned to a spare chair under the window, waiting until Ren sat down before easing himself into a leather chair beside an enormous rolltop desk. " 'Twas quite a goodly haul the *Endeavour* brought in."

"Aye. I would've preferred it to be shorter in duration, but I cannot complain about the deep hold."

"Hardly a whale must be left in the ocean."

"Oh, I think I left a few for some other Nantucket ships."

A frown settled over Rotch's features, and he hooked his thumbs in his waistcoat pockets. He scowled thoughtfully at the floor before looking up.

"I received word there is a problem with distributing lays to my crew."

"Not a problem, exactly. A dilemma,

perhaps. Thy crew has come to collect their lays."

"Aye."

"Unfortunately, we cannot distribute the lays."

Ren was stunned. "The *Endeavour* brought in a full load. Why wouldn't you give my men their fair share?"

"Because of the debt thee has incurred."

"Debt? I have no debt."

"For the new ship that thy partner has ordered. The *Endeavour*'s cargo was offered as collateral, a down payment on the ship." Ren opened his mouth to respond, but Rotch got there first. "Surely, thee knew."

"There must be a misunderstanding. Tristram has told me nothing of this."

Rotch shook his head. "There is no misunderstanding."

Ren thumped a fist on his knee. "I signed no such agreement."

"Thee didn't have to. Thy cousin signed in thy absence. He showed me the power of attorney he held in thy stead. I will let thee and thy cousin work that out." Rotch leaned forward, hands clasped. "In the meantime, how does thee plan to pay thy crew? All day yesterday, they arrived at the countinghouse to collect their lay. We did not know what thee wanted us to tell them."

"I will have to speak to Tristram first." Ren hoped his cousin had a plan, because he had no idea what to do.

Daphne set the children to work on their letters at the long table in the keeping room on Centre Street, in a small house that belonged to Jane, a wedding gift from their father. She'd survived her first disaster of the morning: little Johnny Swain had come to the Cent School with a penny in his mouth, forgot to give it to her when he arrived, and nearly choked when he took a swig of water from the scooper.

How many times had Jane reminded Johnny's mother to put his penny in his pocket? Dozens! And yet she never failed to pop a penny under his tongue as she sent him out the door each morning.

Last year, Jane had started this school for young children, to not only mind children while their mothers were at work, but to also educate them. The majority of their fathers were somewhere at sea, crewing on whaling ships. It was a concept borrowed from England, the Cent School, and it suited Jane well. Daphne had come alongside Jane to help start it, then, intrigued, she stayed, taking part in each day's activities.

Daphne saw Johnny Swain staring out the window. To her surprise, there stood Ren, a quizzical expression on his face. Standing behind him was the Negro sailor. What was his name? Something Old Testament-y. Before she could recall, her mind traveled to Jane's condition. She flew to the door and opened it. "Ren! What's wrong? Has Jane woken?"

Ren seemed startled by Daphne's questions. "I haven't heard anything. I've just come from the countinghouse. Have you heard anything more?"

"Nay. Patience promised she would send word if there is a change."

Ren peered through the window. "What is going on here? Why are my children in this house?"

"I told thee. Last night, I explained that I was taking the children to the Centre Street house."

Ren stepped over the threshold of the open door. Abraham remained outside, hands clasped behind his back. "What is this?"

"This is Jane's Cent School. She started it a year back. Perhaps longer."

"Why?"

"Why did I bring the children? I thought it would be helpful, to everyone. To give thee time to sort out the countinghouse. To keep the house quiet, and to give the children some routine. They're accustomed to being here. We'll be back to the house by midday."

He shook his head. "Nay, nay. I meant . . . why did Jane start . . . ," he shot a look beyond her, ". . . this?"

"The Cent School?" Daphne took in a deep breath. "Our father had given her this house as his inheritance . . . and she decided to use it to start a school."

"But why, Daphne? Why did she do this?"

Oh. *That.* She worked her palms together nervously. "Additional income . . . was required."

"What do you mean?" Ren rocked back on his heels. "Are you saying that Jane did not have a subsidy to draw on?"

Daphne's mind moved quickly. "I'd best let Tristram give thee more details." She glanced at the children. Hitty was underneath the table, tying Johnny's shoelaces together so that he would trip over his own feet. It was her favorite trick, and Johnny, as usual, was completely unaware of the mischief. "I bid thee good day, as I should give my attention to the children." She paused. "Thee is welcome to stay."

Ren, obviously disconcerted, backed out

of the doorway. "I should . . . I must be off." He nodded and waved his hand, as if giving her permission to carry on.

Always the sea captain, that Reynolds Macy.

As Daphne bent down to pull Hitty out from under the table, she thanked God that Ren chose to leave the house and did not persist with questions. She had no desire to remain in this uncomfortable spot — between two cousins, two business partners. If Ren had asked, she would have expressed her own skepticism over Tristram's ambitious project. Jane had given Tristram her blessing to commission the building of the new ship, but to Daphne it was a high-stake gamble, bargaining the *Endeavour*'s haul against the new ship.

It was an argument never fully resolved with Tristram. He had accused Daphne of not having faith in his judgment, not the way Jane did. And what could she say to that? There was some truth in it.

She bent slightly to nudge Hitty to go sit in her chair. As she straightened up, she saw Ren still standing in the middle of Centre Street, as if he wasn't quite sure which direction to go. Then, the black sailor — Abraham! the name popped into her mind — said something as he lifted his hand to point toward Main Street and Ren snapped into action.

It was a surreal moment. The bold and determined Captain Reynolds Macy, gently shepherded along by a lowly black sailor.

MARY COFFIN STARBUCK

1 August 1662

Richard Swain returned to Nantucket on his sloop today with an African slave, having bought him at the Boston Public Market. I knew of slaveholders in Salisbury and had seen Africans before. Not often, but often enough.

I tried not to stare, but I could not help it. The African must have felt my eyes on him, for he turned sharply around and our eyes met. Some kind of connection passed between us, some understanding. He reached a hand toward me, palm up. A small gesture that went unnoticed by others, but it had the power to grasp my soul, for to me it spoke loudly. It said: Help me.

Then Richard Swain gave the African a push to move him forward and he hung his head low, as if he feared what lay ahead.

He should not be afraid, as Jane Swain will be a kind mistress. Richard, I do not know what kind of master he would make. He can be severe and sharp tongued with his wife and children. How, then, fares a slave?

5

Ren and Abraham went down toward the wharf to Tristram's loft, a small rented room above a cordage factory on Water Street. Once again, Abraham deferred, choosing to remain outside and wait for Ren to conclude his business.

Ren climbed the steep stairs to the loft and paused at the open door's threshold. The loft faced Nantucket Harbor with a row of windows that brought in the sea air, clearing out the stink of rendering whale oil that infused so much of the island near the waterfront. Nearly seven years ago, he and his cousin had shaken hands on the start of their business venture in this very room.

He found Tristram seated at his desk — a vastly different desk than the one they had lugged into the small space at the start of their venture. That battered desk had belonged to their great-grandfather Barnabas Starbuck. It was nothing fancy, but there was history in it. This one was a partner's desk, three times the size, made of walnut, with ornately carved legs, and it dominated the room. Tristram's chair was made of forest-green leather with a steep back. For a split second, Ren felt what it must be like to be summoned to meet the king.

His cousin looked up in surprise. "Ren! I didn't expect thee. How does our Jane fare today?"

Ren took a moment to decide how to respond. Before leaving the house this morning, he had sat by Jane's bed and noticed the husky blue on her fingernails had spread from the cuticles to the tips of her fingers. What could that mean? He wasn't sure, but he knew it was not an improvement. "She was sleeping as I left the house."

Tristram's face brightened with relief. "Excellent! Sleep is just what she needs. A day or two of rest will cure her overexcitement."

"Overexcitement?"

"With thy return. That's what Lillian diagnosed. She said Jane was overwrought with thy arrival. Daphne hinted it might be more than that." He seemed sincerely concerned.

Ren hesitated. He wasn't sure how much

he wanted to say, or to whom. His reluctance was not for the protection of Dr. Mitchell, but to shelter the reputation of his beloved Jane. "Mayhap I will find her improved when I finish my business in town and return home."

Tristram nodded as if he understood, but Ren did not think it possible. His cousin's mind was like a hummingbird, flitting from one thing to another, never tarrying too long.

Trist waved at the chair opposite him. "Please, have a chair."

Ren remained standing. "There seems to be a problem at the countinghouse."

"The countinghouse?"

"The countinghouse," Ren repeated, expressionless.

Tristram busied himself with some papers on his desk. "What seems to be the problem?"

"William Rotch said he is unable to distribute lays to the *Endeavour*'s crew."

Trist kept his head down, but lifted his eyes at Ren. "There's a small glitch."

"A small *glitch*? This is a crew that has worked tirelessly for six years. Six *years,* Tristram! And the reason they can't collect their lays, according to Rotch, is because you've already spent the haul by commissioning a ship!"

The tension between them grew as thick as the fog that covered Nantucket on this morning. Tristram bit his lip, pausing, then put the palms of his hands on the arms of his chair and hoisted himself up. "Sit down, Ren. We can talk this through." He hurried to the other side of the partner desk and pulled out a wooden chair. *That* one Ren recognized. "Look, there's a spot waiting for thee."

Ren still refused to sit. He was accustomed to facing trouble on his feet, head on. "You are the one who has talking to do. What of this new ship?"

"I was waiting for the right moment to tell thee. It's all good, Ren. Thee has nothing to worry about."

If that were true, Ren wondered, *then why did Tristram's voice sound so strained? Why did he seem so nervous, so anxious?*

"The *Endeavour* is a doughty old ship. A hulk. Thee has said so thyself. It's a wonder she's lasted these six years. The time has come to sell her and move on."

"I well know the wear and tear of m' own ship." Yet Tristram was not wrong. The *Endeavour* needed extensive repairs before she would be ready for another voyage. But sell her? The thought had never crossed Ren's mind, not once.

"I was hoping the new ship would be here by the time thee returned." Trist's eyes lit with excitement. "And she is a beauty, Ren. A vessel more grand than any coming in and out of port. It's the start of our fleet."

"Our fleet? Tristram, are ye daft, man? One successful voyage does not guarantee the next."

"It was a success, yes, but imagine if thee had sailed on a bigger ship. Imagine the haul thee could have brought in. Ren, listen to me. Spermaceti oil is the export that will make us rich. Ambergris, too. Wealthy beyond our wildest dreams."

"What dreams are you talking of?"

"Ours! The same dreams we've always talked of, ever since we were boys. Sailing ships around the world, chasing the mighty leviathan. Shipbuilding is a booming business. If I hadn't made a decision when I did, it would've been a wait of another year or two." He paused his speech to let Ren take it all in, all the while pacing the small room until he finally stopped moving and stood under the small window. The morning sun streamed over Tristram's head, limning him in sunlight. Briefly, Ren wondered if he'd done it for effect.

"So I used the *Endeavour*'s haul as down

payment," Tristram continued, "to order the building of the new ship."

"You knew nothing of the hold! How long has this been under way? A ship takes as long as a baby to make."

"But I did! The *Deborah* came in last year with news that the *Endeavour* had been spotted in the Caribbean, plowing deep in the water. When word came in, 'twas not difficult to make plans for the future, nor to persuade the right people."

"Who are the right people?"

"The investors! They are willing to wait for their return until after the next ship returns. They have confidence in us, Ren. They understand it takes money to make money." Trist paced back and forth, back and forth. "How can I make thee see the light? Just one more voyage will put us in fine fettle."

"One more voyage?" Ren looked at him, astounded. "Tristram — I have been home but two days. Another voyage could not be farther from my thoughts."

Tristram's face went blank. "Most of the crew has already signed up. I met them on Straight Wharf as the lighters came in from the ship. They gave me their word. All but the first mate and some fellow named Abraham. And thy father. He says he is done loving the sea, that 'tis always an unrequited love. I don't know what he meant by that, but I think he can be persuaded to reconsider."

"Signed up the crew? Signed up!" Ren's voice bellowed throughout the small room. "Before the crew was told they would not be receiving their lay from this last voyage? And you must have *known* all that, Tristram. Have you lost your senses?"

"We'll get it all straightened out."

"Do you have the money to pay the crew's lay?"

A pause. "Nay. I'm a bit short of cash myself these days. I sunk all that I had saved into the new ship."

"How much is the cost of this new ship?"

"Three hundred pounds sterling."

At this point, Ren eased himself down in the hard wooden chair. "Tristram, what have you done?" He felt a trickle of fear run through him. Fear was not an unknown feeling to him. He had sailed nearly to Cape Horn in a creaky old vessel, turning back only when he was convinced the seam of the Pacific and Atlantic Oceans would tear the *Endeavour* in two. Another time, he'd fallen overboard during a severe tempest and could've — should've — died. Yet he had never felt fear like what he'd felt since arriving in Nantucket. Jane's collapse caused a new kind of fear. And now this. Life felt desperately out of control.

First things first. It was the way his mind worked, keeping calm in a panic, quickly arranging the order of tasks. It was a great asset at sea; surely it would carry him through this storm on land. Slowly, he rose from the chair. "I will go to the bank now and see what can be done to pay the crew."

A look of relief swept over Tristram. "Excellent, cousin. They will listen to thee."

"When is this new ship due in?"

"She's a bit late on the tide."

"When, exactly?"

"Next month." He turned to face the window and mumbled, "Perhaps the month after that."

Ren heard.

Tristram whirled around. "The *Illumine.*"

"What?"

"That's the name of the ship. Jane named it. She wanted thee to have this new ship. She gave me her blessing. Wipe that skeptical look off thy face. She did!" He sat down in his chair. "Cousin, forget not . . . . thee was gone for six long years, with hardly a word from thee. Decisions had to be made in thy absence. Thee must understand. Jane did." He paused. "Life had to carry on without thee."

Ren did not disagree, he sympathized far more than Tristram gave him credit for. But it was the shifting of principles that he did not approve of, the borrowing on the future. "Is it true that Jane did not have a stipend for her expenses?"

"Nay, not true! She did, she did. At least . . . up until the ship was commissioned. With Jane's blessing, mind thee." He frowned. "Ren, don't look at me as if I squandered thy earnings. All will be well."

"Nay, Tristram. All will not be well. Six years of hard work has disappeared."

"Disappeared? Hardly! It has been *transferred* to the new ship. Ren, I am trying to plan for the long haul. It takes risk, vision. Thee must not be shortsighted."

Shortsighted. A soft description. Ren wondered how his crew might respond if he told them he could not pay them because he was a bit shortsighted. Mutinies occurred for lesser crimes.

He lifted his chin. "I should keep forging ahead, so that I can return to Jane. Foremost on my mind is distributing the lay to my crew. I must be off to the bank and see what can be arranged."

"Before thee goes, I should tell thee I will be under way to Salem at high tide this afternoon, to see to the *Illumine*. I will be gone a day or two at the most." He smiled brightly. "And when I return, Jane will have recovered, and I will bring thee a full report of our new ship. Nothing but good tidings lie ahead of us, cousin!"

Ren stared at Tristram. His cousin's optimistic nature was infectious, and there were many times when Ren wished he'd more of Tristram's joie de vivre in him. His cousin was a dreamer, with extravagant ideas, and Ren loved him for it. He doubted he would've captained the *Endeavour* without Trist's cheerful confidence in him. Yet he did it, and did it well, and he gave much credit to Tristram for providing the push he'd needed at that critical moment. He hoped his cousin's optimism was fortuitous at this critical juncture, as well. "I pray you have second sight, Trist. Safe travels."

At the bottom of the stairwell, Ren paused, leaning his back against the wall, to gather his thoughts before he went outside and met up with Abraham. His mind was spinning like the wheels of the Old Mill in a squall.

It distressed him greatly that Tristram had commissioned a new ship before waiting until the *Endeavour* returned to Nantucket. They could have lived well off the income from this last voyage. That had been Ren's intention — to remain on island for a while. He would no longer have such a luxury of time but would need to set sail as soon as the new ship arrived from the Salem shipyard and was outfitted — certainly before winter arrived.

This new ship cost three hundred pounds sterling. The cost of insurance alone for the maiden voyage would be at least fifteen guineas. Ren had scarcely a pence left to his name but for the Orange Street house, and he had to find a means to pay his crew what was owed them. A sizable amount. A small fortune. What had Tristram been thinking? Why would Jane have given him her blessing for such an extravagant expenditure?

As he walked outside, into the bright sunlight that had burned off the morning fog, Ren felt bitten by a friendly dog.

All afternoon, there'd been a steady influx of well-meaning relatives to 15 Orange Street, to welcome Ren back and to inquire of Jane's condition. Nearly everyone but Mother, Daphne noted. Cousins Hagar and Kezia sat in the foyer and sipped tea, waiting for their moment to visit with Jane.

They could wait as long as they pleased, for there was no way Daphne would allow those two upstairs to see Jane. They were the gloomiest pair in Nantucket. Each week, they read the obituaries, fully expecting to find their own names.

When Daphne excused herself from listening to the doomful tidings of the elderly cousins, she went into Jane's bedchamber and nearly gasped when she saw that her sister's skin had turned an unearthly pale color. But then, to her delight, she saw that Jane's eyes were wide open. "Jane! Jane, thee is awake!"

Jane tried to lift her head. "Where are my children?"

"They're downstairs, having lunch. They're fine. We've been at the Cent School all morning." Daphne pushed a loose strand of hair behind Jane's ear. "Shall I get them for thee?"

"Nay, nay." Her head dropped back on the pillow. "I don't want them to see me like this."

Daphne sat beside her and reached out to hold her sister's hand. Cold, so cold. She cupped Jane's hand in hers to warm it, noticing how navy blue the fingernails had become.

"Great Mary's book," Jane said, pushing out the words on a breath. " 'Tis thine to keep."

Daphne uttered a small exclamation of

surprise to hear her sister say that, and on the heels of that feeling came . . . embarrassment. Jane must have been aware that Daphne had been reading the journal. "I'm sorry. I found it the other day. I've been reading through it. I know that Father gave it to thee." She tucked the sheets over Jane's cold hands. "Oh sister, 'tis so good to hear thy voice."

Jane's eyes fluttered shut and Daphne thought she'd fallen back to sleep. After a minute or two, her eyes opened and she took in another gasp of air. "My babies." With much effort, she said, "Remember me to them. Remind them how I loved them." She began to pant, shallow gulp. "Daphne, be their mother."

"Jane, thee mustn't talk like this! Thee will recover from this affliction."

"Promise me."

"I do. I promise. But, Sister, 'tis too early for a testament."

"I can feel my life ebbing from me." A tear rolled down Jane's cheek. "Thee must tell them . . ."

"Tell who?" Daphne slipped over to sit on the bed. "Jane, dearest, what does thee want to say?"

Jane's nostrils flared with each breath, as if she was trying to capture every bit of oxygen in the room. "Do not blame him."

"Who? For what?"

Her eyes squeezed shut. "He was . . . trying to help." Her eyes flickered open and she took in a deep breath. "And tell . . ." Her voice drizzled off.

"Who, Jane? I don't know who thee means to tell."

"Ren." She lifted her head slightly. "Ren must exert his mind toward the Light. To relinquish grievances . . . if not for his sake . . . then for the children's."

"He has no grievances, Jane. He only wants thee to be well again."

"Tell Mother."

"Mother?"

She took in another gasp of air. "I forgive her."

"Jane, thee can tell her thyself. Thee will be fine in a day or two. Thee is so strong."

Jane gave a slight shake of her head. "Nay." A bead of sweat broke out on her forehead. "Pretend not with me, Sister." She let her eyelids fall closed and struggled to pull in one more breath. "Each breath feels like . . . when we were children . . . at the beach . . . when we would bury each other in the sand. The sand . . . it's piling up on my chest." Her eyes flickered open. "Soon . . . there will be too much."

Downstairs, Daphne heard a heavy rap on the door. She heard Patience open it and murmur something, then the familiar deep voice of a man. "Jane, Dr. Mitchell has come."

"Get him."

As Daphne hurried down the stairs, she waved to the doctor to come.

Dr. Mitchell started up the stairs, meeting Daphne halfway. "How does she fare today?"

"Better, I think. Much better." She relaxed somewhat, but not completely. "See for thyself." Dr. Mitchell followed behind her to the top of the stairs.

He paused at the doorjamb to Jane's bedchamber, a startled look on his face when he took in the condition of his patient. He strode to the bed, dropped his bag, and pressed four fingers to the pulse of Jane's wrist. He glanced at Daphne. "She's losing strength."

"Nay . . . nay," Daphne said, panic rising in her throat. "Thee is wrong. She is no longer in a stupor."

He frowned, set Jane's hand on the sheet, and took Daphne by the elbow, gently leading her out of the room and closing the door behind her. She stood there, fidgeting like a child, pacing in the small hallway. When the door opened and Dr. Mitchell finally came out, she was alarmed by the defeated look on his face.

"Did she speak to thee? She is no longer confused. I told thee, she is getting better."

He shook his head. "Just try and keep her comfortable. Let everyone in who wants to say their goodbyes."

Daphne's heart started to pound. "Goodbyes? But . . . she's turned the corner! She spoke to me with great clarity."

"About what?"

"About . . . about giving others a message."

The doctor sighed. "I've seen this before, Daphne. Sometimes people get a burst of strength. It's a gift from God, is my opinion, so they can finish up their business."

"But . . . she was talking . . ."

"Lungs can only take so much. When they are pushed too far, they cannot endure. Like a punctured balloon."

Panic tore through Daphne. *Ren.* Where was he? She should get him. And the children. And Mother! But she couldn't bear to leave her sister's side. "Would thee send for Ren? I think . . . he went to see Tristram. Or mayhap he went to the bank." That was hours ago! Where was he?

He patted her shoulder in a fatherly way.

"I'll locate the captain and send him here at once. But thee . . . thee must stay by thy sister's side."

When Daphne went into Jane's room, she realized there was a change from just a moment ago. Jane's face was sheened with sweat. Her breath came in gasps, rapid and shallow, and there was a sharp pulling of the chest below and between the ribs with each intake. Her flesh was white and cold, her lips nearly purple.

"Jane, oh Jane, don't go. Hold on, please hold on. Don't leave us. Ren is coming. Please hold on."

"Fear not, Sister," Jane wheezed, gasping for a breath, "for God . . . is with me. And . . . with thee."

Daphne lay beside her sister and held her in her arms, trying to match her breathing, to sustain her. The gasping ceased, and her breath seemed easier. Then there was a pause, and Jane's breath eased out in a slight puff, as if she was releasing something.

Daphne waited for Jane to take in a breath, but it did not come.

MARY COFFIN STARBUCK

15 September 1662

In the course of a few weeks, a new life has begun on Nantucket Island, and an old life has ended.

Old Rachel Swain passed in her sleep a few days back. 'Twas not unexpected, as she had been knocking at death's door all winter long. But the time had come for the first grave to be dug, and Father chose the field where sits the oak tree that my dear friend Eleazer Foulger and I are so particularly partial to. Fortunately, Father did not instruct others to dig anywhere near the oak tree, but right in the center of the meadow. He called the field "Founders' Burial Ground" and then he marked his own spot! It struck me as a bit morbid, but Father is a practical man.

"Someday, Mary," he said, "my grandchildren will come to this field and remember me."

I looked at him, and he looked at me, and then we both of us started to grin, despite the solemnity of the event. I do not think of my father as a particularly clairvoyant man. Grandchildren! How did he know? How in the world did he know?

6

After an hour or two spent haggling with Ezra Barnard, the manager at the Pacific Bank, Ren finally had a goodly sum in hand to pay his crew their due. But it cost him a profound loss.

Ezra Barnard had refused to extend any credit to Ren or to take out any loan, as if he considered Ren to be a bad risk. " 'Tis not personal, Captain Macy, but bank policy." He would not budge on that.

Ren had reviewed his options. His father would give him the cash if he had any, but he did not. Everything Jeremiah had left was sunk in the *Endeavour.* His mother-in-law had plenty of money, was one of the wealthiest women on the island, but she would not part with a copper pence, not if it benefited Ren.

Tristram had put them in a dreadful position. If Ren could not pay his crew within a reasonable period, he would have no crew.

No sailor would ever sign on with him again. Nor should they — he could not blame them. The crew had risked life and limb for six years. They had earned their lay. And if he could not attract a crew, no investor would back him.

Slanting his beady eyes at Ren, Ezra whispered, "There might be one stone left unturned. My wife has always had a hankering for 15 Orange Street."

A sick feeling roiled through Ren. The Orange Street house had been bought and paid for in full — it was his wedding gift to Jane. It was a modest house for the street, but at least it was on *the* street. The whaling captains' street. He had not wanted her to have any cause for worry during his absence.

But now it had to be sold.

After signing the deed over to Barnard, he went outside into the bright sunlight, blinking as his eyes adjusted to the light. He forgot Abraham had been waiting for him. "Abraham, come along back to the countinghouse. The lays can be distributed now."

Abraham glanced at the bank, then looked at him with that patient look of his. "I can wait on mine, Captain."

That was a kindness, as Ren knew the other crew would not wait. Nor should they.

After he left the crew's lay at the counting-house and walked down Centre Street toward Orange Street, his throat felt tight and his chest was weighted with a strange sadness, as if he were grieving for something that had never been. A thing that never even was, only imagined.

Six years ago, he had kissed his bride and sailed away from Nantucket Island, con-vinced he was doing the right thing. A few years at sea and he would have built a foundation for the rest of his and Jane's life together.

Today, his wife hovered on the brink of life and death, and after all that time away from her — time in which he stubbornly insisted the *Endeavour* would not return without a full hold, thus he let six long years pass by — he was walking away from the countinghouse with nothing left to his name.

But he could not, would not succumb to panic. He had to keep a steady hand on the tiller and a keen eye on the horizon. Tris-tram's cockeyed optimism had put their livelihood in serious jeopardy, but if all went according to his cousin's plan, it might just work. And Jane *had* survived those critical twenty-four hours after her collapse. She was young, strong, determined. Surely, good health would prevail. Mayhap there would be good news waiting for him at the house. Mayhap Jane was improving by the minute. His spirits brightened at the thought and he picked up his steps.

As he approached 15 Orange Street, he saw Daphne sitting on the steps of the house. Memories flashed through his mind. Once he had asked Jane if all Quakers were as quiet as she. "My sister," Jane said, "is not quiet." How true. Daphne was a chatterbox, lively and animated. He felt a special fondness for her, as he was an only child and missed having sisters or brothers of his own.

He recalled how Daphne would wait on the steps for him, just like she was now, to run interference, keeping him posted to Lillian's whereabouts. The sight of her had always brought a smile to his face.

But today, as Ren drew closer to the house, he saw tears running down Daphne's face. Ren clamped his jaw shut so hard his teeth ached.

He knew.

It took Ren a while to wrap his head around the words Daphne had spoken on the porch steps, even though he had no doubt what she was going to tell him. He felt as if he heard them, yet didn't hear them at all. Jane was . . . gone? He grasped her hands in his. "Were you with her? When she died? She wasn't alone, was she?"

Daphne shook her head so hard the tears splashed onto their clasped hands. "She wasn't alone. I was right beside her. Breath for breath. And then she did not take in the next breath. I realized she'd —" her voice broke — "she'd gone."

I can't bear this, he thought. *I can't bear another moment.* And yet, he had to. There was too much to do, too many problems to solve, to allow himself to feel anything. He pushed away the weakness that had started to seep through him. *Not now.* "Daphne, if you don't mind, stay with me to tell the children. I think they will need you to be near. And after that, I'm hoping you could be the one to tell your mother."

"Of course." She nodded dumbly. "Of course."

Telling the children was the hardest thing he'd ever had to do, his voice sounded strange even to his own ears. He could barely get the words out for his throat had grown so sore. All of him had grown so sore. He made himself say the words, that their mother had gone to heaven, and he knew that this day would forever be marked in their hearts. What was unbearable would eventually become bearable, but all their hearts would be scarred. There were some losses you never got over.

Daphne hugged Hitty while they cried together. Henry sat stock-still in the chair; he didn't cry. The boy's reaction worried Ren more than the girl's.

Before they had told the children, Ren had gone to his dead wife's bedchamber and put his lips on her delicate cheek. Her face had taken on the ashen-gray color of a gone-cold fire.

So still, so lifeless. Ren studied the face that had seen him through storms at sea, dreary doldrums, wild Nantucket sleighrides, and safely into harbor at last. He looked at her with the great love that had always been the mark of Macy men. His grandfather had enjoyed the good fortune of a loving wife in the sensible Libby Macy, his father had found a love in Angelica Foulger that few men find in their lifetime. From the first moment Ren saw Jane, walking along Main Street, he had loved only her. Moving again to cradle her face in his hands, memorizing each beloved feature, he said, "Goodbye, my darling Jane." Then his voice broke. "I'm so sorry I failed you so completely. 'Tis the last thing

I wanted to do, was to fail you."

As he sat by the bedside, he thought of what Daphne had told him on the steps of Jane's last few moments, of lucidity and clarity. Of her hard-wrought messages for the children.

Ren had set his jaw and looked away. "Had she no word for me?"

Daphne dropped her eyes to her lap, the brown silk of her skirt rustled as she shifted her feet. "She did. She said thee must exert thy mind toward the Light and relinquish past grievance. If not for thy sake, then for the children. And she said . . . to not blame thee. That thee was trying to help."

No words of love? Of regret for the time they'd lost together? Merely warnings. Tears stung Reynolds Macy's eyes.

He should not feel slighted, but he did. And yet he knew it was his own fault. He had sailed away, leaving Jane to make a life of her own. He shouldn't resent the fact that the life she'd made left no room for him.

He was the one who'd insisted on going whaling. He had no right to go gadding about the world for all these years, only to show up back here and expect . . . expect . . . what?

To have a place at all.

Daphne sent word to her mother, through Abraham, to come to Orange Street as quickly as possible, yet her mother did not come. Instead, she sent word back for Daphne to return to the house by five o'clock, as they were expected for dinner at the Gardners'. Daphne crinkled the paper and threw it into the kitchen hearth.

She needed to go to her mother, to tell her in person. As she opened the front door, she was surprised to see that the fog was gone and the sun was shining brightly. When had that happened? How could but a few hours have passed? Her sister was gone from this earth, yet life carried on as if it were an ordinary day. It felt almost cruel. She walked slowly through the streets, numbly, trying to absorb all that had occurred in the last few days. How could life have changed so quickly? It wasn't fair. It wasn't right!

When she reached her childhood home, hers and Jane's, she thought of how many times the sisters had crossed this threshold. It suddenly occurred to her that one of the saddest things about losing a sibling was that there was no one left to share memories with.

She found her mother in the drawing room seated in her favorite damask chair, sewing on her needlework. Her mother glanced up when she saw her. And like she was commenting on the weather, she said, "Oh good. Thee is home. Hurry and change into thy green frock for dinner."

Daphne turned and blinked at her. No word to ask of Jane, of the children, of Ren. Her mother had spent the last six years pretending she had no elder daughter, no grandchildren. Daphne sat in the chair across from her. "She's gone, Mama. Jane died today. Early in the afternoon, she took her last breath. I was with her when she died. The children were downstairs, having lunch in the kitchen with Patience, like it was just a regular day. But it wasn't."

The words hung there in the air between them, pulsing.

"Did thee hear me? I said that Jane is dead."

The color drained from her mother's face. She rose unsteadily from her chair and came close so that Daphne looked into her smooth, pretty face. She gripped Daphne's arms in a tight clasp, so tight it hurt. "I knew this would happen. When she married that man . . . I knew her life was ruined. That it was over for her."

"Mama," Daphne said softly, "Jane's death has nothing to do with marrying Ren."

"It has everything to do with him." She released Daphne and put her hands to her temples, as if struck by a sudden pain. "She turned her back on me, her father, her faith."

"She never did. She never turned away from thee, not Father, not her faith." Daphne paused, wondering if it would be wise or foolish to say more. But it had to be said. Someone had to say it. "It was thee who turned away from her."

Her mother's shoulders jerked, as if she'd suddenly come awake from a deep sleep. "Thee makes me sound like a monster. Thee is purely hateful to me. Just like Jane was."

Daphne stared back at her. "Jane did not have a hateful bone in her body. She was always trying to interest thee in her children, to bring thee into her life. Thee is the one who refused her. Thee is the one who cares more about what others think than what God thinks."

Lillian clapped her hands over her ears. "Thee hush up! How dare thee speak to thy mother like that! Jane was a different girl before he stole her from me."

129

Daphne took a deep breath to calm herself, and her stays stabbed into her sides again. "Thee is placing all thy anger thee holds against Father on Reynolds Macy. Ren does not deserve thy wrath."

"Stop it!" her mother said, her voice loud and sharp.

"Ren's only crime is that he is a lapsed Friend. I have no doubt he was ever unfaithful to Jane, not like Father was to you."

Her mother hauled back her hand and slapped Daphne so hard across the face that she rocked backward and fell onto the chair. "Do not speak to me of thy father. Nor of Reynolds Macy! Nor of Jane!"

Daphne brought a trembling hand up to her cheek. "Jane deserves to be remembered. And Ren is suffering, Mama." She pushed herself up. "I will remain at Orange Street for a while to help with the children. I'm going upstairs to gather a few things."

"Thee cannot remain at that house without a chaperone! What will others think?"

Daphne didn't care what anyone on the island thought. Wearily, she walked toward the stairs. She put her hand on the newel post, fingering the mortgage button, made of scrimshaw. "Jane gave me a message for thee, Mama. It was one of the last things she said."

Her mother lifted her head but did not turn to look at Daphne.

"Jane wanted thee to know that she forgives thee." Slowly, Daphne walked up the stairs. By the time she had reached the top, she heard her mother burst into tears.

Jane Coffin Macy's memorial service was held two days later, after First Day Meeting. Her body was laid to rest in the Quaker Cemetery on Madaket Road. There would be no monument for her, as the Friends did not believe in such worldly things. It was a flawlessly clear day, and gulls scolded from an azure sky while mourners pressed in a wide, deep circle around the grave. Ren was there, of course, with his children beside him, along with Tristram, Daphne, her mother, and aunts, uncles, and many cousins from both sides of the family. Many Friends had come, as well.

Daphne wore a beige silk dress, as mourning clothes were not permitted, nor was excessive grieving. The Friends did not believe in mourning the dead but in celebrating one's life.

That evening, after the service, Daphne helped the children get to sleep. This third night without their mother. She cupped Henry's face, looking into his sad eyes.

"Why did Mama die?"

"Her body was sick and couldn't get better. But she is well now. She is in heaven."

"Why didn't God make her better?"

"I don't know, Henry. But Scripture tells us that our days are ordained before we are even born. God knew exactly how long thy mother would be on this earth." She tucked the sheet more snugly around Henry, then Hitty.

As she turned to leave, Hitty said in a small, tight voice, "Will thee lay down with us for a time?"

So Daphne turned down the lamp and stretched out beside them, beside Jane's children in the dark, waiting for their breathing to fall into the soft, gentle sign of sleep. Hitty fell asleep first, but Henry lay in bed with his eyes wide open. "Still can't sleep?"

He shook his head.

"Let's go downstairs. I'll make thee some warm milk."

She went into the kitchen and found Ren alone, standing in the middle of the room as if he weren't quite sure how he'd come to be there.

"Ren, can I help thee find something?"

"Nay, thank you." He glanced at Henry. "Should not the boy be in bed?"

Daphne felt it before she saw it coming. Something exploded within Henry. His face grew red and his eyes went wide, and it was like he couldn't hold it in another moment. "Thee did this!" he shouted at Ren. "If thee hadn't come back, Mama wouldn't be dead!"

Henry ran toward the door, but Daphne grabbed him and forced him to face her. "Henry, that is not true. 'Tis a wonderful thing that thy father is here. 'Tis no accident that he arrived when he did."

"She was fine before he came and as soon as he came, she got sick. And then she died!" He choked to a stop. "I *hate* him! I want him to leave and never come back!" Henry jerked away from her and ran upstairs.

Daphne turned to Ren, who stared at the closed door with an expression of helplessness. "Is that really what the boy thinks?"

And now it was Daphne's turn to speak out. In a bold, controlled voice she said, "He's not 'the boy,' Ren. He's not a cabin boy. He's not a crewman. He's thy *son*. His name is Henry and he is thy *son*. And Hitty, she is thy *daughter*."

Ren looked as though someone had wrenched his heart out of his breast and wrung it empty. "Aye, I ken, I ken." He sank

133

down onto a chair, shoulders drooped.

It was quiet in the kitchen, so quiet, she could hear both of them breathing. It made her think of Jane, struggling so for breath, for air.

"Listen," he said, after a while of silence between them. "Six years at sea can make a man lose his civility. I've never been around children much. M' own mother said I never was one. I don't know how to talk to wee ones, other than to sound like a whaling captain." He set his arms on the table and leaned forward. "The girl, Hitty, she answers me in a polite, subdued voice. Henry remains silent, other than just now, telling m' he wished I'd go back to the sea. To tell the truth, I prefer his shouting to his silence." He tried to smile at her, but he couldn't manage it. He steepled his fingers in front of his mouth. "The poor little ones, they must be hurting in a keen way, seeing their dear mother lowered into a grave today."

And he was hurting too. She wanted to comfort him, but she wasn't sure how.

After a long moment, Ren lifted his head. "Daphne, if you don't mind, I think I need to be alone."

She nodded and left the kitchen, then remembered she had forgotten Henry's warm milk. When she opened the kitchen door, she saw Ren lower his head to the small table and cover his face with his hands. His back shuddered, hard. Shuddered with harsh, silent, wrenching sobs.

Quietly she backed up and closed the door.

MARY COFFIN STARBUCK

20 September 1662

Summer has returned to the island after leaving us for a few weeks and, I had feared, was gone for good. Happily, the days are once again quite warm. Hot and humid, even. No one complains, for winter is whispering of her arrival with increasingly early twilights and red-leafed cranberry bushes.

Putting up gardens is what is on the islanders' minds, as we learned a hard lesson from past years. Winters on Nantucket can be very long and very cold.

In Salisbury, we put up our garden but not as extensively as on Nantucket. We must have five times the produce that Mother and I used to put up, and there is still more to do. Tomorrow, all the green beans will be picked and pickled and canned. Catherine pickles everything! All fruits, all vegetables — anything that isn't dried, but for a few apples and potatoes and carrots. She is overly generous with vinegar and salt.

My mouth puckers even as I write. My hair stinks of brine and vinegar, and my hands and arms have burns from hot syrup and beeswax. My mind often floats back to the ease of going to the shops in Salisbury and simply buying what Mother needed. Such ease is not possible on an island. My store is the only shop, and it has far more fish hooks and harpoons than canning spices.

Everyone takes great pride in being self-sufficient. It is satisfying to look at the shelves in the kitchen and see the rainbow of bottled colors among the fruits and vegetables. God has provided so many variations of colors for our eating pleasure! Blackberries, orange carrots, red rhubarb, bright green peas. Treats for the eyes, as well as the bellies.

Salt hay has been gathered from the meadow for the sheep; the corncrib is full of dried corn for the milk cows. The pigs are fattening fast and will be slaughtered in a few months, Esther's aging hens will be bottled, and Nathaniel and his father are spending these September days hunting for deer. In short, the Starbuck household is ready for winter.

Catherine has appreciated my help, and I see that Nathaniel was right. As I put more effort into caring for the Starbucks, she has grown more tolerant of me. As long as I defer to her and let her tell me what to do, we seem to get along fairly well. She is very sensitive, as is Esther, although their sensitivity extends only to their own tender feelings.

It is wearing at times to hold my tongue, but it is a good and needed discipline. It lessens the strain I feel with Nathaniel, for he gets tugged back and forth between mother and wife. All in all, 'tis not an easy thing, this joining to another family. I long for a home of my own.

Someday, Nathaniel assures me, and I have learned 'tis futile to press him any further. My own father was a man of action; no sooner had he heard of a new venture, and he was ordering Mother to pack up. My husband is the opposite. He is cautious by nature, and satisfied with "somedays."

Father has made many mistakes by bending to his impulsive nature. Nathaniel has made very few. The fact that I chose a man like Nathaniel is telling, is it not?

And therein lies my answer. "Someday" will come soon enough.

15 October 1662

This morning, the yard was covered with hoarfrost and the water bucket had a thin layer of ice on top. 'Tis a warning of what is soon to come.

I had thought that with winter approaching, I would have more time for writing, but I've decided that there is less to write about in the colder months.

Today is an exception.

Catherine is beside herself. She received a letter from her eldest child, Sarah Varney, who lives over on the mainland. Sarah has become a Quaker!

Catherine cannot stop weeping. She thinks her daughter's soul has been lost. She is inconsolable.

Peter Foulger came into the store today and did not seem to be in a hurry, which is one of the things I enjoy about him. He always seems to have plenty of time for important conversations, though I know he is a purposeful man with many demands on him. I offered to make him a cup of tea, and he happily accepted, settling into a chair by the stove. I told him about Sarah Varney's conversion. "It is startling to realize that the Quakers are making headway into converting others," I said.

He agreed, and so I posed the question that was on my mind, "Do you agree that a Quaker is lost to God?"

Peter smiled. "They do not think so. Their concern is for everyone else to see and respond to the Inner Light as they do."

That did not satisfy me, and I was hopeful he was not going to leave me with a question to answer my question. He often does.

He sipped his tea thoughtfully. "Mary, have you ever seen a stone archway?"

"I have. In Boston."

"An arch is an architectural marvel. It holds together because the stones are carved to fit together perfectly."

I wasn't sure where he was going with this, but I knew Peter well enough to know that something wonderful might soon unfold to satisfy my curiosity about Quakerism.

" 'Tis that center piece that keeps the arch in place. The keystone." He finished his tea, rose, and handed the teacup back to me. " 'Tis all about the keystone, Mary. Think on that." Then he lifted his hand in a cheerful wave and left the store.

Think on . . . what?

16 October 1662

I woke in the night with the answer to Peter's riddle.

The keystone! 'Tis the essential piece. Christ is our Savior and King, that is the keystone to the theological arch.

Peter was trying to say that if the keystone is properly in place, we need not worry about the other stones.

7

In the days and weeks that followed his wife's death, Reynolds Macy spent most of his time making repairs on the *Endeavour.* It was the only place he felt entirely at ease. He supposed it was a shock to the senses to be on land after six years of the sea providing her own constant rhythm, but he couldn't sleep at the house. He'd slept so many years alone, and now he couldn't seem to do it. So he would toss and turn through the night and leave at dawn's first light. Abraham was always waiting for him on the house steps, no matter how early the hour. They would walk to the wharf, stopping briefly when they passed Jeremiah's small house on Easy Street. The cooper was usually out front, puffing on his pipe.

"Son, you fine?" Jeremiah would ask.

"I'm fine, Dad. You fine?"

"Fine," he grunted. "Just fine."

That was the extent of their conversation,

yet it said much. Side by side, father and son would walk to the dory, Abraham a few feet behind them, and row out to the *Endeavour* for the day's work, staying there until it grew dark.

The first few days, he had tried to discourage both Jeremiah and Abraham from accompanying him. Abraham, Ren insisted, should be looking to sign on another ship. His father should be spending his time setting up the cooperage and hunting for business. There were many coopers on Nantucket, but the demand for casks always outpaced the availability. Jeremiah would have no trouble reestablishing himself. Both men ignored his protests. His father said that barrels could wait. Abraham said he only worked for Captain Reynolds Macy.

Unable to speak, Ren had to fight back a lump in his throat. He was grateful, more than he could possibly say, for such loyalty and devotion.

The hours of daylight were long in August, and they were easily filled up with repair tasks: cleaning and scraping every inch of her hull. Re-caulking seams, holystoning decks before slathering them with thick varnish. Checking each rigger to order new shrouds, sheets, and stays from the sailmaker's shop. Measuring hemp to be woven by

143

the ropemaker.

Ren had made it a point of pride that he could himself perform every task he asked of his crew. He had worked every job on a ship. He'd sailed since he was eight, serving as cabin boy, working his way up, and quickly became familiar with every creak and moan of any ship he sailed on. It was a ship's way of breathing, inhaling and exhaling, he believed, evidence of her unique personality. The creak of her hull, the tap of her sails on the mast, the flutter of the mainsail's leech when she turned up too close to the wind. If a sailor learned to listen, he could hear warnings that might save his life. It was like watching the sky and learning to read signs: certain clouds predicted certain weather changes.

The *Endeavour* was the first ship Ren loved; she had rewarded them trebly. And Tristram wanted to sell her off to the highest bidder, to toss her aside for a new, younger ship. She might be old, but her bones were still intact. An amazing little ship that had traveled so far, up and down the Atlantic Sea, had acted as home for the crew and seen them through a hundred storms. She was a living, breathing vessel.

Breathe. The very word turned his thoughts to Jane, of how she had struggled to breathe. Odd that he had always been attuned to the sounds of breathing; strange that his dear Jane would have died because she was unable to fill her lungs with enough air.

Jane was the first, the *only* girl, Ren had ever loved. She and the *Endeavour* would always be linked together in his mind. Trist had said he was eager to set a date for the next voyage, on the soon-to-arrive *Illumine*. But if Ren sold the *Endeavour,* left her behind for a new ship, would he not be leaving Jane behind too?

Tristram scolded that he was overly sentimental about the ship, that they must keep their heads clear of emotion. And there was some truth to that. A ship was made up of wood and nails.

And yet, and yet . . . Ren did not cast off his first loves so easily.

He grimaced. Too much thinking. He could not shake off the fantods. This was why he felt the need to spend his days on this ship, to stop thinking, grieving, berating himself for being such a poor husband. To make himself so tired from physical labor that he returned each night to Orange Street exhausted, ready to sleep.

Those were the best days, when the only pain he felt was a weary ache in his muscles and bones.

The worst days were when he felt a nearly overwhelming guilt from those last words of Jane's. To not blame himself, that he was only trying to help.

He'd ruined her life. How could he not blame himself?

One morning, Ren planned to stop by the magistrate's office before heading out to the *Endeavour,* so he was later than usual. He strode boldly into the kitchen to scrounge for bread and tea and stopped short at the sight of Daphne seated at the table with the maidservant. As soon as he entered the room, the maidservant jumped from the chair, headed immediately for the water pail across the room, grabbed it, and scooted out the back door. His very presence seemed to alarm everyone in his house. All but Daphne.

He watched the back door close. "Am I so terribly frightening?"

She nodded solemnly. "Very much so."

His mouth quirked up at one corner, amused by her candor but then not at all surprised, and he felt himself ease. "My mother used to say that I could look down-right ferocious when I was serious, which was all the time."

Daphne laughed aloud at that, and he laughed a little too. It felt good, laughing did. "And yet, I daresay I don't frighten you."

"Nay, but then I was raised by Lillian Swain Coffin. Thee seems like a kitten after living with a lion."

He chuckled. "Might a man help himself to a cup of tea?"

" 'Tis already prepared. I'll get it for thee."

He lifted a hand. "Stay seated. I must learn to do these things for myself." He filled a china cup with the lovely amber-colored liquid. Tea was a wonderment, he thought, as he took his first sip. It had a way of calming the soul. He sat in a chair at the small table, facing Daphne. He rarely sat in the kitchen. When he returned late at night, Patience served him in the dining room. It was rather cozy in the kitchen. He glanced at Daphne, scribbling on a piece of paper. "Am I interrupting you?"

"I was going over the household schedule with Patience."

His eyebrows lifted in surprise. "The maidservant can read?"

"She's very bright. I'm trying to teach her all I can about thy household." She put the quill pen down. "Ren, I'm not sure how much longer Mother will let me stay at

Orange Street. She's terribly concerned what others will think."

It hadn't occurred to him what others would think. He took a sip of tea. He was no longer at sea, no longer the captain. He was living on an island, a small Quaker island, filled with rules and regulations. He had to start making some adjustments. "I understand." Though, he really didn't understand the narrow thinking of Lillian Coffin.

This would be the opportune time to tell Daphne that he had sold the house to Ezra Barnard. He *should* say something, but he couldn't bring himself to say it aloud. Not yet. Everything felt so raw, he couldn't add another change to the children's lives. Nor to his own. And the banker had given him two months' notice. There was time. "You're aware of this ship Tristram has commissioned?"

She lowered her eyes. "I am."

"Tristram said Jane gave him her blessing to order its building."

"That is the truth."

He leaned forward on the table, watching her. "Daphne, you don't approve of this ship, do you?"

She dipped her chin. " 'Twas not a question they asked of me."

148

He swirled his tea. "I have heard rumblings that Tristram and thee . . . might soon wed."

She jerked her head up, her brows furrowed. "Then thee is listening to nothing but idle gossip. We have no such plans."

He felt properly scolded. She did not mince words, this girl. Nay, she was no girl. She was a grown woman, with thoughts and opinions of her own. He reached out for an orange, put it to his nose to sniff its fruitiness, put it back and selected another. From the pinched expression about her mouth, mayhap he should leave that particular topic alone.

"Usually thee is long gone by this hour," she said.

"I want to pay a call on the magistrate. I am of a mind to make a charge against Dr. Mitchell."

Daphne's face went blank. "For Jane's death?"

"Yesterday, as I returned the dory to its slip, I heard sailors talk of two stevedores who died that same week, of similar poisoning. Someone must be held accountable."

"The doctor insisted he hadn't given Jane that tincture."

"He admitted he had given her laudanum. The silver flask had an engraved *M* on it, did it not?"

" 'Tis not an uncommon flask."

"Daphne, I need to pursue this. For Jane's sake." Ren drew a circle on the top of the table. He might have been a poor husband, but he was not responsible for the death of Jane. Dr. Mitchell was, though the man would not admit it. He'd tried twice to seek out the magistrate, but his office was always shut tight. The last thing he could do for Jane was to make sure this fraud of a doctor brought no harm to anyone else.

But from the look on Daphne's face, she did not agree. He thought she would say that he must forgive the doctor, that to err is human. But what irked Ren was that the doctor wouldn't even admit that he'd made a mistake. Dr. Mitchell denied any wrong-doing, absolved himself, and kept doling out grains of laudanum.

But apparently that wasn't at all what was running through Daphne's mind.

"Thee will have to wait. The magistrate is on the mainland. I believe he isn't due back for a week or so."

"Blast." Justice would have to keep waiting. But Ren was a patient man. There was a time for all things, that much he had learned from a life at sea. He took a sip of tea, and changed topics once again. "Why has thee helped Jane with this Cent School? I doubt Lillian would approve."

"Mother doesn't know. Well, that's probably not true. There are few secrets on Nantucket Island."

"Don't tell me that you've been lying to your own mother?" He grinned. "I thought Quakers did not lie."

"We don't. There's been no need to lie. Mother never asked where I was going. She doesn't want to know."

A laugh burst out of Ren. That sounded more like Lillian. He tore into the skin of the orange, peeling it off. The sweet scent drifted up. He handed a piece to Daphne with a half jest, "To fend off scurvy," and then began sectioning the rest. He lifted a crescent of orange to his mouth, biting into the sweetness. "But that doesn't answer my question."

Daphne stilled. "I suppose . . ." She ran a finger along the pen quill's feather. "Jane had a saying: 'Love and attention make all things grow.' I suppose the answer is that I want to work in the garden Jane planted."

At that, Ren sobered, and he studied Daphne's face.

The garden Jane planted.

He tipped his head. "The children in the school . . . they are all white. Do not African mothers need help with their children? Wampanoag mothers?"

She frowned. "Jane tried, but it was not feasible."

He arched his eyebrows. "Jane wanted to allow colored children?"

"She did. But too many complained and threatened to disenroll their children. She couldn't afford it."

"And yet the Friends are united in believing that enslavement is wrong."

"True."

"But far from united in what action they should take about the matter."

Daphne stiffened. " 'Tis not such a simple matter."

"Indeed. I have noticed that most Nantucketers benefit from products of enslavement."

He could see her temper flare. "I do not wear cotton clothing."

"Nay, but you do shop at the Dry Goods store. You buy cotton thread, do you not?"

She looked away.

"And what about sugar for your tea? And as I recall, your father enjoyed tobacco in his pipe."

She crossed her arms. "Nantucket abolished slavery in 1773."

"And where do the Negroes live? In a

cluster called New Guinea, far from the white community, near the NewTown Gate, where the barrier is meant to keep the sheep out of town. And immediately adjacent is Gallows Field. And where are the Negroes buried, Daphne? In the Colored Cemetery, far from the Friends cemetery."

He could tell from the look on her face that he was pushing her too far. "I don't mean to place blame on you, Daphne. I know 'tis not a simple matter. I do." Out the window, he saw Abraham help Patience peg wet laundry on the line, smiling as he told her something. Whatever it was, it made her laugh. Ren felt a strange longing well up, and realized he envied Abraham at that moment. Envied his untroubled life.

"He is a good man, this Abraham? He seems quite devoted to thee."

"He is the finest seaman I have ever sailed with." He leaned back in his chair. "He saved my life."

Daphne looked at him. "What happened?"

"We were caught in a tempest, one of the worst storms I'd ever faced. All hands were on deck, trying to keep the *Endeavour*'s rigging in one piece. The deck was icy, tilting and pitching the men. Then a boom broke loose, swung round to hit me from behind and knocked me right over the edge. Abra-

153

ham was the only one who saw me go overboard and helped me get back to the ship. 'Twas a defining moment for me."

"How so?"

"I should not have survived it. I felt as if I'd had a calling from God in that experience, that he had spared me for a reason."

"For what reason?"

"That, I do not know. I had an overwhelming sense that I was saved for a purpose. I don't think it had ever occurred to me to question what God thought of me, not until that moment in the sea, when I was cast overboard and the ship was sailing away from me." He swirled the tea in his cup. "I was alone, yet I wasn't alone. I can't explain it, but something . . . Someone was there with me. That presence . . . it took away my fear." He looked away. He hadn't meant to bring up such an intimate topic. There was something about Daphne that made him reveal more than he intended. Her careful listening, he supposed. He heard Patience's low laughter through the open window. "I have been wondering about a household matter. With the finances in peril, how did Jane afford to pay the maidservant?" When Daphne didn't respond, he leaned forward and said, "Ah. Now I see. You've been her benefactor."

She rose from the table and picked up her half-empty teacup. She stood before him straight as a mast, her face calm and resolute. "I'm not doing anything Jane would not have done for me."

On that point, she was right. Jane adored her younger sister. The two didn't resemble each other, never had. Daphne was taller than most women, sturdy, curvaceous, with thick blonde hair and dark, dark eyes that snapped — they *truly* sparkled — while Jane was brown-eyed, petite, with a beauty that took a man's breath away. Daphne wasn't beautiful in the classical sense, not like Jane, but Ren had to admit she had a striking face. Her dark eyebrows were thick and uncompromising. Her mouth was wide and a bit too full. It was her bones, he thought, those high cheekbones and squared jaw that gave her such a look of strength, of determined resolve. It was a warrior's face, he realized. She was tougher, stronger than he remembered her to be.

"Hitty and Henry, they are my niece and nephew, Ren. I love them nearly as much . . . ," and she choked up on the words, ". . . nearly as much as Jane loved them."

As she crossed the room, he reached out to stop her. "You are a wonder with them, and I know I haven't thanked you properly.

I haven't thanked you at all."

She looked down at his hand on her forearm, covered it quickly, and said, "We are family. No thanks is needed."

Daphne finished reading a story to the children and set them to work drawing pictures on their slates. The morning was warm, so she opened the door and there stood Tristram Macy. "Well, look who it is! Where has thee been?"

"I've been back and forth between here and the Salem shipyard. Just returned on last night's tide."

"But I haven't seen thee since . . ." She stopped abruptly. She was going to say she hadn't seen him since Jane's memorial service, but his eyes suddenly seemed to glisten with tears.

"The weather," he said, looking away. "Summer squalls held me up on the mainland."

The weather had been terrible these last few weeks, wet and stormy, churning the seas. Even the fishermen were complaining, and that took some doing. She moved toward him, first one step and then another. She turned and looked back through the open door. "Would thee like to come inside? Hitty and Henry would be delighted to see thee. They've missed thee. They've asked after thee."

He paused a moment, as if he'd become lost in his thoughts. "Mayhap another time. I have some business to attend to this morning."

"I can imagine. When will the *Illumine* arrive in Nantucket Harbor?"

"Soon." Then he flashed her a flirtatious smile, that smile that belonged only to him, the one that made Nantucket matrons' and maidens' knees turn to water. "I am sorry, Daph. I should have let thee know I was going off island."

Should he have? He never did consult her in his plans, so she didn't expect him to.

"Jane's passing . . . it shook me. I needed to get away. Have some time to think. To grieve. She was like a sister to me."

She was *my sister,* Daphne thought. *I am grieving too. So is Ren, so are the children. What about us?*

"I stopped by to see if thee might know where Ren is. I went to the house but no one answered the door."

Oh. So Tristram hadn't stopped by the Cent School to see her, but to locate Ren's whereabouts. "Ren spends his time on the *Endeavour.* Doing repairs, he says."

"Good. I am eager to put that old lady on

the auction block. She's nearly fin up."

"I don't think Ren considers her to be ready for the ships' graveyard quite yet."

Tristram grinned. "He's got a sentimental streak. But when he sees the *Illumine* arrive in Nantucket under full sail, he will sing a different tune."

That's what worried Daphne. The *Illumine* would sail in, Tristram would outfit it, and Ren would sail away. A troubled look must have crossed her face, as he was peering curiously at her. "I am truly sorry, Daphne," he said, misunderstanding her concern. "I know I should have let thee know I was away. 'Twas inconsiderate of me. After all, we are practically . . ." Before he could finish his sentence, Hitty spotted him, cried out, ran up to him and wrapped her arms around his waist. She grabbed his hand and led him over the threshold and into the keeping room to greet Henry.

Watching them go, Daphne wondered how he was going to finish that sentence. *After all, we are practically . . . what?*

MARY COFFIN STARBUCK

22 October 1662

What are we?

If we're not Puritans, and we're not Baptists, then what are we? I asked Nathaniel that question last night and he said it did not matter because there was no church on Nantucket Island. All that matters is we are Christians, he said.

Of course he's right. There is great resistance on the island to host any kind of clergy for longer than a fortnight. There was a heated argument in the store yesterday between Richard Swain and my father. Richard is campaigning to persuade clergy to settle here, but Father is vehemently against it. If a Puritan minister were to move to Nantucket, I fear Father would be either put in stocks immediately for saying too much of the wrong thing, or he would pack up and move Mother somewhere else. I could not bear that thought.

Nathaniel wondered why I thought it mattered to have a church here. I've been pondering that question all day, and I think I have an answer for him. While it is true that we can worship the Almighty with or without church or clergy, I wonder if a church is meant for even more than worship. At its best, it acts as the hub of a community, lifting standards of behavior, providing a means of help and support.

The problem of Nantucketers, I suppose, is that we have not seen many examples of a church at its best, and therefore, we reject it all.

8

Ren stopped at the bottom of the porch steps at 15 Orange Street and let his gaze roam slowly up the front gray-shingled siding of the house to the rooftop, to the walk. Off-islanders called them *widow walks,* assuming Nantucket wives spent their surfeit of spare time peering out to the harbor to see if their beloved's ship had returned. Islanders scorned that term, knowing the women had no surfeit of spare time. They merely called it a walk, used to hoist buckets of water to the roof should fire break out.

The truth was somewhere in between, as it usually was. Ren wondered how many wives had stood on the walk as widows without knowing it. Whaling voyages and death tolls wove together.

He felt a pride well up inside him at the sight of this house. It was a modest home, but a gift of love to his bride. He had planned carefully so Jane would want for nothing.

Instead of providing her with security, he had unwittingly left her in a precarious position, without the community of Friends to support her. He had assumed Lillian would relent on reading Jane out of Meeting, the way mothers and daughters make up after a row. But Lillian, he should have realized, was not like other mothers. She was quite fond of her grudges, nursing them like little pets.

He breathed deeply as he entered the house, filling his lungs with the sweet scent that had grown familiar to him these last few weeks. It was the scent of Daphne, a trace of lemon verbena that she left behind. It made him think of warm spring days, when the whole world seemed full of expectation and promise.

He heard her before he found her in the sunroom, reading a book to Henry and Hitty. He smiled at the sight, each child nestled beneath one of her arms. The sunroom was beautiful, with windows on three sides that filled the room with morning light. Jane had declared it to be her favorite room. He cleared his throat and she looked up. Hitty gave him a shy smile, Henry scowled. "Might I speak to you a moment, Daphne?"

She frowned. "It will have to wait. We are right in the middle of a story about a pirate who is plotting to highjack a ship on the high seas."

"Stories can wait."

"So can sea captains."

His eyebrows lifted. He was not accustomed to someone who did not instantly obey his request, nor someone who spoke back to him. "I'll be in the kitchen."

He was hoping a teakettle would be boiling on the hearth, but alas, the kitchen was empty, the fire gone cold. He was on his own. He struck a flint, cupping the flame until it flowered, and set it underneath kindling in the fireplace. Satisfied that the fire was under way, he filled the kettle with water from the pump in the yard and set it on its trammel. And still Daphne had not come.

Was he to make his own tea? He hadn't made a cup of tea since he was a cabin boy. He couldn't remember how it was done! Drumming his fingers on the tabletop, he waited for Daphne to join him. When the water started rolling in a boil, he gave up waiting. He scooped tea out of the container and put it in a mug, then poured water over it.

He looked up when the kitchen door

opened. "Better plan for rain tomorrow," Daphne said, as if he had asked. "There's a strong west wind blowing, and a west wind always brings wet weather." She caught the puzzled look on his face and peered into his mug. "What has thee done? It looks like thee is drinking tea leaves."

He swirled the concoction in his mug. "I have not had much experience in the kitchen."

"Clearly not! 'Twill taste much better if the leaves are strained." She took the mug from him and dumped it out in the swill bucket.

Strained! That was the step he'd forgotten. He leaned far back in the chair and crossed his boots.

He cleared his throat, produced a smile, but Daphne didn't smile back. He wondered what had made her so tetchy tonight. "Look here, Daphne, there's a more pressing concern at the moment than thickly brewed tea. I've had to . . . the house . . . *this* house . . ." He took a deep breath and spit it out. "I've sold the Orange Street house."

She froze, mid-pour, and pivoted around to face him. "Thee has done *what*? Why?"

"The banker offered me a price that . . . I could not refuse." There was both a truth and a lie in that statement, for Ren could not have refused any price.

She finished pouring water through the strainer. Without looking up at him, she asked, "Where will thee go?"

"I will find a place to let." He should have been scrounging the island. Ezra Barnard's two months notice had begun weeks ago. His father had offered his house on Easy Street, but Ren declined. His father's small house was near the wharf, redolent with the pungent odor of rendering whale oil, and more of a cooperage with a bunk in the corner than a home. It was no place for two small children, plus him, plus the maidservant. He hoped Patience would remain with them, but he wondered. She was a fine servant, quiet and competent, and would have no trouble finding work elsewhere.

Daphne set the teacup in front of him, and he glanced up at her, then took a second look. Her eyes were glistening with tears. "Why? How? How could thee sell the children's home? *Jane's* house?"

"Please don't look at me that way." It surprised him. Daphne struck him as a practical woman. "I know your sister was dear to you, but her memories will stay in your heart."

She nodded her head, but the tears kept coming.

Oh no. He wasn't accustomed to handling tears, or women. Especially not women with tears. "Try to understand." He set his teacup down. "Daphne, I must be wise about my circumstances. I don't know how much Tristram might have told you, nor if Jane was aware of this, but Tristram used the *Endeavour*'s haul as collateral to commission a new whaler. There have been unforeseen delays." He blew out a puff of air. "I could not pay my crew their lay. No investor will consider providing additional funds to outfit the new ship until it is complete. And of course there is one delay after another." He looked away as he added, "I had no choice but to sell the house."

She slipped into a chair at the end of the table and wiped tears off her cheeks. She kept her head dipped when she spoke. "Tristram stopped by the Cent School this morning, looking for thee. He told me that thee plans to captain the new ship as soon as it is outfitted."

"Aye, well, apparently that's the plan."

"Don't tell me thee has considered taking the children along."

His eyebrows shot up. So *that's* what was troubling her. The thought of the children leaving the island. "Nay. If anything . . . I suppose . . . mayhap you could . . ."

She lifted her head in defiance. "Raise thy children for thee? While thee is jousting with whales?"

Her voice had a sharp edge to it. This wasn't going well. He should have brought Tristram along with him for this conversation. Trist could speak of difficult matters in such a way that women didn't end up mad at him. He sighed. He was not blessed with the gift of conversation like his cousin.

She leaned forward, hands clasped together on the table. "Ren, when thee told me about the time thee fell overboard, that thee nearly died — should've died — thee said that God spared thy life for a purpose."

"Aye, I said as much. But I have not yet discerned the purpose."

She lifted her hands in the air. "This! This is thy purpose!"

"What is *this*?"

She squeezed her eyes shut as if astounded by his obtuseness. "To be a father to thy children. A true father. Not an absent one."

"Am I not trying?" he snapped. By the look on her face, no, he wasn't trying. Not hard enough. More gently, he added, "And how does one go about that with a lad and lass who will not speak to me?"

"Start by taking meals with them. Here, in the kitchen. As their mother did."

Such a thought shocked him. "Did Jane not eat separately in the dining room?"

"Nay. She ate here, with the children."

"In the *kitchen*?" Like a servant?

"From the start. She preferred it. And then . . . later on . . . she closed those rooms off in the winter."

Later. Ren's stomach tightened. *Later* meant after Tristram used Jane's stipend to commission the ship. His own wife did not have the fuel to warm or illumine this house during a bitter Nantucket winter . . . while he was chasing down that very fuel across the oceans.

Daphne smoothed her silk skirt and the rustling sound snapped him back. "I have another thought. Take them to the *Endeavour*. Show them thy ship. Tell them what it's like to chase a whale on the open sea. What boy or girl would not want to hear such a gory and gruesome story?"

"Gory and gruesome? Why, 'tis nothing of the sort. 'Tis a hunting expedition, skillful and practiced. A harmony of movement between man and beast. Why, 'tis a magnificent moment for a man, to sight a pod of great slow-moving creatures, making their way north to the cold seas they love." He caught her smiling at him. "I see thy point, Daphne."

168

The *Endeavour.*

He would do it! Soon.

It was so simple! How had Daphne not considered it the moment Ren told her that he had sold the Orange Street house? She woke before dawn, dressed quickly, and hurried downstairs to catch him before he left for the morning. Even still, she nearly missed him. He had his hand on the front door as she came down the stairs.

"Ren! Hold on a moment. I think I have the perfect solution to thy problem."

He spun around at the sound of her voice, surprised to see her. "What problem is that? I should say, which one? For there are many."

She hid a smile as she came down the stairs, amused by his stance. He stood dark and tall against the white door, with his shoulders thrown back and his legs splayed wide, as if he was on a rolling deck of a ship. "Hear me out. There's a house to live in . . . and it already belongs to thee."

"I'm listening."

"The Centre Street house! Father gave it to Jane after thee set sail. He wanted to provide some insurance for her because he knew Mother had cut off her inheritance. That house, 'tis yours to use."

"The place where Jane's Cent School is housed?" Interested, he leaned against the door. "But Lillian . . . surely she would object . . ."

"It was Father's to bestow. My mother would never consider living in it. Too small, too humble."

He gave her a wry grin. "Not too humble for a poor sea captain and his two children."

"Thee might want to see it again. It has no kitchen, only a keeping room. Bedrooms are upstairs, but they are small. There is a lean-to in the back. 'Tis old, Ren. The original part of the house was built nearly one hundred years ago."

"Sounds grand compared to the captain's quarters of the *Endeavour.*" He folded his arms against his chest. "You're confident that your mother would not object? Raise a ruckus?"

"Leave my mother to me." She smiled. "I'll tell Patience. We'll start packing today."

"Hold on, hold on. What of Jane's Cent School?"

"What of it?"

"I wish it to continue. How did you put it? To keep Jane's garden growing."

"If thee does not mind sacrificing thy keeping room after breakfast each morning, then Jane's Cent School shall continue."

He nodded. "I do not mind in the least."

"Consider it done then."

He reached out to take her hand, covering it with both of his palms. "Daphne, I . . . am most grateful."

Their eyes met, perhaps a beat too long, until Ren dropped her hand as if he'd touched a hot stove.

Daphne hurried upstairs, trying not to think about the pressure of Ren's touch on her hand. She filled her mind with tasks to speed the move to Centre Street, first of which was to find Patience and make a plan. The door to Jane's bedchamber was open and she stopped to close it. She did not want the children to see the empty bed as they came downstairs.

Grief was an odd companion. At times, Daphne was so busy she hardly thought of Jane. Then a quiet moment would arrive and a wave of grief would roll over her, almost buckling her. The mornings at the Cent School were blessedly busy, for it was there that she was most keenly aware of Jane's absence.

With her hand on the doorknob, she paused. The room was dark, with curtains drawn to keep the sun from fading the rug. As her eyes adjusted to the dimness, she saw that Patience had been in here recently. The bed linens were gone, the room had been swept and dusted. She wondered how Patience had the fortitude to come in here without being asked to. She knew how devoted Patience was to Jane.

Patience had been a house servant to the family for as long as Daphne could remember, and a minder to both girls, at least until Jane's marriage. Prior to her elopement, Jane was also considered to be Daphne's minder, "and a poor example at that," Mother often said since.

At the time, Daphne was fifteen. Patience would never admit her true age, but Daphne thought they were closer than she wanted to reveal. Patience wanted Daphne to think she was the minder, but the truth was that they had a mutual understanding: managing Lillian.

Daphne discovered that truth one day when she had been at 15 Orange Street. It was not long after Ren had sailed off, mayhap two or three months later. Jane was horribly nauseated with her pregnancy and Daphne stayed with her all day long to hold a cold cloth to her head, or empty her buckets, and keep her company in that big empty house. When Daphne finally went home, she smelled awful and looked worse.

Mother took one sweeping appraisal of her and erupted. "Where has thee been?"

Daphne stared back at her, at a loss for what to say. Jane had sworn her to secrecy, convinced their mother would assume they eloped only because she was with child.

Patience stepped right in. "Madam, do you not remember? Today is Miss Daphne's day to take food baskets to New Guinea."

Mother's irritability instantly tempered. "Well, go bathe before thee spreads illness throughout the household."

"Of course," Patience and Daphne said at the same time and then passed each other a little smile.

From that moment on, Daphne knew she had an ally in Patience. If Daphne was over at Jane's, she could count on Patience to make excuses for her. "I believe Miss Daphne went down to market to buy you those fresh oranges you like so much, madam," she would say when Mother asked for her and, magically, oranges would appear from the kitchen. Or . . . "Did not Miss Daphne say something about delivering quilts to the Wampanoag village?"

Mother did not dare question Daphne's charitable activities, because she was delighted that her daughter was doing something noble, something she could brag about at gams and gatherments. Something to distract other Nantucket hens from asking about Jane and her embarrassing elopement to the lapsed Quaker sea captain.

From Daphne's point of view, it was delicious to have someone to keep secrets with after Jane left home. But it wasn't just skirting around Mother. It was wonderful to have Patience, wise beyond her years, someone who looked at Daphne and loved her just the way she was, who saw purpose to her life beyond bringing prominence to her socially minded mother. Patience gave her all that.

But then her father died, suddenly and dishonorably, and on the same day Lillian Coffin fired Patience. No reason, no explanation.

Daphne helped Patience pack her few belongings, followed her outside to the street, rehired her, doubled her salary — Daphne's entire monthly allowance — and sent her off to Jane's house to live. Not a moment too soon, either, for the twins were born six weeks early — causing additional mortification for Lillian Coffin.

Something changed after that tumultuous time. Unlike Jane, Daphne was no longer afraid of their mother.

Daphne walked inside Jane's bedchamber

and turned in a circle in the middle of the room. Mayhap it would be best to leave this house, filled with memories of Jane. The children would start fresh with their father at Centre Street, a home they already felt comfortable in. Her eyes landed on the nightstand, to the drawer that held Great Mary's journal. Each day, she had found a quiet moment to come in and read a few entries from the journal. She probably should have started at the very beginning rather than the middle, but she was caught up in Great Mary's current story. The journal brought her comfort, and helped ease the sorrow she felt about losing Jane. She let out a deep sigh, opened the night-stand drawer, took the journal and slipped it into her pocket. She certainly did not want it misplaced in the move to Centre Street.

MARY COFFIN STARBUCK

25 October 1662

Just when I thought things had come to a peaceful place with Catherine and Esther, I am faced with a new challenge: Edward! My father-in-law has not often been at home, as he has spent much of the summer months on the other side of the island with the Wampanoags. He has learned their language and is translating parts of the Bible for their benefit.

When Edward is home, I pepper him with questions about the Wampanoags, their way of life, what they think about. He enjoys my interest in his work. At least, I thought he did, until last night, when Catherine shushed me at dinner. I have grown accustomed to her shushes and do not take them to heart as I first did, but last night she added in a very snippy tone, "Why must you talk so much?"

"Because she is a female, Catherine," Edward said. "All women talk a blue streak. It's in their nature." To my shock, Catherine laughed and passed him the bread.

I did not find Edward's remark to be at all amusing.

Why do men dismiss women, as if their thoughts are trivial and not at all important? And why would Catherine find it humorous?

Later, in the privacy of our bedroom, I said as much to Nathaniel. He wondered if I had ever considered that not every thought I have need be expressed. Of course I'd considered that! 'Twas not the first time he had said as much to me. 'Tis true for me, as 'tis true for others. But it's the casual dismissal of my gender that I object strongly to.

And then there's Catherine's constant shushing. That, too, is deeply annoying.

When I asked Nathaniel why his mother shushed me whenever I shared an opinion, yet she does not object at all when Esther speaks her mind, he said, oh-so-gently, "Esther is her baby girl, Mary. Soon you will have a baby of your own. Can you not see how vehemently you would defend him or her?"

As I have felt flutters from my little one, like butterfly wings in my belly, I have realized his meaning. My heart has softened in understanding.

He is a wise man, my husband. I am blessed to have a man who likes to hear my thoughts, even when they differ from his.

9

Ren rolled up the design papers for the new ship and set them back on top of Tristram's desk. He could find no flaw with the design, though he was looking carefully. Just as well, he supposed, for Tristram's ship was nearly completed.

Tristram's ship. Strange, Ren thought, that his mind framed it as such. His cousin bestowed the ship with the name *Illumine,* an interesting choice Jane had wanted. It meant to light the path.

Indeed, he was pleased to see that the ship was soundly built, and well it should've been, for Tristram had contracted the preeminent shipbuilder of New England to undertake the project. The *Illumine* was much larger than the *Endeavour*'s simple square rigging and blunt nose. This broad-beamed ship would present more sail to the wind to move the ship swiftly, and her hold would store five hundred barrels and then some. It was not faulty thinking on Tristram's part — a larger hold would make a significant difference. Such a hold meant the ship could seek out new whaling grounds, for the industry was growing. As Tristram had often pointed out, there would be no need to hurry home on such a ship.

Ah, there was the rub. The source of Ren's unrest. A larger ship meant longer voyages. He'd already been away from Nantucket for six years. It took that long to fill the hold. Six long years. How could he leave again? Even if the next voyage were to last but a few years, Henry and Hitty would most likely be ten or eleven years old when he returned. He was already a stranger to them. What then?

Two months ago, if anyone were to ask Ren how he envisioned the rest of his life, he could answer without dropping a beat: "To spend my life sailing the seven seas." It was not the pursuit of wealth that drove him as it did most Nantucket whaling captains. It was the sea itself. He was at home on the ocean. He loved everything about it. What most sailors considered to be tedium, he viewed as endless variety. He liked having the full, awful responsibility for the crew rest on him. He was never happier, never more alive than when he was guiding his ship safely through a tempest. In a way, he took pleasure in reading the sea, mastering her moods.

Fool that I am, he realized, *thinking I was captain of the sea, of my life, in complete control. I never was.*

As he turned onto Orange Street, he heard a child's voice and saw Abraham and Henry out in front of the house, playing with a hoop and ball, and his heart hitched. He slowed as he approached, and his heart dropped further still as he heard the topic of questions Henry was peppering Abraham with: all about harpooning a whale. The sound of his son's voice caught up in animated conversation nearly undid Ren and he stopped to lean against a fence post. With a twinge of guilt, he reviewed again Daphne's remark that he had been spared from death for a purpose, that being a father to his children *was* his purpose. He had mulled that insight over and over; he intended to take the children out to see the *Endeavour* as she had suggested. He liked the idea of it, but had not gotten round to it. Partly, he'd been preoccupied with repairing the ship, with preparing for the move from Orange Street. More so, he had to admit, he felt uncomfortable around children.

Henry spotted Ren down the street, dropped the hoop, and ran into the house. The boy seemed just as awkward around him as he did around the boy. Abraham picked up the ball and walked up to him, waiting until Ren addressed him. "Abraham, thank you for taking time with the boy."

"My pleasure, Captain."

"You have a way with little ones, Abraham. You'll have to let me in on your secret."

"There is no secret, sir. Children require time."

Ren took the ball from him. "Love and attention make all things grow, eh? Something like that?"

Abraham beamed. "Exactly that, Captain, sir."

A memory floated through Ren's mind, long forgotten. He was four or five, close to Henry's age, and had timidly asked his own father to toss a ball on a summer afternoon. He remembered being promptly rebuffed, for his father did not particularly like children. In fact, he had never even called him anything other than Jeremiah. Not Father, not Dad, not Papa. Jeremiah preferred his given name, which made things simpler once they crewed together on ships. Simpler, but not sweeter.

Jeremiah was softer now, in his middlin'

years, and they had grown to understand and respect each other. But as a boy, Ren remembered vowing to himself that he would not treat his own children in the same dismissive way his father had treated him. And yet . . . mayhap he was doing just that. It was a nettlesome thought.

The smell of cinnamon spiced the air. "Dare I hope that sweet smell is coming from my house?"

Abraham smiled, a large wide grin. "Sir, I believe Patience has made an apple pie for supper's end."

Ren glanced up at the shingled house with blue shutters. It was a place he loved for all it represented. His first true home on land, a lovely and stately abode. Despite his gratitude for the availability of the Centre Street house, he had to hide his dismay at its shabbiness when he toured it the other day. Most of the furniture from Orange Street had to be sold off, as little could fit in the Centre Street abode. "I hope you will stay and join us. Our last night spent in this house, for tomorrow is moving day." He grinned. "Methinks a certain maidservant might enjoy your company, as well."

The sailor's brown eyes went wide, and if Ren wasn't mistaken, he blushed. Ren laughed, and so did Abraham, and they walked up the steps.

Later that night, Ren stood in the small yard behind the house, gazing up at the darkening sky, dotted with a few stars. The air was still, hot and humid, and fireflies flickered in their dance in front of him.

Without consciously trying, his eyes sought out the North Star, fixed in the sky. Wherever Ren was, at any time, day or night, even in the middle of the ocean with no land in sight, he always, always knew where he was and where he was going. For the first time in his life, he had no clues to navigate. He had no idea, deep down, where he was, nor where he was going. It was an unsettling awareness, one that he tried to tamp down throughout the days but seemed unable to in dark of night. He went to the well in the center of the yard. After drawing up the bucket, he leaned against the curved stone wall and drank from a tin cup left out for the purpose. When Daphne came outside to join him, they watched the fireflies flicker in their dance.

" 'Tis a wonder that insects can light up from within," he said.

" 'Tis a wonder that illustrates what is in all of mankind. We all have that Light within."

He took a deep breath. "Mayhap . . . to

varying degrees."

She cupped a firefly with her hands. "Some, I think, do not acknowledge the Light that is within them. Some let it smolder, but even then, all it takes is a spark to cause the Light to flare up again. But then there are those who . . . snuff out the wick."

He watched her as she lifted her hands to release the firefly that blinked away on its flight.

"I would like to hear more about the time when thee went overboard. How did Abraham reel thee in?"

"Ah, that. There was so much commotion going on, thundering and lightning, I didn't think anyone saw me fall. But Abraham saw. He has a rare ability to see the full picture, even as he's fully occupied with his own work. He cut the closest whaleboat loose, so I was able to swim to it and grab on. Even still, trying to return to the ship seemed an impossible task. The headwind pushed me farther away. Finally, Abraham threw a harpoon at the center of the whaleboat, nailed it spot on, and dragged me back to the ship."

"When?" Daphne's eyes flashed briefly at him. "When did this happen?"

What you noticed first about Daphne, Ren

thought, was the way her dark eyes would snap. They truly snapped, the way sparks flew off a struck flint. He'd never seen eyes quite like hers — they could send a jolt down a man's spine, those eyes of hers. "Oh, let's see, I suppose a year ago."

She lifted her hands to cup her face. "Oh my goodness . . ."

"What is it? Why are you surprised by that?"

"About that time, word came in that the *Endeavour* was feeling blue."

"Feeling blue? M' own ship?" When a ship was said to be feeling blue, it meant the captain had died.

"A blue flag had been spotted, a blue line painted along the side of the ship. The town crier went through the streets, calling out thy name in the death toll. When Jane heard thy name called out, she was inconsolable. Utterly distraught, unable to sleep, refusing to eat. I was the one who fetched Dr. Mitchell. He measured out but a grain of laudanum, I remember that distinctly. He mixed it well in some kind of spirits to mask the bitter taste. She slept for two days, and when she woke, she was herself again. A few weeks later, a whaling schooner arrived into Nantucket with more accurate information. 'Twas not the *Endeavour*'s captain that

185

died, but the *Enterprise*'s. This ship had spotted the *Endeavour* from afar, and knew she was sitting low in the water."

"The *Deborah*. Tristram filled me in." He looked straight at Daphne. "Did Jane's laudanum use continue after that? Please be candid. I want the truth."

"Not that I was aware of."

"See here, Daphne, do you mean to say y' never noticed if Jane seemed . . . floaty? Preoccupied? If the pupils of her eyes were constricted? You were with her nearly every day."

"I did not see signs of indulgence. Truly, I did not," she hastened to add as he gave her a skeptical look. "Patience might know more."

"I asked. She would not answer me. She seems . . . uncommonly devoted to Jane."

"Patience has been with our family for as long as I can remember. She would not betray Jane."

"Is telling the truth a betrayal?"

"I think . . . Patience's silence is her way of telling the truth." Daphne fingered the ends of her capstrings. "I remember how distraught Jane was after hearing of thy death, and the laudanum . . . it helped her cope." She tilted her head. "She loved thee, Ren."

186

He couldn't speak for the longest while, couldn't voice what those words meant to him. He hadn't realized how he had needed to hear them until they were said aloud, and it felt as healing as balm to a wound. Finally, he broke the silence. "I've not had a chance to take Henry out to the *Endeavour*, but after the move to Centre Street is sorted out, I plan to. I suppose I could take Hitty too, if she might have interest —"

"She will. They're both learning to sail my sloop."

"You have your own sloop?"

"A small one. I keep it docked off my mother's house."

Interesting, how Daphne and Jane always referred to their childhood home as their mother's house, as if they were but house-guests. While most everything had changed for him as he returned to the island, some things had not changed at all. It felt oddly comforting. He ran a finger around the top of the tin cup. "Daphne, I don't suppose . . . well, would y' come along with us?"

She looked shocked at the thought. Then she lifted her head to look at the stars. "I would love it."

Someone, long ago, had planned this snug little cottage well, Daphne thought, as she helped Patience unpack a crate of kitchen tools. The keeping room was positioned with a southern exposure, one window facing the road and one in the back, so sunshine flooded the room most of the day — at least it did when fog wasn't blanketing the island as it did three days out of four. Patience had scrubbed the house clean and opened the windows to let it air out.

The Centre Street keeping room was about half the size of the Orange Street kitchen, but Daphne preferred it, though she wouldn't be staying here. She had moved back to her mother's house, at Lillian's strong and repeated urging, and she let her mother believe she had obliged her. The truth was that there was no place for her to stay in this small house.

Much furniture from Orange Street had been sold to accommodate the small house. Daphne worried the children might feel distressed to leave their childhood home, but they seemed very at home in Centre Street. Hitty said the house smelled of tea and lemons now. Henry was pleased that it was closer than their Orange Street house had been to the wharves — his favorite place to be.

After the kitchen was unpacked, Patience took Henry and Hitty with her to the small garden out back, to hoe the weeds. Abraham offered to help dig, so the four of them set out. Daphne watched them out the window, noticing how at ease Abraham and Patience seemed with each other, often laughing together over something. It occurred to her that she had never heard Patience speak of a man in her life, so when she came back into the kitchen, she asked her directly. "Has thee ever wanted to have a family of thine own?"

Patience was searching in a crate for a tin of biscuits for the children to snack on. She looked up, her face lightened with quiet laughter. "Miss Daphne, I cannot tell you my private business."

"But why?" Patience knew everything about Daphne, everything about her family. Why would she ever keep secrets? What secrets were there to keep?

Patience's hands went still for a moment, and then she said, "Because some things are more complicated than you want to see."

Of course, Daphne knew that. Of course she did. *Like what?*

5 December 1662

I was working at the store when I heard shouts come from Capaum Harbour. Nathaniel was with me, as was his mother, for they had come to pick up some supplies that my brother James had brought from the mainland. We went outside to see what was causing such a ruckus. It turns out Richard Swain's slave had run away, but was caught hiding in James's sloop.

Richard had bound the slave and forced him to walk behind his snorting horse, like he was taking home an animal from auction. As they passed the store, Richard raised his hat to us. His hand knocked all the bags that hung off his saddle horn to flop against his horse's side, spooking it. The horse reared and the slave was yanked off his feet. I hurried to help him up, but Nathaniel grabbed me and held me back. "Do not get involved, Mary."

I shrugged off his hold. "But he may be hurt."

"Do what your husband tells you," Catherine said.

I looked to Nathaniel to soften his mother's sharp tone. He did not: he was watching Richard, whose gaze was fixed on the slave. The poor man was lying facedown in the dust, kicking his legs to try to roll onto his side. Richard had an odd look on his face, as if he enjoyed the man's helplessness.

I have never much given thought about slavery, whether it was right or wrong, moral or immoral, approved of or abhorrent to God. Not until today.

'Twas a very unsettling experience, all around. I did not speak for the rest of the afternoon and evening. I could not.

2 February 1663

Peter Foulger once told me that I was a brave person. I have never thought of myself as a brave person, though my mettle had not truly been tested now.

All day, I had the strangest sense that I was not alone, though I knew I was. Edward, Nathaniel, and Jethro were out hunting and would not return for a few days. Catherine and Esther were spending the day with Jane Swain, due back before nightfall. I have been feeling under the weather lately, and was grateful for the peace and quiet. I went outside to feed Esther's chickens and let them out of the henhouse, to get a bit of sun as the weather has been uncommonly pleasant this week.

On my way back to the house, I heard the sound of a log falling from the woodpile in the shed. It could've been an Indian dog, or some other animal. I could have left it at that. There was plenty of wood in the stack against the house. I didn't need another stick.

And yet . . . I couldn't shake that odd feeling I'd had all day, that I was not alone. So I took a deep breath, held it, and walked over to the woodshed. I pushed open the door and peered in.

The light reached only a foot or two inside the woodshed, then it was dim, leading to darkness. For a moment, I could see nothing as my eyes adjusted to the dim light. There was a narrow gap between wood and wall, for access to the stacks of piled wood. In that gap stood a man.

I stared at him and he stared at me. Heart pounding, I recognized him as Richard Swain's Negro. He had seemed so big to me when I'd seen him those two times, but I realized with a start that he was the same height as me, and I am not considered to be tall.

"I beg you," he whispered. "Do not turn me back to the master."

I did not know what to say! I backed up,

out of the woodshed, and hurried to the house. I paced around the kitchen, unsure of what to do. Though it was early in the day, I decided to prepare the meal, as cooking and baking always helped me settle my mind. As I set the kettle of beans on the hearth, I wondered if the Negro was hungry. When had he last eaten? How long had he been in the woodshed? When the cornbread had finished baking, I cut a large chunk of it, smeared it with butter and honey, added a few pieces of bacon that were meant for the bean pot, and wrapped it all in a handkerchief. I thought of the thin clothing he was wearing, of how cold and dark that shed was. In our bedroom, I went through Nathaniel's clothes and grabbed a sweater that he rarely wore, for the scratchy wool gave him a rash, and some stockings I had knit for him that were much too big. At the last moment, I pulled one of the quilts off our bed and wrapped everything inside like a parcel.

I ran out to the woodshed, opened the door, and dropped it inside, then ran back to the house. When I reached the door, I felt foolish, for the Negro meant me no harm. If he had wanted to hurt me, he'd had plenty of opportunity, all day long.

In the afternoon, as the sun was setting, I realized I'd forgotten all about the chickens. If Esther found out that I'd let them out in the yard, I'd never hear the end of it. Those chickens were her babies. I wrapped my woolen shawl around my head and shoulders, and ran to the henhouse. The hens were all inside, all accounted for. The Negro had done it for me.

Not five minutes later, I heard the voices of Catherine and Esther come up the path. The first words out of Esther's mouth were news about Richard Swain's runaway slave. "He says he will offer a reward for the slave's return! Two pounds sterling, he said. I looked for signs of him as we walked home." She clapped her hands together. "I would like to have two pounds."

I stirred the beans as she spoke and kept my gaze fixed on the bubbling pot. "And did you find any signs?"

"Nay. Not one. But I aim to keep looking."

"Why did the slave run?"

Catherine snorted, surprising me with her answer. "I wouldn't want to be a dog of Richard Swain's." She took the lid off the bean pot to stir the beans and frowned. "They're burned! And you've made enough

for the King's army. What were you thinking?"

I don't know. All day, my thoughts were
like barn swallows, swooping in and out
without any destination in mind.

I did not sleep well. All through the night,
I kept waking up, my mind filled with one
thought: "There is no way this can turn out
well."

10

Ren had been caulking cracks in the *Endeavour*'s top deck seams when he heard a voice call up to him. He went to the side and peered over. There was Tristram, waving his broad-brimmed hat at him from the dory down below. "Throw over a rope."

Ren threw down the climbing rig and watched as Tristram made his way up to the railing. He gave him a hand and yanked him onto the deck. "What brings you here, cousin?"

Tristram brushed off his pants and straightened his gray double-breasted top-coat. "Lillian Coffin just paid me a call. She believes it is high time I propose marriage to Daphne and wanted to apply a bit of pressure." He grinned. "Seemed like a very good time to make haste to the *Endeavour*."

Ren kept his eyes on the tips of Tristram's polished black boots. "So," he said, thinking that his cousin had become quite a dandy, "you do not agree with Lillian's assessment?"

"I . . . suppose . . . I do . . . ," he said slowly, distractedly. "But," he grinned, "what is the need for hurry?"

"Lillian's fortune, for one."

"Oh, cousin. Does thee think I would marry any girl for money?"

"Daphne's not just any girl."

Tristram stopped. "Nay, she is not. Daphne is . . . well, she's Daphne. One of a kind."

"She'd make any man a fine wife."

Trist gave Ren a hard, tight smile. "I did not row all the way out here to discuss the impending risk to my beloved bachelorhood. Nay!" And he gave his cousin's shoulder a little shove, relaxing his face. "I come bearing tidings."

"Good tidings, I hope. I'm weary of bad news."

"Excellent news. The *Illumine* is nearing completion, but for some details in the captain's quarters that I thought thee might like the final say on. After all, the cabin will be thy home for the next few years. I hoped we could go together to Salem to inspect it."

Ren hesitated, crossing his arms against his chest, shifting his weight from one leg to the other. "I've been thinking on this, Tristram. I think you should captain the *Illumine* for her maiden voyage."

Trist's face, alit with delight only seconds ago, suddenly lost its smile. "Me?" His voice rose an octave.

"You wouldn't have to stay out long, mayhap six months or so. Seek out right whales. They're slow and cumbersome and stay in a pod. Most every sailor cuts his teeth on a right whale. There's a reason they were given that name."

"Me?" he repeated dumbly.

"Or go north, capture minke whales, if you can catch them. They're small, but plentiful. They can be evasive, I agree, but I'll give you an advantage that few seamen know. When a very big squall is in the makings, the minkes launch up in the air like a cannon ball, and give away their position. Most ships batten down the hatch, but *that's* the time to hunt."

Tristram's face blanched. "And then thee has a very big squall to deal with." He stood silently for a long time, hands tucked under his crossed arms. "What's changed thy mind? Why wouldn't thee want to go?"

"I do want to. But I can't leave the children after what they've been through. Not so soon after Jane's death."

198

"Yet they will be well cared for. Daphne will mind them. She's like a second mother to them. This island is full of second mothers. I myself was raised by my two dotty great aunts."

"It's just that . . . Jane's death came so suddenly. So unexpectedly."

Tristram grew solemn, turning the brim of his hat around and around in his hands. He swallowed before saying, " 'Tis hard to understand why God took someone so young."

"I'm not at all sure 'twas God's doing." Now was the time, Ren thought, to tell Tristram of his suspicions. "I'm convinced Jane was poisoned."

"Poisoned." The hat held in Tristram's hand slipped to the deck and landed with a soft swish. "Poisoned? How could that be?"

"Apparently, she'd been taking a sedative from Dr. Mitchell, just for now and then, mind you. Unfortunately, 'twas a tainted tincture."

"Tainted?" he echoed in a half moan.

"Far too much ethanol was added. Something was awry in what she took. Filled her body with poison. Caused her to go into respiratory distress." He glanced at Tristram. "I'm not wanting that information to get around town, please understand. For Jane's sake."

Tristram gripped the rail, shocked by the revelation. For a long time, he didn't speak, didn't move a muscle. Then he cleared his throat. "Of course, of course. I won't speak of it. Not to anyone."

"As for Dr. Mitchell, I plan to talk to the magistrate when he returns from the mainland. 'Tis another reason that compels me to remain on island for a spell."

"Magistrate?"

"To press charges against the doctor. I have no doubt he's the one who gave her the tainted tincture. I recently learned that two others succumbed to the tincture. The very same week that Jane died."

"What?" Tristram's eyes went wide in alarm. "Where did thee hear of that? I've heard nothing of the sort."

"My father learned of it. Two stevedores. You don't hear of such things, Trist, because you only leave the loft to go to Salem and fuss over that ship of yours."

Tristram loosened his collar. A bead of sweat ran down his temple and along his cheek, though it was not a particularly warm day. "Two stevedores, thee says?"

Ren bent down and picked up Tristram's hat. "If Mitchell is the one who doled out that tainted tincture, I'll see that he pays for it."

"What does that mean?" His eyes widened as understanding dawned on him. "Don't tell me thee means to see him hang!"

Ren handed Tristram's hat to him and took his time answering. "I don't know what the punishment would bring — that's up to the court."

"The magistrate would never accept the charges. Dr. Mitchell has been a Nantucket fixture as long as I have been alive. And the only islanders who end up getting hung are Wampanoags. Thee would be wasting time and effort." He squeezed the brim of his hat. "I strongly encourage thee to drop the matter."

"I cannot. I will not."

"But Ren, Jane is gone! What good would it do? What purpose would it serve, other than satisfy a husband's need for revenge?" Tristram's voice was nearly pleading.

"I simply can't tolerate the thought that another might suffer because of what he freely doles out as harmless. I've seen too much damage from what the poppy sauce does to sailors. 'Tis an evil. I won't rest until justice is served. I owe Jane that much."

But then a deep grunt interrupted. "Ren?" Jeremiah gave a wordless greeting to Tristram with a nod of his head. "Found a rotten board down in the bilge," he said. "Need yer help to figure out what t' do."

The rotting bilge board discussion took longer than expected, and when Ren returned to the upper deck, he was surprised to find Tristram still aboard, standing at the bow of the ship, staring out at the gray-green water. The bow was pointing away from the harbor, out toward the ocean. "Still here? I thought you'd rowed back by now."

Tristram kept his eyes on the ever moving water, frowning.

"Are you all right? You look a little . . . seasick."

Tristram startled and seemed to come to his senses, like he just realized where he was and who he was with. "Cousin," he said, squaring his shoulders and lifting his chin, right before punching his right hand into his left palm, making a sound like a pistol shot, "I've decided I will take thee up on thy offer. I'll captain the *Illumine*'s maiden voyage."

Sixth Day dawned sunny, warm, with a gentle southwestwardly wind. After the last child was picked up from the Cent School, Daphne left Henry and Hitty in Patience's care and hurried to her mother's house to change her clothes. She'd been excited about the trip to the *Endeavour;* she'd been looking forward to it all week. Ships fascinated her, and she was eager to see what it might feel like to be on a whaler. She'd never been invited onto a whaler before. She was almost disappointed that the day had been so sunny and calm, the sea so still.

Her mother met her at the door. "Daphne! Thee is finally home."

"I can't stay long," she said, probably too quickly.

Her mother narrowed her eyes. "Thee is up to something."

"Nothing new, Mama."

"Look at me," Lillian said, and Daphne did as she was told, to avoid a scene that would only delay her plans. Experience had taught her that it was always best to go along with her mother, or at least let her think so. "Hear me, daughter. Tristram Macy is paying a call tonight and thee *must* be at home to receive him."

Daphne narrowed her eyes. "How does thee know what Tristram plans to do?"

Her mother replied without looking up. "I saw him in town this morning."

"Thee saw him — where?"

Here Lillian did look up, a challenge in

her blue eyes. "It matters not where."

"Oh Mother, did thee go to his loft again?"

Lillian gave Daphne a cat-that-swallowed-a-canary smile. "He said he is most eager to have a private chat with thee. That he has tidings to tell."

Tristram Macy suited her mother's criteria perfectly: he was island-born, he was well-educated, good-looking, and unlike most Nantucketers, had no ambition to be a sea captain. Tristram minded the home office and did not have a longing to escape to sea, which delighted Lillian Coffin. She wanted nothing more than to clip every bird's wings.

Daphne looked at her mother's smiling face, buoyed by bright hope for her youngest daughter. "He said that?" She'd hardly seen much of Tristram in the last few weeks, not since Jane's passing. If he'd wanted a private chat with her, he could've always sought her out. He knew where she was.

"Indeed!"

"Well, he will have to come another day. I've made plans with Hitty and Henry."

"Plans that will have to be postponed."

Daphne clenched her teeth. "That's just not possible."

Lillian reached over and squeezed her hand, pressing her thumb and fingers down hard over her palm. "Make it possible. Thee has been spending all thy time with those children. It is *thy time,* Daphne. Do *not* miss this opportunity." She leaned closer, her eyes sparkling. "I believe Tristram is finally prepared to propose."

Daphne pulled her hand away from her mother's tight clasp. "I'm not at all confident that is the direction Tristram's thoughts are going. He's grieving, Mother, over Jane." *Unlike thee.* "And he's quite distracted with his new ship." She walked over to the window and noticed a beautiful blue hydrangea bush in full bloom. Jane had loved hydrangeas, the iconic island flower.

She turned and found her mother frowning at her, then sighing a deep, long-suffering sigh. "Why must thee act as if any young man I approve of is not good enough for thee?"

Because they aren't, Daphne thought. *Can't thee see, Mother? All they want is thy fortune.* "Would it really be so terrible if I did not marry Tristram?"

Her mother clutched her arms as if made cold by the thought. "Don't say such a thing, Daphne. Don't even give voice to it. Thee are destined for each other. It has always been that way. Everyone has always seen thy bond. Why can't thee see it?"

That was the problem. Daphne *did* see it.

It was true she and Tristram had a unique bond. They had been close friends since childhood days. Tristram's stutter, Daphne's stoutness, both mercilessly teased — their vulnerabilities had brought them together, giving them a shared, unspoken understanding. "What if we don't love each other the way a husband and wife should, the way Jane and Reynolds did?"

Daphne thought she saw a quick pain flash in her mother's eyes, but no sooner had the thought filled her mind, and the look was gone.

"Thee has schoolgirl notions about marriage, daughter. I won't allow thee to marry unwisely, not like thy sister did. Foolish longing for passion leads only to heartbreak."

"Not every marriage need end like thine, Mother."

Her mother cinched her lips together at the sting.

It wasn't kind, to deliver truth with a barbed point. Still, Daphne had no desire to take back her words because finally, finally, she had said something her mother was listening to.

But her mother was not so easily swayed from her original intent. "Wear thy blue silk dress for Tristram. 'Tis his favorite."

Daphne sighed. In her stubbornly infuriating way, her mother had beaten her again.

Ren waited as long as he could for Daphne to return to Centre Street, until it was clear she was not returning. Lillian's doing, he suspected. He had not seen much of Daphne this week, not since the move, when she had moved her belongings back to her mother's house. He found himself missing her — for the children's sake, of course, as she was an enormous help and source of stability to the children. But if he were honest, he missed her for his own sake as well. Daphne was a merry person to be around, always industrious, full of plans. Full of light and good cheer.

He finally decided to go ahead and take Henry and Hitty out to the *Endeavour,* despite their loud objections to the outing because Daphne wasn't with them. They spoke not a single word as he rowed the dory out to the ship. They sat across from him, eyes fixed on the water, with a look on their small faces as if their fate was doomed. He did not mind so much, for it gave him an opportunity to study them. He noticed the tiny springing curls beneath Hitty's bonnet, her brown eyes that reminded him of Jane when she smiled — which wasn't terribly often. Henry had a soft round face and intelligent eyes that took in everything. Something powerfully sweet started to swell in Ren's heart, so much so that he had to blink back tears. How much he had missed! He knew too little of these two.

As he gave them a tour of the *Endeavour,* he could sense their curiosity growing. At one point, as they walked along the upper deck and the bow of the ship lifted in a wave, Hitty reached out for his hand and he felt his heart expand. Henry worked carefully to avoid showing interest, but as Ren let him hold a harpoon in his hands, he could see the lad's natural inquisitiveness rise despite his best effort to tamp it down. When he took them down to the forecastle, he pointed out the hammock that belonged to the cabin boy. "I was not much older than you are now, Henry, when I sailed on m' first whaling voyage. My father was the ship's cooper, and I was cabin boy."

Henry peered up at him, pushing his glasses up on the bridge of his nose. "Thee was once a boy?"

Ren swallowed a smile. "Indeed I was." Though he did not remember many carefree days of childhood, not like he hoped for his own children.

"What about school?"

"None."

"No school!" Henry let out a whistle, impressed. "That sounds perfect."

"I was educated at the Academy before the Mast." He grinned. "On the sea, among the sailors. 'Twas a constant schooling."

Hitty sat on a hammock and swung back and forth. "What did thee do as cabin boy?"

"I coiled ropes so the captain wouldn't trip on them."

"Grandfather Jeremiah!"

"Later, Jeremiah was captain of this very ship. But I'm talking about another time, when I was cabin boy for another ship, and another captain. This particular captain would punish any sailor who left a rope untidy."

"How would a sailor be punished?"

"For an uncoiled rope? Tied to the mast for a full day, with the sun beating down on him."

"Did thee ever leave a rope uncoiled?"

"Once. Indeed, once I did, but Jeremiah intervened and I was not bound to the mast. After that, I was especially careful to do the captain's bidding. I served the captain his meals, and he liked them hot. I learned to serve him quickly, to avoid a scowl that often led to a lashing. I swabbed decks and holystoned them. Mostly, I was given the lowliest chores on the ship."

Henry poked his glasses up. "What else?"

"When a sperm whale was captured and killed, the crew towed it back to tie to the ship, and it would be flensed. The blubber would be stripped, like peeling an orange. Then the head was cut from its body and raised onto the deck. The teeth were pulled."

"For scrimshaw!" Hitty said. "Abraham carves scrimshaw."

"Aye. Scrimshaw is carved with a sail needle, or a knife, and filled in with ink or soot."

Henry squinted his eyes. "Pulling teeth doesn't sound like a lowly task."

Nay? Well then, how about this? "A hole was cut into the whale's skull, just big enough for a boy."

Hitty gasped, then cried out, "For thee!"

Ren laughed. "Aye!" He stopped himself, wondering if it was wise to continue, if such gritty knowledge might make them queasy. He could almost hear Daphne's voice, scolding him, reminding him they were but children. And yet Henry and Hitty stared at him with rapt attention, waiting for him to continue. " 'Twas my task to stand in the whale's skull and scoop out the valuable spermaceti oil in a bucket."

"How much?" Henry asked.

"One time I counted 582 bucketfuls. I slipped and splashed and was thoroughly drenched with blood and oil. By day's end my hands were blistered and raw."

Hitty looked at Ren thoughtfully. "Did thee have to stand in the whale's head for each one thee caught?"

Henry scoffed. "Only sperm whales have liquid wax in their head. That's what's used for candlemaking."

Hitty scowled at him for butting in, but the boy's knowledge was correct. Ren, watching Henry and Hitty inspect each corner of the forecastle, said to himself, *Why, I do believe they like this old hulk of a ship!* They were enchanted by it, awed by stories of the whaler's life. And he loved them even more than before with this awareness of their deep connection. It was in their Macy blood, this love of the sea.

Hitty turned to him. "Where did thy mother sleep?"

"Ah, well, that's a tale for another day." The story of Ren's mother was a complicated one.

Only one thing marred the day. They had climbed the companionway and up onto the upper deck, drinking in the fresh scent of the damp, salt air after being on the musty lower deck. When Hitty caught sight of the setting sun, a glory of red and gold and orange, she spun in a series of pirouettes, like a ballerina on a stage. Something inside of Ren broke as he watched his young daughter dance for joy on the upper deck of the *Endeavour.* To his surprise, words spilled out from his heart. "I've missed you. Both of you. I've missed so much."

Hitty stopped abruptly and turned at his words, her gaze searching his face. "We've missed thee too, Papa," she said.

"*Thee* was the one who left," Henry quickly thrust out. "Not us."

What could Ren say to that? It was true. He had left Jane to face life alone. But on the heels of the sorrow he felt for missing out on his children's early childhood, it dawned on him that Hitty had called him Papa. *Papa!* For the very first time.

As the sun dropped on the horizon, he rowed the dory back to the wharf with a promise to take them out again. He carried Hitty home and she fell asleep on his shoulder. Tears stung his eyes as he laid his cheek atop his daughter's head. Patience opened the door before he could knock, as if she'd been watching through the window for them. Out of the corner of his eye, Ren saw Abraham stoke the hearth fire and gave him a nod. It pleased him that something sweet was stirring between Abraham and Patience.

Ren took Hitty upstairs and laid her gently on her bed, then let Patience take over the bedtime ritual. Henry did not look *quite* so hostile when he bid him good night.

It was a very good day.

Tristram did not arrive at Lillian's house until long after nine o'clock in the evening. Annoyance flooded Daphne. She could have gone with Ren and the children out to the *Endeavour,* returned back, helped get the children to bed, and still be waiting for Tristram.

Were it anyone else at the door, looking the way he did, Lillian Coffin would have the servant send him on his way. But for Tristram Macy, she welcomed him warmly, ushering him into the drawing room where Daphne sat reading. As Trist came out of the shadows of the foyer and into the brighter light of the drawing room, Daphne took note of the dark stubble on his chin, the tie that hung loosely around his neck, the open collar of his shirt, the disheveled hair. And no hat! Anyone else and Mother would have upbraided him for his sloppy carelessness. Not Tristram, though, and especially not tonight.

Mother had chattered nonstop all through dinner, nervously straddling the fine line between giddiness at the thought of Daphne finally, *finally* getting betrothed . . . and fear that her daughter would do something to ruin this glorious, long-sought-after moment.

Tristram smiled brightly when he saw her, swaying slightly as he stood by the door-jamb. "Daphne, thee looks lovely on this s-s-summer evening." He took great care to cross the room and helped himself to the whiskey on the sideboard. He poured a generous amount in a cut-glass tumbler, cradled in his palm, then lifted it in a mock toast to her. He tried to smile but it came out all wrong. He took a long gulp of his drink. He paced around the room, looking at trinkets, refilling his glass, slurping down the amber liquid. Two drinks. Three drinks. "These knickknacks — they are from thy f-f-father's whaling voyages?"

Daphne nodded, slightly bewildered by his anxious behavior, not at all acting like his usual swaggering self. "What thee is holding in thy hands — he called it his monkey's spoon. Father picked up a monkey on some island and discovered it liked to steal his eating utensils. One day it grabbed that spoon and climbed up the center mast.

When Father ordered it down, the monkey threw the spoon at him. See the dent in it?"

Tristram squinted his eyes and peered at the spoon. It was a sizable dent, but he seemed to have trouble focusing. She took the spoon away from him and set it back where he'd found it.

"It must s-seem odd, to live in a h-house where thee mustn't touch anything. Like . . . a museum."

Daphne had never considered her mother's house in such a way, but now that Trist pointed it out, it probably was odd. His own upbringing had been helter-skelter, raised by elderly maiden aunts, as his mother had died in childbirth and his father was a seafaring man, rarely in port. Trist had to make his own way in this world. Daphne envied him such freedom, but he scoffed at her admiration.

"Thee doesn't know how s-s-s-sweetly blessed thee has been, Daphne Coffin."

She took a closer look at him. She hadn't heard his stutter in years; it only returned when he was under great stress.

"T-T-T-To never have a worry about the future, that is a r-r-remarkable thing."

She supposed there was some wisdom in that, but she knew that inherited wealth brought complications of its own. And she could not deny that she relied on her mother's generosity. What would she do if she had no financial resources, like Trist? It occurred to her that *this* was the panic Jane had lived with, was why she started the Cent School. Maybe this was why laudanum had slipped in to become a part of Jane's life, if Ren's theory proved true.

At some point, Mother popped her head into the drawing room to see what was going on. Daphne smiled like everything was fine and she smiled back, happy to see it was all working out.

The mantel clock chimed and was joined by the grandfather clock in the hall. Half past nine! Too late to go to Centre Street and apologize to Ren for missing the trip to the *Endeavour.* She felt a flash of familiar annoyance. Why did she always seem to be *waiting* on Tristram? Finally, she addressed the purpose for his visit. "Mother said thee had tidings."

"T-T-Tidings?" His cheeks turned as red as autumn apples. He wavered, and reached out a hand to grab the black marble mantel capping the rounded arched fireplace.

"She said thee was coming by with news." She couldn't keep the snippy sound of irritation out of her voice, though she didn't try very hard.

He wiped the corners of his mouth. "News?"

She sighed. "Tristram, it seems as if we are paddling a canoe in opposite directions, so the canoe has nowhere to go but to spin around in a circle."

He gave her a funny look, blinking his eyes rapidly. "Thee has a w-way of . . . putting me off m-my stride."

As they studied each other, they both knew there was no more pretending.

He smiled suddenly and tossed back another healthy swallow of whiskey. Then he tugged the hem of his double-breasted waistcoat, as if steadying himself, and cleared his throat before moving — lurching! — toward Daphne to sit beside her on the settee. So close to him, she could catch the smell of whiskey on his breath and notice how bleary his eyes looked. She frowned. He was drop-dead drunk.

"Daphne, my darling." He reached out for her and pulled her close to him, kissing her. It was not their first kiss, but this kiss was clumsy, without tenderness. And the taste and smell of whiskey revolted her.

She untangled herself from his awkward embrace. "Oh Tristram, let's just . . ." But she didn't know how to finish. Let's just *what*? "Why don't I get thee a glass of water?"

She didn't wait for him to respond. By the time she returned from the kitchen, he had stretched out on the settee and was sound asleep.

She thought of waking him, of pushing him out the front door to let him stumble his way home. Hopefully, the town crier would spot him, hurry to the sheriff, and have him sleep off his bender in the Nantucket gaol. The image pleased her.

Instead, she blew out the candles in the bowl-shaped reflector of the hurricane lamps — the Coffin fortune had begun with whale hunting, but no Coffin would use it, for the price of whale oil was too dear — and left Tristram snoring away on the settee.

Upstairs, as she opened the door to her bedchamber, eager to untie those awful corset stays that poked her so mercilessly, she stopped abruptly, surprised by a person in her room. "Mother!"

Her mother was seated in the reading chair, waiting for her, a glint of hope lifting her brows. She dropped the book on her lap. "Well?"

Daphne shook her head. "Not tonight."

At times Daphne felt she could almost see

her mother's disappointment in her, like fog rolling in from the sea before settling heavily over the room.

Her mother stared at her for several seconds before her voice came, quiet and hurt and angry. "Thee is determined to spoil things for me."

"I'm not trying to spoil anything, Mama. Tristram was tired tonight, 'tis all. He'd had a long day, he said."

Her mother contemplated her across the shadowed room. Her hands gave away her nervousness — they were gripped together tightly. " 'Tis just as well." She rose and sighed tiredly. "Thee looks a bit peaked this evening as well. 'Tis that brown silk. It washes thee out. I told thee to wear the blue dress, did I not?"

"Did thee? I'd forgotten."

Tenderness covered her mother's face. "Mayhap I only thought to say it. Do not worry, Daughter." She tutted, patting Daphne's shoulders. "All is not lost. Tomorrow, we will regroup."

As her mother headed down the hall to her own bedchamber, Daphne breathed a sigh of relief that Tristram's heavy snores floating up the stairwell from the drawing room went unnoticed. When he woke, if he

woke in the night, he could let himself out
the door.

MARY COFFIN STARBUCK

4 February 1663

The Negro has a fever. I went to the shed late last night, waiting until Catherine and Esther had retired to their beds. The wind was fierce and the lantern wick nearly blew out twice as I crossed the yard, my boots crunching on the winter-brittle grass. 'Twas such a cold night, I felt worried about the Negro, that he might freeze to death. Yet I also hoped he had fled and gone elsewhere to seek shelter. Even still, I carried an extra quilt with me. When I pushed the door open and shined the lantern inside, I saw him huddled in a dark corner, shivering and sweating. He is younger than I'd first thought, not much older than Jethro or Esther. I put a hand on his warm brow, and he closed his eyes as a child would with his mother's touch. It made me think of whether his mother had done the same for him, and where she is now. I did not stay long on that image, for I feared that he had been stolen from her and the thought was quite disturbing to me. I cannot imagine being parted with my own babe, and I haven't even met him yet. I already love him so dearly though.

The runaway's fever felt warm, but not

burning up. I brought him some water from the well and covered him with the quilt. Just as I slipped out of the woodshed to hurry back to the warm house, I heard the Negro whisper, "Thank you."

5 February 1663

I have not slept more than a few hours at a time since the Negro arrived. Throughout the night, I kept jerking awake, certain I'd heard Richard Swain's horse clatter into the yard. It turned out to be nothing more than a loose shutter, banging against a window in the wind.

Even in the daytime, I cannot relax. I keep noticing clues of the runaway's presence — less eggs for Esther to find among the hens each morning, the changed location of the scooper near the well. Clues are all around us. I marvel Catherine and Esther seem not to notice and yet they do not.

Why can I not still my troubled thoughts? What is this Negro to me?

This afternoon, after closing the store, I stopped by my parents' home. Mother was kneading dough, punching it, lifting it up, and punching it down again. I knew she was upset about something. Bread dough is made early in the morning . . . unless Mother is upset. It is her remedy.

She was quick to fill me in, even as she punched and poked the poor ball of dough. It has to do with the anticipation of new settlers to the island this spring, and whether they are deserving of full shares of property or not. Father says no. He wants complete control of the island left in the hands of the first proprietors. He feels a half-share status is more than generous. Mother believes a half-share status will only discourage newcomers. She longs for more female companionship, as do I.

I listened as long as I could bear to watch that beleaguered ball of dough get beaten and punched, until I could bear it no more. I took my leave, claiming I should return to the Starbucks' before darkness fell.

I walked home heavyhearted, burdened, and disappointed. This morning, I had prayed for some insight about this Negro and fully expected to receive it. This afternoon, I am even more confused about who belongs here and who doesn't. I feel all at sea about the future of our island. I know there is no such thing as paradise this side of heaven, but a little part of me hoped we had found a corner of it.

Tired as I was, I lay wide awake in bed, imagining conversations that might be illuminating, to shed light on my dilemma with the Negro.

Nathaniel, if he were here and not out hunting, would tell me that this is not our problem, but Richard Swain's.

Were I to ask Father for advice, he would tell me to walk right over to the Swains' and tell Richard that the Negro is hiding in the woodshed. To Father, it would be nothing more than returning a runaway horse or cow. Merely property.

What would Peter Foulger say, were I to ask for his opinion?

I think I know Peter well enough to know. He would turn the question back to me, and ask why I felt such turmoil. I can hear his voice: "What might God be trying to teach you, Mary?"

The answer would be that I had never considered all men to be equal in God's eyes until I saw the pain in that Negro's eyes, until I spoke to him, and cared for his needs.

And if I do believe such a thing, what do I do with that belief?

11

Daphne slipped out the door of her mother's house to hurry to Ren's Centre Street house as early as she dared to arrive, as fast as she could go with those horrible corset stays gouging deep into her ribs. How she hated them! But she didn't want to miss Ren before he left for the ship.

"Daphne!"

She whirled around. "Tristram!" She waited for him to catch up. "What is thee doing here?"

"I never left."

"Looking for more to slake thy thirst?"

His eyes widened in hurt, as if she had slapped him with her words. "I was waiting to speak with thee this morning . . . though I didn't expect thee to be slipping out the door at first light." He rubbed his face and she thought he looked terrible, world-weary, with bloodshot eyes and rumpled clothing. And he reeked of a boozy smell too. "I wanted to apologize. I thought thee might be angry with me. For . . . overindulging." He tipped his hand to his mouth in pantomime.

She wrinkled her nose in disgust. "I was. I am! Why would thee come to my mother's house in such a state? Soused! Like a low-rank sailor."

He lifted his shoulders and shrugged in such a way that Daphne sensed an echo of the charming, lighthearted boy he had been. The boy she had admired and envied for his devil-may-care attitude, the boy she had loved and adored.

"I was nervous. I came to speak to thee about our . . . future."

Her anger started to slip away. "We can discuss it some other time, Tristram. There's certainly no need for haste." How her mother would shudder to hear those words spoken aloud!

Relief flooded his eyes, which did not surprise her. For whatever reason, she knew he was not keen to wed, despite her mother's steady prodding. But then what next poured out of Tristram's mouth did surprise her. More than surprise, it disoriented her because it was the last thing she expected from him.

"But there is reason enough to hurry. 'Tis

time we made plans, Daph. I want us to be married before I sail away."

She squinted in confusion. "Before thee sets sail? Where to?"

"I'm going to captain the *Illumine*'s maiden voyage. I thought thee knew. Nantucket's small for secrets. I was sure Ren would have told thee."

"So Ren isn't leaving?"

"Nay. He wants to stay on island, at least until next spring, so he said. But I am doubtful. He seems to have lost the fire in his belly for seafaring."

"Oh, that's wonderful news!"

"Which news?" Tristram narrowed his eyes in confusion. "That I'm leaving? Or that he's staying?"

"I meant . . . 'tis wonderful for the children's sake. They need him here." She tried to redirect the conversation. "When does thee plan to embark?"

"As soon as possible. To return before winter sets in. So we could wed in December."

"December? *This* December?"

"Too soon?"

"Of course it's too soon! Mother would never allow it. Far too suspect. She will require a year's engagement, at the very least. Mayhap longer." Her mother could not, would not be dissuaded from believing Jane's elopement was done to save face, to hide a pregnancy. And it was not true! But Daphne would go overboard in the other direction, just to avoid unnecessary backlash.

He gave her a patronizing smile. "But I'm not marrying Lillian. I'm marrying *thee.*" Before she could object, he added, "Trust me, I thoroughly understand thy mother's way of thinking. So then . . . we will compromise. Promise me we will wed as soon as I return from the maiden voyage."

The sun rose over the trees behind Trist, casting its first rays on the day. "Let's give it some serious consideration." She was anxious to be on her way, to catch Ren and explain about her absence last night.

"Daphne, I'm not fooling around here. Thee said it thyself, we are like a canoe stuck circling in the water. It's time we started to paddle together, in the same direction." He grabbed her shoulders, wanting her to face him. "Don't look at me as if I'm prattling away in Chinese. I am asking thee to be my wife."

Behind Tristram was the grand house, and Daphne caught sight of her mother standing at an upstairs window, watching them, hands clasped as if in prayer.

Here it was. The moment she — and her mother! — had been waiting for, yet now that it was here, she didn't know what to say. Or what to feel.

She risked a look at him.

He was limned by the sun behind him, adding to the moment's solemnity. His eyes, albeit bloodshot by last night's overindulging, were the clear blue of pond ice, his hair, albeit musty and in need of a combing, the brown of polished mahogany. He was considered a handsome and charming man by all who knew him. Were he to have benefited from inherited wealth like so many others had, he might have been considered Nantucket's most eligible bachelor. Even without the inheritance, he came from solid ancestry, from one of the island's founders, Thomas Macy. And his skillful and determined avoidance of matrimony only added to his intrigue.

Daphne had known Tristram all her life. They'd always felt at ease in each other's company, always free to share whatever was on their minds, but right now, she had no idea at all whether she wanted to marry him. Did she love him? Did he love her?

"Daphne," he said again, impatient now, "don't keep me hanging off the mast here." But he didn't really expect her to turn him down. No one did.

She tried not to look past him to the upstairs window in the grand house, but she couldn't help herself. Yes, her mother was still there.

He took her hand up to his mouth and pressed his lips to the inside of her wrist. He looked up at her, his blue eyes full of expression, of longing, of eagerness. Mayhap he did love her the way she wanted to be loved. "Yes," she said, surprised by the conviction in her voice. "Yes, of course I will marry thee, Tristram Macy."

Daphne arrived so early that no light was on in the keeping room of Centre Street yet. She knocked gently on the door until Ren opened it, a surprised look on his sleepy face. "I'm so sorry, Ren. I tried to leave yesterday afternoon, but Mother, she . . . she shanghaied me. I couldn't break away."

"No need to apologize." He backed away from the door to let her in. "It worked out rather well."

Oh. Daphne felt a tinge of disappointment, though she wasn't sure why.

"It's you I have to thank, Daphne. You pointed out to me what was needed." Ren fanned the flames of the fire and set the teakettle on the trammel. "Look how self-sufficient I've become. Soon I won't need you or Patience."

Another tweak of disappointment. "Where is Patience?"

"Today is Saturday. Her day off." He poured her a cup of tea. "The very day, I've been told, that you promised to take the children clamming."

Daphne bit her lip. How kerfuffling! She *thought* it was only Sixth Day. She *thought* the children would arrive in an hour's time for the day's Cent School. She felt a rosy bloom creep up her cheeks. She'd woken Ren up for no good reason. She thought of telling him about the conversation she'd just had with Tristram, that they were now officially betrothed, but something held her back. She would let Tristram tell him. "I'd told Henry and Hitty that I would take them clamming over in the salt marsh during low tide on Seventh Day."

Ren took a pitcher off the shelf, filled the tea into the small, screened scoop, and poured boiling water over the filter. He waited patiently — as long as he could — before pouring the tea into two china cups. Clearly pleased with himself, he handed Daphne a cup of hot, pale-colored tea. "I've had a serious hankering for clam chowder

231

lately. Might anyone object if I tagged along?"

Daphne sipped her tea to hide her smile. The tea tasted like hot water, but her disappointment in the day vanished like the steam rising from her cup. "I think not."

Ren found clamming rakes in the yard, and after a hurried breakfast of bread and soft-boiled eggs, the four of them walked over to the marsh. Salt breezes swept across the sand, carrying the fragrance of bayberries and beach plums. Henry and Hitty set right to work. They pulled off their shoes and stockings, and ran down to the water's edge to start digging. Ren set them up with buckets, and showed them how to find clams: as soon as the undertow pulled a wave back, revealing a soft sand, dig when a bubbling hole emerged. Clams!

Daphne stayed a few rods distance, holding a clamming rake, watching them. Something had changed between Ren and his children. Or was starting to change? Whenever, whatever, it pleased her to see their comfort grow with each other.

Ren walked back toward her and plopped down on the sand. He scooped sand in his hand and let it fall. Something was on his mind, she had learned that much about him. "I heard the magistrate will return to

Nantucket by week's end. I plan to speak to him about Dr. Mitchell. He is still seeing patients. I have come across him a number of times."

Nantucket was a small town, with only one doctor. Did Ren really expect anything different? But she didn't respond, not until he finally looked up at her. "Does thee truly intend to grasp this nettle?"

"A nettle? Hardly that."

"Friends are known for peace. Jane put much effort into mending the world."

"And yet I would not honor Jane if I let this pass over. I don't believe in that kind of Quaker thinking — don't ask, don't tell, don't even think about it. Jane deserves better." Hitty and Henry had lost interest in clamming and chased after each other by the water's edge. "My children should not be growing up without their mother. The doctor should be held accountable for this."

Daphne made a swirl in the sand beside her with her finger. "Dr. Mitchell is a kind man."

"I don't argue that. But kindness isn't what's on the stand here. The issue is causing harm to a patient, someone who trusted him. Surely you can see my point."

Could she? Because she didn't seem to be able to. "I think any man is capable of making mistakes. Mayhap he caused Jane's death, mayhap not. Surely, it was not intentional."

"What if it was a careless error? Do you want him to go unpunished? To harm another Nantucketer?"

"Of course not. But he was candid with thee. He didn't deny that he had given her laudanum, but he believes Jane found this tincture elsewhere. What good would come from destroying Dr. Mitchell's reputation? He has served Nantucketers for years. He's done far more good than bad."

"Not just bad, Daphne. Evil. The poppy sauce is an evil. Sailors think it harmless and soon they are bound to it. I will not allow it on my ship."

"Jane took it willingly, Ren. Thee must admit that much." He refused to face that truth. "What would it serve to bring charges against Dr. Mitchell? Ultimately, what would it give thee? Peace of mind?"

"Peace of mind that no other Nantucketer would succumb."

"And what if the doctor is telling the truth? What if he did not give Jane that particular tincture?"

"All the evidence points to it. It came from the same flask Mitchell gave her. His initial is engraved on it."

"What if Jane *had* procured it herself?"

He straightened his back and leaned in. "Do you know something you're not telling me?"

"Nay, I did not even realize she was indulging but for that one time . . ." She sighed. "I'm not sure thee will find what thee is looking for by prosecuting Dr. Mitchell."

"Justice. That is what I want for Jane. So she might rest in peace."

"Jane *is* resting in peace. 'There is fullness of joy in the presence of God.' "

He said nothing, only kept his gaze fixed on two sandpipers by the water's edge.

"Mayhap, this pursuit of justice isn't for Jane, but for thee."

He snapped his head around. "For me? How so?"

"Mayhap . . . peace of mind? Assurance that thee is not to blame for Jane."

"Blame?"

"Thee might feel responsible for the undue stress Jane had been under."

He held her gaze a moment longer, then looked away. "Other sea captains' wives have had to make do alone. Was Jane so very unhappy?"

"Nay, I believe — I *know* — she was quite content. She loved her children, she looked forward to thy return. But," she paused to watch a gull swoop down and pluck at a sand crab with its pointed yellow beak, "she did not share everything with me." Great Mary's journal, given to her by Father, for example. It sorely irked her that Jane had not shared news of such a meaningful gift with her.

It suddenly occurred to Daphne that Jane might not have considered the journal to be as meaningful as she did. When she had found the book in her sister's nightstand, it was still bundled tight by a string, tied in a particular seaman's knot that was characteristic of their father. Try as they might, she and Jane had never been able to reproduce that knot. It dawned on her just now . . . Jane had not even read the journal! And if so, why ever not?

Ren dug his hand into the sand, movement that startled her back to the present. "Unhappy without the Friends, I meant." He lifted his handful of sand and splayed his fingers, so that sand poured out. "I took that from her."

"She *gave* that to thee. 'Twas her choice."

He glanced up at her. "But it was a hardship, was it not? More than I would have thought."

"Aye, I do not deny it. 'Tis a hardship to

be read out of Meeting. Especially when our own mother led the charge." Another seagull circled above them, squawking, before flying back to stalk the ocean. "Jane had a hope thee might join her when thee returned." She looked over at Henry and Hitty. They had grown bored of chasing each other and returned to the task of clam digging. "Would thee consider it? For their sake?"

" 'To mind the Light,' she told you on her death bed. So that's what Jane wanted of me?"

Daphne winced at the memory. When would she be able to think of Jane without recalling those desperate, confusing last few moments? "She did. But not just to appease her. She would only want it to come from thy heart."

Ren rubbed a hand over his closely trimmed beard. "I am not tolerant of hypocrisy."

She smiled. "No doubt thee will find plenty of hypocrisy in the Nantucket meetinghouse if thee is looking for it. We live on a sin-wracked island. Happily, God has not abandoned us. He is still richly present in our lives." Ren brushed sand off his pants and she wondered if she had said too much.

"The tide is coming in." He called out to

the children to bring their buckets, for they must be on their way home, and they gave him a disappointed look. "I will consider it, Daphne. If for nothing else, think of the look on Lillian Coffin's face when her pagan son-in-law strolls into Meeting." He regretted the words as soon as he caught the shocked look on her face. "I am sorry. That was uncalled for."

A laugh burst out of Daphne, and she clapped her hands over her mouth but couldn't stop giggling. His face broke into a smile, and she couldn't help smiling in return. She would not have imagined having such easy, candid conversations with Ren. And then it was the strangest thing — she suddenly felt as though she could have talked to him, laughed with him, for a long, long time. She made herself look up, wondering if he had the same thought. Their eyes met. Met and held. And then he touched her face gently with his fingers. She heard her heart drumming in her ears; it seemed to have run amok, her heart, run aground, gone astray. And then, like all such moments, it came to an end.

"Sand," he said.

"Hmm?"

"You have sand on your face."

Abruptly, he stretched to his feet, took her

by the arm to help her stand, the children came running up, and then they were on their way home.

Late afternoon, Ren arrived at the cordage factory, feeling thoroughly satisfied with his conversation with the magistrate — back on Nantucket at long last! — that resulted in pressing charges against the doctor. He took the stairs two at a time to reach the loft and found Tristram seated at the ornate partner's desk, surrounded by paperwork.

Tristram looked up at him with a scowl. "Where has thee been? I expected thee hours ago."

"Clamming. With the children. Daphne had promised to take them, and I tagged along to help."

Tristram frowned, pointing to a stack of folders he had put on Ren's desk. "While I'm gone, thee must conduct some trading matters, and finish up contracts to outfit the *Illumine*."

Ren cocked his head to one side. "I would have thought you'd be grinning from ear to ear to go get this ship of yours and sail it into Nantucket Harbour. And yet you seem all at sea."

"There's been rather a lot to take care of while thee was off on a morning frolic. I've got much to order: ropes and tar and leather and candles. Food supplies, clothing for the crew. More, apparently, than thee can bother thyself about."

Ren startled at Tristram's impatient tone. "You're not bothered Daphne and I took the children clamming, are you?"

"Thee spends a good bit of time with Daphne."

"With my children, you mean. Daphne is my children's aunt. She's been a tremendous help to me." He tipped his head. Trist's suspicions sounded much like Lillian's influence. "Don't tell me you're jealous."

Tristram stopped and looked up. "Should I be?"

"Of course not! Daphne's always been your girl. Everybody knows that. I can't understand why you haven't made it official. I'm sure Lillian is most eager to have you in the family."

Tristram did not respond.

"So why haven't you?"

Tristram stared at him, a curious look on his face. "Thee just spent the entire morning with Daphne. Did she not speak of me? Of us?"

"We talked, but not of you. We talked mostly about Jane." He thumped his fist on the partner's desk. "About pressing charges against Dr. Mitchell."

Tristram swayed back in his great chair, as if Ren's words were a blow to his body. "Cousin, I have advised thee to let this matter rest."

"Never."

"Why must thee rock the boat?"

Rock the boat? As if he was creating a nuisance? "For the sake of my wife, that's why."

Tristram said nothing to that, though Ren sensed there was something on his mind. Chin tucked down, he picked up the quill and dipped it in the ink, then added his signature to a letter. "Thee will need to get the crew to sign articles, twenty-one men. And no greenhands, I beg thee. Experienced hands only."

"Tristram, it will cost twenty thousand dollars to outfit a ship. Where will that money come from?"

"That's why thee must sell the *Endeavour,* as quickly as possible."

"I've told you I don't want to sell her. Besides, she wouldn't bring in much."

Tristram set down the quill. "Let me take care of finding money. That's always been my job and I do it well."

Ren might take issue with that. "How? Or

rather, who? Who do you plan to persuade to give you money to outfit a ship that you don't even have?"

"If thee must know . . . Lillian."

Ren coughed a laugh. "Lillian Coffin will only loosen her purse strings if you marry Daphne." When Tristram picked up the quill to continue signing a letter, it dawned on Ren that he did have such a plan in mind. Well, why should that be a surprise? Daphne and Tristram had been thick as thieves, growing up together, arguing frequently but always mending their quarrels. It shouldn't bother him . . . but it did, and he couldn't say why.

"And thee must seek out a cooper to sign on." Tristram glanced up. "Would thy father be willing to reconsider?"

"Doubt it. I'll speak to him, though. He hasn't opened the cooperage for business yet. He's been helping me on the *Endeavour.*"

"And I still haven't found a first mate. Apparently Myron Gardner is now a wealthy man and has no need for whaling. Thee ruins people with thy generosity."

Ah, Myron Gardner. He was a fine first mate, but had grown tired of the sea. "What about Abraham? He's a fine navigator. He served as my second mate this last year on the *Endeavour.* I would not hesitate to make him my first mate."

Tristram didn't even look up. "Very amusing."

"I'm not jesting."

Tristram leaned back in his chair. "I can't think of a single captain on this island who would sign on a colored officer."

"And yet they are all Quaker captains, are they not?" Ren picked up the folders. "I don't understand you Friends. You say one thing, you do another."

"Be practical. Nantucket crewmen would not take orders from a Negro officer."

"They would if the captain said to."

Tristram frowned. "Thee will get to work on these matters, yes? If thee refuses to sell the *Endeavour,* then at least leave her repairs alone for now. She will still be sitting in the harbor in a few weeks, after the *Illumine* has set sail."

"My mind is at rest after my conversation with the magistrate just now. As I was walking down to his office, I saw a light inside. He has finally returned to Nantucket! I explained the situation and the magistrate said he would be willing to look into it. He needed a bit of time to get organized, he said. Then, it would have his full attention."

"Just like that?" Tristram said in a weak

voice. "He did not require convincing?"

"Nay."

"Stuart Mitchell was willing to bring charges against his own relative?"

"Stuart Mitchell? Is that the name of the former magistrate?"

"Former?"

"I heard the old magistrate had gone to visit his sister in Boston and fallen, shattered his hip. He won't be returning for the near future." Ren let out a sigh. "Thank heavens for that. I did not realize the old magistrate *was* a Mitchell. No wonder you and Daphne tried to talk me out of it. The new magistrate is a young fellow, educated at Harvard. Eager and ambitious. Named Linus Alcott."

Tristram blanched. "An off-islander?"

"He said the governor of Massachusetts appointed him. He's a Friend, if that makes you feel better about Nantucket's corrupted legal system."

Tristram stilled, then gave him an odd look. "Ren, what if Dr. Mitchell did not intentionally do wrong?"

Ren shrugged. "What of it?"

"Thee would ruin the reputation of a man who has tried to help others, all his life."

"You sound like Daphne. Wrong is wrong. If a doctor prescribes a poisonous prescription, should he not be held accountable? Is a man, any man, not responsible for his actions, whatever his intentions?"

"Ren, I beg thee" — and indeed, Tristram was pleading — "think carefully on this. Thee might send a man to the gallows."

"Me? I would not be sending him anywhere. The law makes those decisions."

Though clearly troubled by the conversation, Tristram had no answer for him.

At first Daphne didn't hear his steps on the quahog-shell drive that led from her mother's house, and then she did. She looked up and saw Tristram striding toward her, hat in hand. She smiled. He hated hats and often left them behind, wherever he was. When he was but a rod away, she said, "Hello, there. Has thee been waiting for me at the house?" Had she forgotten that they were to meet?

"I wanted to bid thee farewell. I'm off to the mainland."

"Thy ship! 'Tis ready at last?"

"Nearly. Soon enough. It needs a bit of finalizing. Some tweaking."

"How thrilling, Tristram!" But he didn't look at all thrilled. Sunlight glinted off his forehead and made him look sallow and pasty, as if he might be feeling poorly. "If I were in thy shoes, I would be over the moon with excitement to captain a new ship."

He glanced out beyond her toward the water. "I would give it up in a minute, if I could."

She tilted her head. He stood before her, nervous and tense. "Trist . . . why so ill at ease? Thee should be on top of the world. The *Illumine* is waiting for thee in Salem, thee is soon to captain thy first voyage. What more could thee want?"

"Thee. I want thee." He dropped his hat on the ground and took hold of both her hands. He spoke as if his voice hurt, his heart pleading in his eyes. "Come away with me."

She sucked in a sharp breath of shock and surprise. "Come away with thee?" It sounded stupid to repeat, even to her own ears, but she was *that* boggled.

"Let's leave Nantucket and start fresh somewhere new."

Leave Nantucket? "Has thee gone mad?"

"We could start over again. Have a new life."

"This? I don't want to leave this all behind. This is . . . my life. My family. My niece and nephew. The Cent School. They count on me. They need me."

"And Ren?" He pushed the name out so it sounded like a hiss in the air.

"What *about* him?"

Tristram's eyes were on their joined hands; his palms felt hot and sweaty. "Can thee not leave him behind?"

She yanked her hands out of his. "What has come over thee?"

His face was white. "I'm sorry," he said in a strained whisper. "I'm just . . . it's overexcitement. The new ship, the voyage. I'm just feeling a little . . . panicky. 'Tis a bit terrifying to leave the island without a return in mind." His hands, still held out toward her, began to shake and he let them fall to his sides. "Thee knows how I'm a landlubber at heart."

Her heart softened at his distress. "Just a few months' time, thee said. Just the maiden voyage, to work out the ship's quirks."

He made a show of checking his pocket watch, giving himself time to recover, then flashed her a grin, though pain shone in his eyes.

"Enough serious talk on this beautiful afternoon," she said, a little too brightly. "Come in and visit with Mother. The sight of thee will bring her great joy. It always does."

He glanced up at the house. "I've already had a long chat with her."

She stilled. "Thee told her of our conversation earlier this morning?"

"I did. Should I not have?"

Daphne looked up at the house. "I just . . . wanted to be with thee. Never mind. She was delighted, I presume?"

He smiled, though it didn't quite reach his eyes. "Over the moon," he said, echoing her words. "I must be on my way. I set sail for the mainland at high tide."

"So soon? Well, then, safe travels, Tristram. I will stand on the walk and look for the shiny new *Illumine* to sail into Nantucket Harbor."

He did not return her smile. "Might I have a kiss to remember thee by?"

"Melodramatic as usual," she said, laughing. "Thee will be back behind that ridiculously large partner's desk before thee knows it, counting thy money." But she saw that his eyes were glassy. She leaned into him and brushed her lips across his. He reached out to crush her against his chest and whispered in her ear, "Farewell, fair Daphne." He released her, holding her hand an extra moment before letting it go.

MARY COFFIN STARBUCK

7 February 1663

Richard Swain came by the Starbuck house today to ask if anyone had news of his runaway slave. As he asked questions of us, he never stopped moving about and peering at things. I said nothing, letting Catherine take the lead, but had an uncomfortable feeling that Esther suspected I knew something and wasn't telling. And she would be right.

Richard asked if he could have a look around the property, and of course, Catherine agreed, though I suspect he might have done so whether she complied with his request or not. We watched him through the small window as he walked across the yard, eyes scanning the landslip, before he went into the barn. He was in there for a very long time, so long that I started to worry. The Negro disappears during the day and I do not know where he goes. But Richard came out of the barn. I held my breath when he opened the door to the woodshed, but he only peered inside, then shut the door.

" 'Tis a wonder he doesn't take the logs out one by one," Catherine said.

"No doubt afraid of spiders," I said. I'm

not sure why that popped out of my mouth, but 'twas my mother's ready excuse to avoid a trip to the woodshed.

Esther shuddered and wrinkled her nose. "Me, too."

Satisfied that his runaway was not to be found hiding on Starbuck settlement, Richard Swain rode off on his poor, patient horse, and Esther set the table for dinner. When she brought me a plate, she filled it extra full, and gave me a sharp look.

"What is this?" I asked.

"You seem to be unduly hungry of late."

I did not know how to answer her, and yet she was waiting for a response from me. Her natural suspicion made her study me with narrowed eyes. In this case, though, she was on to something.

Each evening, as I go outside to draw water from the well, I take a sack filled with food, whatever I can manage to take without drawing Catherine's attention — a heel of bread, some slices of ham, apples. Each morning, I find the sack empty, neatly folded where I had left it.

It was Catherine who came to my defense. "Oh Esther, can you not see? Sometimes you miss what is right before your eyes."

Esther looked at her, confused. "What?"

Catherine smiled. "Mary is going to have a child. In just a few months. Have you not noticed how wide her girth has grown?"

She looked me up and down, shocked, and I blushed from her wide-eyed stare. For such a keen observer, Esther often overlooks the obvious. However, I do not think my girth has grown so especially wide. As 'twas a timely and helpful remark, I did not take offense.

All evening, Esther has treated me as if I was made of spun sugar and might crack into thousands of pieces. Throughout dinner, she has spoken of nothing but babies.

This babe is already bringing me a blessing. I have not seen a side of Esther to enjoy until now.

8 February 1663

I thought the Negro might move on after Richard's visit, but he is still here. I don't know what he is waiting for.

I don't know what else to do for him, besides provide food. And keep his hiding place a secret.

9 February 1663

Richard Swain nailed a notice on the door of the store, declaring that anyone who provides aid to the fugitive slave is breaking the law, and will be fined or imprisoned or both.

What law? Nantucket Island has no laws yet.

I ripped down that notice and used it to start the fire on this cold morning.

I had thought our little island could escape the plagues of the mainland. The Wampanoag Indians are treated with respect. In turn, they treat settlers with respect. Why could not, or better still, should not, a Negro be treated similarly?

Esther has asked me many questions about having a baby, and I have freely answered. My older sisters were often a source of private information for me, of matters that made my mother blush. I think it is best for a woman to know what to expect from her body, and I sense that Catherine has not prepared Esther for what lies ahead, for the time when she blossoms into womanhood. I let her put a hand on my tummy while the baby was particularly active last night, and her eyes went wide with delight. She wondered how it felt to have a baby inside, rolling and jabbing.

"It feels nice," I told her. "Like I'm starting to get to know him already."

Her interest in the baby has caused me to wonder if Esther and I will get on better after the baby arrives. Alas, it seems that the baby is the only area of interest she has in me. Yesterday, she remarked (in that oddly suspicious way she has, as if I've done something wrong) on the enormous quantity of wood piled by the door. "The way you keep stacking that pile, you sure are worried about running out of wood."

And she is right! I keep that pile so high that she or Catherine will not feel a need to venture out to the woodshed and stumble into a runaway slave, as I did. But to Esther, I replied, "Sister, I know you are frightened of spiders, and there is an abundance of them in the woodshed."

She has not spoken of the woodpile since.

12

Summer settled over Nantucket the week after Tristram left the island. As Daphne headed home after a happy day spent at the Centre Street cottage, she took a deep breath of the salt-scoured air, smelling the tang. She looked around her as if she'd never seen the sea before, never seen the white birches flashing silver in the sun, or the bay spilling sea foam and seaweed onto the shining beach. She had never felt a summer breeze like this, so soft and hushed, or heard a thrush singing quite so sweetly.

And never in her life had Daphne seen her mother as angry as she was at the moment she met her at the door of the grand house, eyes glowering. "Thee has been spending time off with Reynolds Macy. And don't deny it."

"Spending time with Ren?" Daphne colored and turned away. "Mother, I've been spending time with my niece and nephew.

Thy grandchildren! The ones thee won't acknowledge."

"Stop lying! And stop using those children to hide behind. Thee is creating a scandal right out in public!" Her mother turned, went into the drawing room, sat down in a chair, and covered her forehead. "What if Tristram hears of this upon his return? To learn that his betrothed has disgraced him in his absence."

"Disgraced him? A scandal? Who calls it a scandal? I've done nothing wrong!"

"Thee fancies Reynolds. Thee has been doing wrong with him since —" Her eyes narrowed on her accusingly. "Since when? The day Jane died? Or even before?"

Daphne winced. She could think of no way to answer that would satisfy her mother.

Her mother sighed heavily. "Thee always has fancied him. I remember how thee would wait on the stoop until Jane returned from her trysts with him."

"That was years ago. And the reason I would sit on the stoop was to warn them that thee was home."

"Thee is sounding more and more like thy father. Deflecting the truth . . . while he was off with . . . ." She pinched her lips together. "He'll turn thee, Reynolds Macy will. He'll make thee walk wayward. Just like he did Jane."

"Ren never turned Jane, Mama."

" 'Tis exactly what I feared would happen. That man is poison to our family. He turned Jane away from me, and now thee." Her mother clenched her fists, and Daphne wasn't sure to whom she was talking — to Daphne, or to herself. "I won't let it happen. Not this time. Not again. He will not win this time."

Sickened, Daphne looked away, wondering if everyone in town was thinking the same suspicious and dark thoughts about her and Ren. Already, the joy of the day was fleeting away.

Stepping into Tristram's shoes was a bit more difficult than Ren had imagined it to be. First, the Friends — who controlled the island's economies — were reluctant to do business with him. Despite having been born on the island, being a descendant of one of the first settlers, despite his father's long history as a cooper, Ren was a nonobservant Quaker and therefore not considered to be one of them. Even still, he persisted. He knew that money talked. If he waved it in their faces long enough, they would do business with him. And they did.

But only on their terms.

Friends did not haggle over prices, something Ren found unnerving. There was an underlying Quaker assumption that the value of goods or services was intrinsic and not dependent on whether it was in demand or not. In every port he had traveled to, he was accustomed to fierce haggling, a game of wits, in which each side was adamantly right and convinced the other party was morally suspect. Even the crew, before signing articles, would bicker and demand a higher lay. It was the way of business, of a free economy. However, the first deal he had tried to make was at a chandlery, not ten rods from Tristram's office. The ship chandler was Quaker. Ren had offered a very low price for a large quantity of candles — ships consumed large amounts of candles on voyages — and the man had looked at him indignantly and politely but firmly declined the offer. Ren had fully expected him to bargain for a better price. He left the chandler puzzled.

It was Abraham, wise Abraham, who set him straight. He had accompanied him to the chandlery and had been patiently listening by the door. "Captain, sir, I believe the Friends set a price and do not budge on it."

"But how do I know it to be a fair price?"

"The Quakers do not cheat or lie. They

quote a fair price, Captain, sir."

How did Abraham seem to know of such things? More importantly, how did Ren not? He was embarrassed by his own ignorance. Tristram had handled all these details, from signing the crew to outfitting the ship. Head to toe, bow to stern, Tristram often said, to remind Ren of his value. And now he did not need reminding.

A storm soaked Nantucket Island for the next few days, finally exhausting itself. Ren woke to a sky that was colored robin's-egg blue, with white cottony clouds, and a breeze wafting light and soft as down feathers. A glorious island day. Ren and Abraham arrived home as the children were waiting for their noonday meal at the table. "Hello, children. Where's Patience?"

Hitty pointed out the back window. "Aunt Daphne and Patience are trying to fix the rope that goes down the well. Henry broke it."

That was all it took for Abraham to make a beeline out the back door to help the women.

"I didn't break it," Henry growled. "It's old. It snapped. Hurry up and eat, Hitty. We have to go."

Ren remained by the door. "Where are

you two off to?" He found himself increasingly curious about these two. They weren't typical of children he'd been around, though he had to admit that most of the children he'd been around were street urchins in foreign ports.

"Aunt Daphne is taking us sailing this afternoon," Hitty said, and Henry frowned at her.

Ren barely stifled a grin. He was shortening his days on the *Endeavour,* finding excuses to return to the Centre Street cottage more often. He was surprised to realize he liked coming home, even if Henry did greet him, more often than not, with a scowl. The snug little house was an inviting place, clean and tidy, full of tantalizing aromas that lingered all day from Patience's cooking. As Daphne came through the back door and into the keeping room, they nodded to each other.

Ren asked, "You're taking them sailing this afternoon?"

"I am."

"She promised," Hitty volunteered. "She's teaching us to sail. I'm an excellent sailor. Henry is not."

"I am too," he muttered back, and gave her a kick under the table.

"He's not. He's not at all patient. And he

doesn't listen to the wind."

"I do too," he snapped in a tone that suddenly reminded Ren of his father, Jeremiah. *Interesting,* he thought. *So that's who Henry takes after.*

Between bites of bread, Hitty said, "Last time Aunt Daphne took us out, he nearly ran us straight into a fisherman's dory." She grinned. "The fisherman was so scared he dropped his net."

"That's enough out of thee, Hitty." Daphne gave her a look, then turned to Ren. "I'd promised them a sailing lesson on the next perfect afternoon. Today's mild weather makes it the day to take advantage. 'Tis a perfect sailing day — blue skies and a steady, gentle wind."

"But on which vessel?"

"I have a sloop. It's moored to my mother's dock."

Ren's hand hovered over his hat on the wall peg. He turned to face the wall as he took off his overcoat. "Might you be needing the help of a sea captain with a bit of spare time this afternoon?"

An awkward silence fell over the keeping room. He dared not turn around. He knew enough about his children to know that Henry was shaking his head no and Hitty was considering it and Daphne was frowning at both of them. He was fairly confident Daphne would win. And he guessed right.

"We'd be honored to have the captain come aboard," she announced in a nautical tone, and he heard Henry barely stifle a groan. "We're hoisting sails at fourteen bells."

He spun around and grinned at her. "Aye, aye." He glanced at the grandfather clock. He grabbed his hat off the wall peg and pulled on his coat. "I'll see you all at the sloop at two o'clock."

"But where is thee off to now? If thee is late on the tide, we will leave without thee."

"I won't disappoint. I'll be waiting at the sloop." He stopped, pivoted around slowly. "But what of your mother . . ."

"What of her?"

"What if she sees me on the dock?"

"She isn't home this afternoon. Something about wedding preparations."

This *wedding*.

Ren learned of Tristram and Daphne's plans to be wed through Jeremiah, of all people, who'd heard it from a sailor on the docks who was courting one of Lillian's housemaids. At first, he didn't believe it, so he asked Daphne and she colored red like a tomato. "I meant to tell thee," she told him, brushing it off as if it was nothing. As if Ren was not family, but a casual acquaintance. "We decided last week, in a bit of a rush, just as Tristram set sail for the mainland."

While it was an expected event, hearing of it created a maelstrom of emotion within Ren. All kinds of conflicted feelings for Tristram swirled through him: old loyalty, new rivalry. *Ridiculous!* he thought, thrusting jealousy aside.

But for Daphne? Confusion, disappointment, mingled with loss. A great loneliness overwhelmed him. Yet he had no claim on her, no right to discourage the engagement.

He supposed it came down to change. He'd had too much of it, as had his children. He wanted things to stay the way they were. He liked Daphne's presence in his home, he liked how comfortable the children were with her, he liked hearing stories of the day's events of the Cent School. He liked . . . Daphne. She made him a better man.

His father had a sage response for such nettlesome, complicated matters in life. "It is what it is," Jeremiah would sigh, and Ren felt that just about summed up this situation.

This wedding.

Lillian, a devout Quaker, had shrugged away constraints for modesty to spin it into the social event of the season. Daphne rarely spoke of her upcoming wedding without embarrassment.

All those thoughts ricocheted through his mind as he walked down Centre Street and increased his stride on Main Street to hurry to the magistrate's, waving to his father as he passed him. He was seated on a bench in the sun next to an old salt, exchanging fish stories. Jeremiah looked . . . quite content.

The magistrate, Linus Alcott, had sent word that he would like to meet with Ren at his earliest convenience. "Come in, sit down," he told Ren, extending his hand for a shake. "I believe we have a case to pursue here, and everyone on Nantucket will have thee to thank for it."

It made Ren slightly uneasy, though he couldn't say why. "Really? You've studied the evidence?"

"Solid facts are what I found. I'm going to draw up a warrant this very day and send the sheriff after the doctor." Alcott brushed the palms of his hands as if dusting off flour. "Off to gaol, where he can do no more harm to the citizens of Nantucket."

Ren stilled. Into the Nantucket gaol? It was a grim place, dark and dank, the stuff of local lore. "Surely you'll set an amount for bail."

"I certainly will!" Alcott scoffed. "Too high for him to pay, at least without doing some serious scrounging."

Ren rubbed the back of his neck. "Could not the charges be drawn without arresting him?"

"Not for homicide."

Murder? Ren shifted uncomfortably in his chair. "Even if it was accidental?"

"That's for the court to decide." Alcott rose from his chair, a signal Ren recognized as dismissal, and reached a hand out. "This is an important case for the island, Captain Macy. Thee is brave to pursue it."

That was too easy, Ren thought, as he left the magistrate's office. It shouldn't have been that easy. He left the meeting both confused and disheartened. What was it Daphne had said? He was grasping a nettle. The sting made its way all through him.

As he hurried toward Lillian's house, far up Main Street, he decided not to say anything to Daphne about Dr. Mitchell, not quite yet. He needed time to think this through, to ponder why the magistrate seemed almost eager to arrest the doctor. Ren wanted justice for Jane, but he wanted it done for the right reasons. There was something — dare he think it? — too ambitious about this magistrate.

He picked up his pace. He wanted to be waiting on the dock for the children, to keep proving his word to them. Last evening, Hitty asked him when he was sailing away again. When he told her that he wasn't going to leave, that Uncle Tristram was going to captain the new ship, she didn't believe him. She told him that Uncle Tristram insisted men were made for land, fish for the sea.

Daphne was right — these two children were not easily fobbed off. They weren't going to give him their hearts if they thought he wasn't a permanent fixture in their life.

Despite Daphne's reassurance that Lillian was off island, he still felt jumpy as he walked past her grand house, down the quahog-shell path toward the dock that jutted into the cove. He hadn't seen Lillian but for Jane's memorial service, where she ignored him as he tried to politely speak to her. Most likely she had been avoiding him. He would be easy to identify on the island. His clothing was not the typical garb of a Quaker man, but that of a whalemaster.

He prepared the sloop, untying its cleats and unfurling the sails. Sunshine beat down on his head from a hazy sky. The air was thick and still, the few sailboats out on the cove bobbing like fishing corks. The wind was picking up as the sun warmed the air. A perfect day for sailing. He lifted his head and sniffed, to see — nay, to feel — which direction the wind was coming and felt a return of well-being flood through him, of healing. How he *loved* being on the water.

He wondered where Daphne and the children were, for by now it was well past two. Finally, he walked down the road to the turnaround and saw figures approaching from a distance. He squinted to get a clearer view: Patience was with them, as was Abraham, who carried a hamper in his arms. As they came a little closer, he could see Henry's head tipped up, no doubt peppering Abraham with questions. A few nights ago, he overheard their conversation in the keeping room while he was at the top of the stairs. Henry was asking Abraham about harpooning a whale. Ren could not deny that it irked him, hearing his own son asking whaling questions to another, when he obviously had an interest in it. It wasn't Abraham he was jealous of, it was his son's attention, even admiration, that he would like to have. Was that such a bad thing? Most every son he knew on Nantucket had an admiration, even an awe, of their seafaring fathers. But not Henry.

"You are Captain Reynolds Macy?"

Ren whirled around to face a man — tall and burly, with greased black hair beneath his dirty hat — standing in front of him, his hands on his hips. "I am."

"I'm on the hunt for a fugitive slave."

Ren stiffened. "You're on the wrong island. Nantucket has no slaves."

"Doesn't matter where I am. I have a valid legal claim to bring him back to his master."

Ren appraised the man. A white scar slashed from his forehead down across his cheekbone, causing one eyelid to droop, adding to his look of malice. He reminded Ren of a sailor who once had been a prison guard. He'd not been a reliable sailor, as he didn't like taking orders from anyone. "And . . . you are . . . ?"

"Moser. Silas Moser."

"Bounty hunter." He knew of him. Everyone did.

He grinned. "That's right." He pulled out a paper and unfolded it. "You recognize him?"

Ren looked at the paper. It was a sketch of a black man, advertising a reward for his return. Wide, brown eyes, a broad nose, a round loop earring on each earlobe. He turned it over and saw it was torn from a Boston newspaper. Ren's jaw flexed. "Why are you asking me?"

"Word is you got a black man on your ship. That you picked him up in the Barbados, a year or so ago."

"Where would you have heard such a thing?"

"Don't matter where."

Exactly what Ren thought he'd say. Though, it was hardly a secret. Any sailor on the *Endeavour* could have seen the advertisement, could have sought out a bounty hunter to receive a cut of the reward. "So you've come to the island to find him? That's quite a distance."

"He's a valuable slave. Skilled. His master was a seaman."

"If the master was a seaman from Barbados, I assume he takes part in running the Triangular Trade." It was a deplorable practice to Ren. He'd seen many such ships sailing on the Atlantic. Enslaved Africans would be imported to the American colonies as the labor force was needed for cash crops, which were exported to Europe in exchange for manufactured goods.

"Don't matter what he does. He wants this boy back. Supposed to be a real smart boy. Right there, in the paper, it says that."

"Too smart, mayhap, to be enslaved by another man?"

Moser narrowed his eyes. "Not too smart

268

for me to find him and haul him back to his master."

Ren folded up the paper and handed it back to him. "Moser, you'll have to keep looking." As Moser dipped his head to fold the paper back up, Ren glanced over his head to see Daphne and the children approaching.

Abraham and Patience were no longer with them.

Ren seemed preoccupied as he hoisted the sails and cast off from the dock, as did Henry. Something had happened to change this outing from a lighthearted afternoon, just moments ago, to a gloomy one. Daphne sat in the cockpit with her hand on the tiller and tried to think of a way to lift everyone's spirits. "Captain Macy, would thee like to take the helm today?"

He looked at her as if he'd forgotten she was there. "I would. But I need the help of two small helmsmen, if you happen to know any."

A tiny smile lifted the corners of Henry's mouth.

Ren noticed.

"I'll take the rudder," Hitty said.

"Hold on. Do the two of you know basic commands of sailing?"

"I know them all," Hitty said.

"She doesn't," Henry said, adjusting his glasses. "Like what commands?"

"Such as . . . have you noticed the 'lay of the land' "?

They peered at him. "If you don't know the lay of the land, you're in danger of foundering the ship." Ren pointed to the shoreline. "If the land is flat and sandy, like it is there, it means the seabed is shallow and sandy too."

Henry nodded. "Give us another."

"An easier one," Hitty added.

"Hmm." Ren rubbed his beard. "How about, 'All hands on deck.' " When they looked curiously at him, he explained. "The seamen must hurry to their positions."

"Another," Henry said. "Give us another. Aunt Daphne didn't teach us these."

Daphne was flabbergasted. She had tried so hard to pound proper sailing terms into those two . . . and it seemed all for naught! Though she had to admit there was something romantic about ship's jargon compared to a tiny sailboat's.

The corners of Ren's eyes crinkled. "I see we're going to need to take some time to learn the ropes."

"I know that one," Henry said. "It means learning how to tie a knot."

"Partly. On a ship, it means to learn the use of many ropes. Like this one." He neatly tightened the main sail. "For now, I'm securing the sheet and centering the boom. We don't want the boom" — he pointed to the spar on the after side of the mast — "to swing back and forth. That's how I went overboard once. Hit by a jibing boom."

"Was that when Abraham saved thy life?"

"Aye. 'Tis something I'll never forget."

Daphne was just about to ask him a question about it when Hitty pointed out another sailboat. "Oh look! There's my friend Mattie and her papa. Can thee sail close to her boat so she can see I'm holding the rudder?"

"Nay, lass. There's no room for pride in sailing."

Hitty scowled, pulled her blouse down over the pudgy roll of her waist. She let out a sigh as if life was hardly worth living under such a condition, and Daphne could see by the confused look on Ren's face that he was wondering if he'd said the wrong thing.

"You might have noticed by now that Hitty can be a wee bit dramatic," Daphne whispered, and he gave her a grateful smile. "Do not worry. It will pass soon."

And just as suddenly, Hitty's mood lifted and she was jumping up and down as a gust

271

of wind filled the sail and the sloop started to skim along the water. Her head tipped up at the bloated sheet. "Oh Papa, 'tis a butterfly's wing!"

Suddenly the sloop had tilted so far over, the sails seemed to be skimming along the white-capped water. Daphne hauled hard on the jib sheet as the sloop came about, cleating the line fast with expert hitches. The wind blew strong and steady, and they sailed up into it, close-hauled and nicely trimmed. When she sat back down, she realized Ren had been watching her.

"Well, Daphne, I am duly impressed. You've a deft hand. I would hire you for my crew."

A smile stole over Daphne's face, although she carefully kept that face turned away from him. She'd had to take her bonnet off because of the wind, and most of her hair had come loose to blow about her. She coiled her hair in a knot and pinned it with a stray pin, hoping it would stay tucked in.

They stopped for a picnic at Tuckernuck, a small island off Nantucket where there were more sheep than people. Patience had filled the hamper: bread slathered with thick butter and jam, sliced apples, cold lemonade, and shortbread cookies. The children ate quickly and ran to explore the inlets.

"Who taught you to sail?" Ren said. "As I recall, Jane was not a sailor."

"She never enjoyed it. But I loved it. Father had me out on the water as soon as I could walk. I was sailing my own little dinghy by the twins' age. Father used to say I had salt water in my veins." She handed him a slice of apple. "What about thee? When did sailing become thy great love?"

Ren leaned back on an elbow, stretching his legs out, crossing his ankles, and told her of his first position as cabin boy. "I was eight years old," he said. "My father was cooper for a ship and lied about my age so that I could join the crew, as long as I told no one we were related."

"Did not thy mother object?"

"Indeed. She objected loudly, as I recall. But 'tis no easy thing to change the direction of two Macy men when their minds were made up."

"But thee was only eight years old!"

"An eight-year-old boy can do the work of a man."

"But every child deserves a childhood. Surely, thee will not expect as much from Henry."

He smiled. "Worry not." He shielded his eyes to watch a sandpiper run along the water's edge. "And then there are some men who prefer to remain a child."

"Such as Tristram," she said and he laughed.

Sitting on the beach with Ren felt nothing like sitting next to Tristram. Daphne found herself acutely aware of Ren: every remark, every toss of his head or roll of his shoulders or flick of his wrist. She had never been self-conscious around Tristram. Truth be told, she had never paid such close attention to Tristram as she did to Ren.

As Hitty and Henry chased after seagulls, Ren asked Daphne what had happened to Abraham and Patience. "They were coming along for the picnic, were they not?" They'd barely made a dent in the hamper's contents.

"Abraham suddenly remembered he had an errand to do for thee. Patience chose to go with him."

"I do not believe there was an errand, but a reason to go." He sat up. "Daphne, did you happen to notice the man I was talking to in front of your mother's house? He said he's a bounty hunter."

"Hunting for . . . what?"

"Not for what. For whom. He's after Abraham."

Shocked, she gave him a sharp look. "I

wasn't aware Abraham was a runaway slave."

"Nor was I." He leaned his elbows on his knees. "Though I admit I am not surprised. He is a clever man. I'm hoping Tristram will take him on as an officer. At first discussion, Trist seemed unwilling, but I will wear him down. When he returns, that is."

"Will thee be able to keep Abraham hidden until Tristram embarks?"

"I'm going to have to."

"Ren . . . what if the bounty hunter finds him first?" Daphne heard a noise behind her and realized Henry had been listening to them. She twisted around, hoping he hadn't heard or understood too much. "Does thee need more to eat?"

Henry shook his head. "Is that man going to take Abraham away?"

Ren's gaze was on Henry's. "Son, I'm not going to let that happen."

For the first time Daphne could recall, Henry's eyes remained fixed on his father's face.

MARY COFFIN STARBUCK

10 February 1663

Nathaniel, Edward, and Jethro have returned with a large sack filled with cottontail rabbits, four snow geese who had lost their way . . . and a harbor seal found in the near shore waters off the coast!

How I would love a new pair of gloves, lined with rabbit fur.

Catherine, Esther, and I have been plucking goose feathers for a cradle mattress for the coming babe. The house stinks to high heaven of rendered goose fat. The smell is in my hair and my clothes.

Nothing goes to waste. Tendons and sinews from the animals are used to make thread. Bone slivers will be transformed into sewing needles.

Nathaniel has always been so enchanted with the sea — fishing, whaling, sailing — that I had almost forgotten what a skilled hunter he is. He has a keen eye and steady hand. And such patience.

With those traits in mind, 'tis a surprise to me that he has not noticed any signs of the Negro. I have not told him, for he is very preoccupied with the tasks at hand. Soon, I will tell him.

Or should I not?

~~What I truly wish to happen is for the Negro to move on to someone else's woodshed. Then I would not have to think anymore of this troubling concern.~~
I should. I will tell Nathaniel.

12 February 1663
The Starbuck men have scarcely come inside these last two days, but for hurried meals, before returning to the barn and working late into the night. Catherine questioned their slowness in preparing the seal, but they only shrugged their shoulders and exchanged boyish grins.

They are up to something, those three.

How could they not notice the Negro? He is still there. I am careful when I bring food out to him, waiting until after dark, pausing until I hear evidence of their activity in the barn. I know the Negro is aware of their presence, for he vanishes by daybreak and returns late at night.

I still haven't told Nathaniel about the Negro. While I might have hoped that he would move on, I have come to understand that he has come to me for a reason. He is dependent on my help, and he is expecting me to find a way out.

After another night of tossing and turning, I got out of bed and stubbed my toe on something hard. Wide awake, Nathaniel lit a candle to show me what I had stumbled on. There by my bedside was a wooden cradle, set upon two curved legs, with even and smooth dowels all along the sides. So that's what has occupied those three Starbuck men these last two days!

" 'Twas Jethro's idea," Nathaniel explained. "While we were out hunting, he asked me what the baby would be sleeping in. I hadn't given thought to that. So we started to make plans to work on a cradle right away, while winter allowed us a few extra hours."

A few extra hours! Hardly that. They spent two days crafting this beautiful cradle, with hearts cut out on the front and back pieces. "Our baby will know he is wanted and welcome, with such a fine bed to rest his little head."

"Or her head," Nathaniel said. "It would please me greatly to have a daughter. One who looks like her mother, with chestnut hair that shines like fire in the sunlight."

I climbed back into bed with a full heart.

13

Rain had started at dawn's light. Ren was aroused from sleep by the sound of someone hammering on the front door, as if he were trying to break the door down. He braced up on an elbow and listened.

"Captain Macy! Open up! I know he's in there!"

Ren rolled to the edge of the bed, searching for the flint. When the wick caught, he glanced up to see Henry in the wavering candlelight, standing at the open bedroom door.

"It's that bad man. He wants to take Abraham away."

"I told you I wouldn't let that happen." The banging on the front door started up again. "I'll take care of him, son. You get on back to bed."

Ren slipped on his pants, yanked a sweater over his head, and made his way down the wooden steps to the door, barely aware that

Henry was on his heels. Abraham stood by the fire, eyes wide. "Out the back door, Abraham. Head to the docks and mix in with the other colored dockworkers. They'll protect you. Wait there until I come for you."

He waited until he heard the back door click shut before he strode to the front door. "I know he's in there, Captain Macy! I've been told he comes and goes out of yer house. I've got a legal right to him."

Ren opened the door and unceremoniously hauled Moser inside. "What's the meaning of banging on my door at this hour?"

"Where is he?" Moser shook Ren off and pushed past him to walk into the keeping room, then turning the door open to the small storeroom.

"You've got no right to come bursting into my house at this unholy hour."

"I've got every right! You're impeding justice." Back in the keeping room, Moser eyed the bedroll still laid out by the fire. He bent down and put a hand on it. "Still warm."

" 'Tis mine." Patience had slipped down the stairs unheard and unseen. She stood next to Ren with her head held high. " 'Tis where I sleep."

Ren was amazed at the transformation of

280

this young maidservant. Gone was the timid, chin-tucked, shielded-eyes look. Why, she was downright forthright in her stare at Moser. Something about her reminded him of Daphne.

Silas Moser glared back at her. His expression told Ren he didn't believe a word of it. "I'm going upstairs."

"My children are sleeping. You'll not go up those stairs." Ren blocked his path, but Moser tried to push past him. Ren clutched his lapels, then ground out his next words through clenched teeth. "You'll not take another step without a warrant signed by the magistrate. Now get out of my house."

"I know he's here."

"You're wrong. Now, get out and stay out."

"I'm coming back with a warrant. With the law."

"See that you do, because that's what it'll take to get past me."

"You might be a big man on the water, but you ain't so big on the land." Moser spit on the floor by Patience's feet, then stomped through the door. Ren closed the door behind him. When he turned around, he saw Hitty standing at the top of the stairs in her nightgown, shivering.

"Papa, what did that man want?"

He went halfway up the stairs to her. "He's mistaken, Hitty. He thought we had something that belonged to him, but he's wrong."

"He said he's coming back."

"Never you mind that. I've dealt with plenty of men like him. I won't let him harm you or Henry."

Without warning, Hitty burst into tears. She ran down three steps and threw her arms around Ren's neck. Startled at first, he didn't know what to do, then he did what came naturally. He lifted her up and embraced her. "There now, darlin', there's nothing to be afraid of." He carried her downstairs and into the keeping room, surprised to see the morning sky had lit the room. Patience had already tucked away Abraham's bedroll and was stirring the hearth to prepare a meal. Everything seemed normal again, though it wasn't. Ren's mind went through the sequence for the day — he would need to see the magistrate before Moser did and find out what Nantucket Island's current laws were regarding runaway slaves.

But for now, his daughter needed comforting. And she had called him *Papa,* not *Captain, sir.* That alone was worth the morning's trouble. "Hitty, hush now. You'll wake your brother."

She took a deep breath, and lifted her head. "But Henry's gone."

"Gone? What do you mean, gone?"

"I don't know. I woke up when I heard the ugly man's voice and Henry's bed was empty."

Alarmed, Ren swiveled around to see Patience. "Did you see Henry go?"

"No, Captain, sir."

Hitty started wailing. "He's gone! That man stole Henry!"

"Nay, nay, child. Calm yourself. Your imagination is running amok." But then Ren remembered Henry had been on his heels as he went down the stairs. The boy must have slipped out the door and gone to the docks with Abraham. "I think I know where Henry is. Are you all right to stay with Patience while I go looking?"

She nodded and he set her down in the chair, then took the stairs two at a time to change as fast as he could and hurry to the docks.

Ren tipped his hat to cover his face from the rain and tightened the cloak around his neck. He hurried toward Straight Wharf to make sure the dory had been taken, but to his surprise, there was a crowd gathered despite the rain, eerily somber. And among the crowd, he saw Silas Moser.

Rain pounded as Daphne hurried to Centre Street, dripped on her face from her bonnet rim even as she tried to protect the books in her arms with her cloak. The front door was left wide open at the Centre Street house, yet no one was at home. Daphne dropped her armful of books from her father's library on the table in the keeping room and went back outside. Two boys were running past the house when she called out to them. "What's thy hurry?"

They stopped abruptly, round faces bright with excitement, even with the rain coming down hard. "A dory capsized. Down in the harbor."

"Whose?"

"His." One of the boys pointed to the house. "Captain Macy's."

"Thee must be mistaken." The words were a whispered lament, and her fingers covered her lips. Reactions tumbled through her in swift succession: *there's got to be some mistake . . . it's too early for Ren to have left for the* Endeavour *. . . he couldn't possibly have capsized . . . he knows how to sail through any storm . . . there must be a terrible mistake.*

But a moment later she hiked up her skirts

and flew down the street, crossing deserted Main Street, and ran on toward the gray churning water of the harbor. The closer she came to the wharves, the greater grew her terror, for she saw a crowd gathered there, despite the rain, all faces turned toward the bar. On the calmest day there were breakers over Nantucket Bar; when the wind came in from the north, pushing the ocean toward the shore, as it did now, the waves grew steep.

She shouldered her way through the crowd to Patience, who stood under a tree with Hitty pressed tightly against her. "What's happened? I heard that Captain Macy . . ." Her voice drizzled to a stop.

"No, mistress. He is there." Patience pointed down toward the end of the wharf, to a group of men preparing to go out in a fishing boat.

And then Daphne saw Ren, and her knees turned to water. Praise God, those boys had been mistaken!

She looked at Patience with relief and quickly realized something else was awry. "What is it?" A terrible thought clutched her.

Hitty looked up, tears running down her face. "Henry's dead!"

"No, little miss. We do not know that he is

drowned." Patience held Hitty close against her, to shelter her from the rain and from hearing unnecessary conjecture from others. "Captain Macy is down at the end of the dock, Miss Daphne. Speak to him."

Daphne swallowed and made her way down the dock to Ren, listening to people mumble about the missing son of Captain Macy. When he saw her, he hurried to her and pulled her to the side, out of others' hearing distance. "Abraham took the dory to the *Endeavour* this morning and I believe Henry followed him." He told her of Silas Moser's visit to the house this morning.

"They are together, Abraham and Henry?"

"I don't know." At last he choked, "I don't know where else the boy could be," as if unable to comprehend how an incredible thing like this could have happened.

"Ren, is thee confident they took the dory? Could not it have slipped off its cleats during the rain?"

"All I know for sure is that the dory has capsized. And this . . . this was found." He held out Henry's small black broad-brimmed hat, dripping water. She nearly faltered at the stricken look that darkened his eyes. "But there's no sign of his . . . of a . . ." He couldn't put voice to the words. "We're going out with nets to try and

286

find . . . them."

Daphne had seen this sight many times before — searchers scouring the harbor with fishing nets, seeking missing fishermen. She studied the squared shoulders of the men as they prepared for the gruesome task. Her mind couldn't accept that Henry could be out there, nor could she imagine Abraham allowing a dory to capsize. After hearing stories of him from Ren, she knew he was too smart a sailor, too savvy for such a novice mistake. "Abraham was with him?"

Ren put a finger to his mouth. "Shhh. Quiet. I believe so. But others do not know that. They must not know." He glanced at Silas Moser, who kept his eyes on them both. Then he turned back to Daphne. "Tell me, is there any chance . . . does Henry know how to swim?"

"No. Not really."

His gaze shifted to Hitty, standing under a tree with Patience.

She didn't have to guess what he was thinking: *Please, God. Not another death for the little girl to bear.* "Ren, remain hopeful until all hope is lost."

Someone in the fishing boat called out to Ren to come and he clutched her arm, an anguished look in his eyes. "Take Hitty home. Don't let her witness this." He

287

handed her Henry's hat and walked back, chin tucked, shoulders slumped, to the clump of men standing by the fishing boat. As Ren climbed into the boat, she turned and headed back down the dock. Murmurs of sympathy surrounded her as she edged toward the start of the dock.

"I'm so sorry, dear."

"Such a pity."

"The sea has no mercy, not even for a child."

Daphne gripped Henry's hat even more tightly as these pitying words swirled around her. Each person meant well, she knew that, but something deep down inside her refused to accept what seemed to be factual. She simply could not believe that Henry and Abraham were gone, without a trace, other than this sopping wet hat.

A thought flitted through her mind, then returned. She picked up her skirts and nearly ran to the tree where Patience stood with Hitty. Patience wore a stoic look, but Daphne could see her hands were quivering. Hitty had tears streaming down her round cheeks.

Daphne crouched down and grasped her shoulders. "Dry thy tears, Hitty. 'Tis not time to cry yet."

The little chin trembled. "Then when?"

288

"I'll tell thee when. But not now. Not yet."
She stood and looked back toward the wharf
to see where Silas Moser stood with a clump
of men. His back was to them. "Come with
me," she said. "Quickly."

"Where are we going?"

"I'll tell thee on the way. Better still," she
said as she picked up her pace on Main
Street, "I think thee might soon be able to
guess."

Not twenty minutes later, they stood at
the small dock that jutted off the back of
Lillian Coffin's property. Daphne's sailing
sloop was gone. Far out on the horizon, she
spotted a small single triangle of a sail, bobbing up and down among the waves.

MARY COFFIN STARBUCK

15 February 1663

'Tis an odd and uncomfortable thing to keep a secret from my husband, even if my intent is for his own good. I have thought of sharing my secret with him, the words have nearly spilled from my lips on a number of occasions, but they have stopped on my tongue.

Nathaniel would feel compelled to take the matter to Richard Swain and I do not feel such a compulsion.

True problem solving, Peter Foulger once told me, finds a solution that satisfies everyone.

And there lies my conundrum. We are a small community on Nantucket and must depend on each other to survive if we hope to thrive on this island. Surely, trust amongst each other must be a guiding principle.

And then there is Richard himself. He is a forceful personality. Even my own dear, blustery father, who has locked horns with nearly everyone and considers himself the patriarch of the island, even he has taken pains to avoid an entanglement with Richard.

Yet if I confess to Richard Swain of the

Negro's hiding place, how can I make peace with myself? For after many sleepless nights, much heartfelt prayer, studying the Holy Scriptures, I have come to a soul-certainty that slavery is against God's intentions for mankind. God created each one of us in his own image, male and female, right from the beginning of time. Each one. If we go against the laws of God, what else matters? For it would be far worse to displease God than to displease Richard Swain.

I suppose that is the answer I have been searching for. I cannot return the Negro to Richard Swain. I cannot.

That brings up another dilemma. If I help the Negro run away on this island, where can he run?

14

Ren spent the rest of the morning searching with the fishermen for some sign of Henry and Abraham, stretching nets between dories, dragging, pulling, hauling up empty nets. Again and again, time after time, the nets came up empty. The weather only worsened as the day wore on, and yet they did not stop searching, these fine, brave Nantucketers.

It was Jeremiah who finally convinced Ren to call it off when streaks of lightning began in the gloomy sky, and the searchers reluctantly agreed, turning their bows toward shore. "Tide's starting to turn, slowly creeping up," Jeremiah said. "No sense waiting here. Go home, go to your family, get dry clothes on. Have something to eat. I'll stay here and send word."

The news, Ren knew, would be grim either way — whether bodies came in on the tide or not.

He didn't know how he could face Hitty, or Daphne. Or Patience. If only he could turn the clock back, to that moment when Moser banged on the door and, in the chaos, he overlooked noticing that Henry had followed Abraham out the door. He was swamped with remorse.

Ren caught sight of a woman standing on the dock, a distance apart from the sailors. He squinted, thinking for a shocking moment that it was Jane waiting for him, then he recognized the small figure to be Patience, with a black shawl clutched tightly around her shoulders. When he reached the dock, his father called out to him to hold up. He waited impatiently for Jeremiah to climb out of the boat.

His father put a hand on Ren's shoulder and steered him to a man tying a boat to the cleats. "This is the fisherman who spearheaded the search."

Ren reached a hand out to him. "I thank you. I thank you for your help." His voice was perilously shaky. "I don't even know your name."

"Mitchell. Dan Mitchell."

Ren jerked his head up. "Be y' kin to Dr. Mitchell?"

"Aye. His grandson."

The two men eyed each other and Ren

was fairly confident he knew what was going through Dan's mind: the doctor, he had heard just last night, had been hauled off to gaol by the sheriff, accused of being responsible for Jane Macy's unfortunate death as well as the death of two stevedores. "Again, I am grateful to you."

"It's what we do for each other on the island. We help each other."

An eddy of discomfort made its way through Ren, but now was not the time to examine it. He nodded to Dan Mitchell and hurried down the dock to Patience. He searched her face, hoping for news, but her face was inscrutable, as usual. Was that good? "Have you any news of Henry?"

"Captain, Miss Daphne asked that you come to the house. Straightaway."

Ren turned to his father. "Come with us. Please."

Father and son started down the deck, aware that Patience would not walk beside them even if invited to. Ren scanned the few faces that remained on the dock in the beating rain. He was looking for Moser who, thankfully, was nowhere in sight. Ren thought he might tear the man apart. A sympathetic hand here and there touched his shoulder as he passed by. Not now, Ren wanted to say, shrugging off their pity. Not yet!

They strode up Main Street and hurried down Centre Street to the narrow gray saltbox when he heard Patience call out from several rods behind him. "Captain! Captain! Not to the home. To the house."

He stopped and waited for her to catch up with him. "To Orange Street?"

"To Miss Lillian's house."

Jeremiah's eyebrows lifted. "Say what?"

"To Lillian Coffin's house?" Ren repeated disbelievingly. He stared at Patience. "You must be jesting."

"No, sir. Miss Daphne is waiting for you there."

Ren could not bring himself to move. He could not face Lillian today, not on his best day and certainly not on this worst of all days. "I want to change into dry clothes."

"No, sir."

"No?"

"Miss Daphne said to not delay."

Thunder rumbled around them, and still he could not make himself budge. At last he could put it off no longer, so he started back toward Main Street and up the road to the grand house. When he arrived at the massive front door, he took off his dripping wet peacoat and set it on the ground. He smoothed his hair down, took a deep breath, and just as he knocked on the door, Daphne opened it, a smile lighting up her face. "Ren! Hurry! Follow me."

"What's happened, Daphne?"

"Come. See for thyself."

He followed behind her, Jeremiah and Patience trailing behind him. There, in the kitchen, seated at the trestle table next to Hitty, sat Henry. And standing against the wall, in the shadows, was Abraham.

Seeing Henry there, safe and warm, something cracked in Ren's heart. And something in that sight broke Henry too, for he jumped off the chair and was on his feet.

"Dear God," Ren started with a sob, "my boy, my son." He went to Henry and bent down on his knees, pulling the boy tight against his chest. "You're safe."

His eyes met Daphne's and they shared the moment without words — the two people on earth who loved this child with all their hearts.

Then he noticed his father and Lillian, standing by the back stairs in silence, each considering the other, with a peculiar inquisitiveness in their eyes. Lillian, fingering the stiff lace at her throat, with her smooth, pale cheeks flushed with pleasure, and a shine of excitement on her face. His father, stoic as always, though his eyes had grown tender.

Over bowls of clam chowder, Henry told his father the whole story of how the capsizing of the dory had transpired. Daphne remained quiet at the far seat of the dining room, silently absorbing the turn of the day's events with such joy in her heart. Henry was here, safe and sound, as was Abraham. And her mother, while not welcoming, was not cold or, worse, hostile. She thought it had something to do with Jeremiah's presence, though Daphne had no idea why. Lillian suggested that the two of them take their nourishment in the drawing room, and Jeremiah accepted the invitation without hesitation. As they left the room, Ren's dark eyebrows lifted quizzically and Daphne answered back with a shrug.

" 'Twas Abraham's idea to capsize the dory and trick the bounty hunter," Henry explained. "We saw him coming to the wharf. So Abraham had the idea of tipping the dory over and swimming to shore."

"But, son, thee can't swim!"

"Abraham can. I clung to his back. We did just fine." He looked so delighted with himself that Daphne couldn't stop smiling. "Then we ran to Aunt Daphne's sloop and sailed it. We thought about going to the *Endeavour,* but there were too many people near the wharf. They might've seen us. We sailed out in the cove until the storm got worse, then we figured the coast was clear."

"The *Endeavour*?" Ren said. "Why would thee have thought to go there?"

"Thee said that no man can board a ship without permission. I thought Abraham would be safe on the *Endeavour.*"

"Henry," Ren said, but it was all he could manage. He leaned over and wrapped his arms around Henry, holding him tight, so tight. "Thee did the right thing. Certainly, thee has a brave and generous heart, Henry Macy. I am proud to be thy father."

Henry squirmed to get out of his embrace, tried to pull free, but Ren tightened his grip and finally the boy stopped fighting. There was no denying the pleased look on Henry's round face.

A curious thought circled through Daphne's mind: Did Ren even realize he had picked up the Quaker speech?

By the time sunset spilled over the island, the storm had blown through and the sky was filled with streaks of gold. The sandpipers hurried to their nests while the piping plovers played their last evening song. The wind disappeared, and the gentle lap of the water against the dock seemed the world's only sound. Daphne had slipped out the door to follow the path through the trees to the beach where her little sloop was docked. It had been left with sails lowered but not furled, sheets tangled on the deck, and she was too dedicated a sailor to leave her sloop in such condition overnight.

"Daphne, I'd like a word with you."

She turned and waited for Ren. He walked down the shell path toward her, his boots crunching as he approached. He brought himself right up to her and she felt oddly nervous. Why? Why should she suddenly be uncomfortable around Ren?

"Henry has given me a fine idea. I can hide Abraham out on the *Endeavour* until we get things sorted out with Moser and the magistrate." He looked at her sloop. "May I borrow it tonight?"

She smiled. "Of course," she said. "Of course! Patience and I will gather food for him." She wished she had more to offer. There was no male clothing at her mother's house. After her father's death, her mother ordered everything he once wore to be given away.

Ren stopped and let his gaze roam slowly up the two-story house. "Daphne, it is best if as few people as possible know of Abraham's whereabouts." He hesitated.

"Thee means my mother." She lifted a hand when he started to explain. "I know. My mother can be . . . quite unpredictable. Worry thee not. I will distract her when thee departs." All she would need to do is ask her about wedding preparations, or where she and Tristram should live after they marry, and her mother would become thoroughly absorbed in endless details.

"That might not be necessary," Ren said with a grin. "It seems she and Jeremiah have much to discuss. I didn't realize they were acquainted."

"Nor did I. But then, how could they not? They were both born on island."

The wind came up from the water and tore at her untied hair covering, pulling it free of its pins. Ren's eyes followed the swirl of her loose hair as it lifted in the wind and she reached up to capture her hair, coiling it around her wrist. She knew they should return to the house before someone went looking for them. They should . . . and yet they both stood unmoving, as if they might have been the only two people on earth, until a seagull wheeled and cried overhead, breaking the moment. They hurried up to the house and into the kitchen, to find

Abraham teaching the children to carve scrimshaw.

As the coming night cast its dark shadows, Ren made a noisy show of taking the children home for a hot bath and bed. As soon as he, Jeremiah, Abraham, Patience, and the children crossed the threshold of the massive front door, Daphne took a glass of warm milk to her mother in the drawing room and peppered her with questions about the wedding. In reality, Patience swept the children off to their Centre Street home, while Ren, Jeremiah, and Abraham quietly went down to the dock behind Lillian's house to set sail for the *Endeavour* on Daphne's sloop.

Gaslight flickered in the transom above her mother's door. Impatiently, Daphne waited until it went out and she knew her mother was comfortably settled in for the night. Then she tapped down the stairs, clicked the door shut behind her, and crossed the green lawn rather than risk the crunch of quahog shells.

When she got to the edge of the lawn, she turned and looked back to make sure the light in her mother's corner bedroom had remained snuffed out. The full moon shone down on the two-story house, square and solid, typical of the homes of the day. As a young bride, Lillian Swain Coffin had commissioned and oversaw the building of it, ensuring results that would make it the most stately home on the island. Sea breezes and snowstorms had weathered its shingled walls to a delicate silver gray. The house was enchanting, grand and majestic. It was also cold and empty.

Daphne turned her back on the house and hurried down the road toward town, toward the cozy Centre Street house, covered with pink roses, that she loved so well. Ren hadn't returned yet, so after letting Patience know she was downstairs, she set a teakettle on the trammel to boil and waited.

An hour later, Ren opened the door and stopped midstep when he saw her. His face softened, becoming tender and solicitous, then he recovered his surprise and went straight to the fire to rub his hands. "What a day. Full of twists and turns."

"Did anyone see thee?"

" 'Tis a night with still waters. We made haste, there and back again."

She poured a mug of tea and handed it to him. "At least thee is ending tonight with a problem solved."

He cupped the mug with both hands, relishing its heat. "Not solved, Daphne. Just postponed." He sat down at the table. "I'll speak to the magistrate tomorrow about a legal way to stop Silas Moser."

"Tomorrow is First Day. The magistrate will not be in his office."

Ren sighed.

"But he will be in Meeting. Thee could speak to him there."

He threw his head back dramatically, his eyes scanning the ceiling above. "Heaven help us! Women are always finding sly ways to get their men to Meeting."

Their men, he had said. The words warmed her. But to him, she feigned innocence, making her eyes go all wide and innocent. "Hardly that. I'm just telling thee of an option to see the magistrate. Thee could always wait until Second Day . . . if thee thinks Abraham's situation can wait." She knew the answer.

He ran a finger around the rim of the tea mug. "Long ago, my father took me to a Quaker meetinghouse. On Arch Street in Philadelphia."

She waited, knowing there was a reason he was telling her this information. Ren did not draw from his past without reason. When he didn't continue, she prompted him. "There are many Friends in Philadelphia. 'Tis a large meetinghouse, I've heard."

"Very large. Crowded, too. But there was

an empty pew. Any idea why?"

She said nothing, but waited.

"They said it was the Negro pew. For black Quakers. None came, mind you. My father wanted me to see. To remember the irony that Friends who claim equality for all would separate black members in that way. They deserved God's love but not social equality with their white neighbors."

She kept her eyes on his. "Is that what has kept thee from God?"

"Nay, Daphne, not from God. Only from a meetinghouse. The sea is my church. The ocean preaches the best sermons."

"I don't disagree with thee. God's nature is to communicate, though not always in words. An evening sunset like tonight's fills me with wonder of his glory."

Ren rose and refilled his tea. "There's something I don't understand about being a Friend."

Daphne looked up.

"You sit in silence. Why?"

"We are listening."

"For what?"

"For God. For his guidance. It's easier to listen to God in silence, much less distracting. The quiet allows one truly to listen to what is deep inside. We call it 'waiting in expectation.' "

"Doesn't your mind wander off and down the street? I would be making a list in my mind of all the repairs still to do on the *Endeavour*."

Daphne nearly laughed, but caught herself. His question was an earnest one, she could tell by his eyes. So often, his eyes could be guarded, or even slightly mocking, but other times, like now, his eyes were soft, open. "Sometimes I think about the children at the Cent School. Or about sailing on my sloop. It takes time to clear the mind of everyday thoughts." She tried to think of words to explain what she felt during Meetings. "When my mind does clear, I turn inward and sink into a deep stillness. There is peace there, and a strong sense of being held by the Inner Spirit, or the Inner Light."

"Silence is the same anywhere, is it not?"

"It helps to be with others also waiting in expectation for God's guidance."

He rose and went back to stand by the fire, facing it, legs splayed wide. It was his customary stance, as if he was absorbing the roll of the ship on the waves even though he was on solid ground. He let out a defeated sigh, asking, "What would that mean? To become a Nantucket Quaker."

He startled her at times, the way he thought, the things he said. She had hoped he would come but once to Meeting, and yet Ren didn't do anything halfway. She appraised his worldly clothing. "To start, I suppose, with different clothing."

He glanced down at his shirt front. "Oh no . . . not the somber clothing and ridiculous-looking hat."

"And speech. Soon, I believe, thee will find the outward changes bring about the inward ones. To seek the Light within."

"Mayhap that is the problem with many Friends. They should have started with seeking the Light first, and worry last about the outward appearance."

"Thee is speaking of my mother, I believe. Not all Friends are like her. Most aren't."

"And yet they did not befriend Jane."

"Mother is an elder. 'Tis not many who dare to brave her censure." Daphne knew it could be brutal. Outside, she heard the town crier walk through the street, calling out the hour. "I must go." She grabbed her cloak, and suddenly Ren was beside her, wrapping it around her shoulders, so close that only a hand's space separated them.

"I'm grateful to you, Daphne, for this day." His voice sounded rusty, as if he hadn't used it for a long while.

Her head fell back as she looked up at him. There was something so compelling about his face, or mayhap it was his eyes. Brave but somehow broken eyes, and she could not pull herself away from them. He stared down into her upturned face, and she waited with her heart pounding loud, feeling a rushing well of excitement rise inside her.

For what, Daphne? Waiting for what?

Then the moment ended when his eyes glanced up the stairwell. " 'Twas a day that could have turned out quite very differently."

Of course. Of course! The children.

Ren burst into his father's small cooperage as early as he dared. "Drink yer coffee, old man. We're going to Meeting."

Jeremiah nearly spilled his coffee all over the barrel that served as a table. "We're what?!"

"If I go, you go. You're to blame for not taking me to Meeting as a lad."

"I took y' to Meeting. I clearly remember."

"Once." Ren pivoted in a circle to scan the room. "Have you anything that resembles Friends' clothing?"

Not budging from his stool, Jeremiah swallowed down the last of his coffee. "I'm sure I've got some funeral clothes around here somewhere."

Ren appraised him. "Did that shirt you're wearing used to be white?"

His father looked down. "Is it not still?"

Ren scoffed. "Where do you keep your clothes in this shanty?" As Jeremiah pointed to a cupboard, Ren added, "I'm hoping you've got something to wear that isn't made of cotton."

"Save yer lecturing, boy. My mother dragged me to Meeting every week. Until I left on a whaler, I'd never missed a First Day Meeting."

Ren crossed the room to open a wardrobe and root through the pile of clothing stacked within. "As I recall from your stories, you were fifteen years old when you signed on, and you've missed plenty First Day Meetings since."

"Tell me why you're suddenly minding the Light?"

"Two reasons. First, I want to talk to the magistrate about a legal way to protect Abraham. Second, apparently, I've got some character rehabilitation to do."

Jeremiah's bushy eyebrows lifted. "Yer character's just fine. In fact, I've always considered y' to be something of an old schoolmarm."

"On island. My on-island character."

"Ah. Well, that's not new. Lillian has

308

always thought your character was suspect."

"It's not Lillian I'm worried about."

"Aha! Now I see. 'Tis Daphne."

"You see nothing. Daphne believes this is best for the children's sake." Ren turned from the wardrobe and tossed a white collarless shirt at Jeremiah. "And while we're on the topic of Lillian Coffin, would you mind filling me in about the two of you? That's one tale you've left out."

A red blush started above Jeremiah's chin whiskers. "Nothing to tell."

"Something. There's history between the two of you." For an instant Ren saw a vulnerability in his father's eyes, a regret, as if a brittle shell had cracked open.

"We go way back, Lillian and me."

"How far back?"

Jeremiah pulled off his graying tunic and slowly put on the white, badly wrinkled shirt. "You know this island as well as I do. We knew each other as children."

"That wasn't the kind of look you gave each other."

"We were . . ." He scratched his whiskers, stalling, until Ren cleared his throat in impatience. "We had an understanding."

Ren stared at his father. "Did you break her heart?"

Jeremiah scrunched up his face. " 'Tis a

309

long story."

"We've got time."

"Let's just say . . . when I returned to Nantucket, a summer when Lillian had a certain expectation of me, and mayhap many others as well . . . I met your mother and I was a goner."

"I'll be a monkey's uncle." Ren's laugh was low and ragged. "So *that's* why Lillian despises me. All these years, I thought it was because I was a lapsed Friend. It was because my own father jilted her."

"It wasn't just your everyday jilt," his father said in a rusty voice.

Talking like this, venturing near deeper-to-the-heart topics than sailing, it wasn't something Jeremiah did often. Ren knew his father was uncomfortable, but he wasn't going to miss a chance to understand more about his parents' courtship. He knew it had sent shock waves through the island, a Macy marrying Captain Phineas Foulger's daughter from an off-island marriage Foulger had kept carefully hidden from all Nantucket. "How so? A jilt is a jilt."

"Not this one."

Ren saw the tightness of his father's throat as he swallowed.

"I chose a woman whose skin was a few shades darker than Lillian's. Y' got yer mother's blood running through you, maybe more than mine. Y' look like her, y' think like her. And you know how this island feels about the color of skin, for all their high and mighty talk." A brightness of tears was held back in his eyes as he gruffly added, "Y' know how they treated your mother." He fell silent for several long, long seconds. Then came the words, scarcely perceptible, "Angelica was a saint. Didn't deserve what she got."

Ah, you old sea dog. You're not as tough as you want everyone to think. "You might've told me."

Jeremiah shrugged. "Wouldn't have changed anything. Yer still a lapsed Quaker and stubborn as a mule." He slapped his hands on his knees, a signal that the rare intimate moment was over. "She's looking well preserved, that Lillian. Held up rather well over the years."

Ren ran a hand over the back of his neck, pondering what a curious turn of events this was. They were mind-boggling thoughts. The grandfather clock chimed and he startled, grabbed more clothes, and tossed them at his father. "I won't be a lapsed Quaker after today, if you'll stir your tired ol' stumps and make haste. Change your clothes. We'll stop by the loft to borrow some hats from Tristram's collection."

Jeremiah groaned. "Not the flat hat."

"Aye, we are wearing the flat hats. The full picture."

His father scowled at him. "And you say this isn't to impress Daphne."

"I told you. This is for the sake of the children."

"Balderdash. Jane never got y' to Meeting." His father brought himself right up to him. "What's going to happen, then, when Tristram returns back and finds you've stolen his girl? I can give y' a Yankee guarantee he won't like it and yer big business expansion plans will blow up."

Ren tried to force a smile, but his lips felt stiff. "Why don't you save your jabber so we can be on our way?"

His father's words pricked, surprisingly so. They echoed his own unwanted thoughts.

Not twenty minutes later, they arrived at the meetinghouse. As Ren led Jeremiah to a back bench pushed up against the wall, every head turned to watch them, astounded. From the front, seated on the elder's bench, he felt Lillian's hard stare. Out of the corner of his eye, he spotted Daphne among the head coverings on the women's side, Hitty beside her. Daphne was preoccupied with making some kind of hand motion to someone across the room. And then, suddenly, a little hatted figure rose from the center of a bench, bumped and wiggled and pushed his way down the row of men to reach the aisle, then came to plop down beside him.

Henry.

Daphne braced herself for a harsh conversation with her mother as they walked home from Meeting. Lillian was never without opinions after Meeting. Normally, she would list the many indiscretions she had observed during Meeting: William Gardner nodded off again; Hester Foulger felt the Spirit move her to speak twice, which was two times too many; Barney Blakey scratched himself publicly in a very private place, on and on and on. Daphne would point out that if her mother would turn her attention to hearing from God rather than spotting indiscretions, she might get more out of Meeting than complaints. And then her mother would turn her sharp tongue in Daphne's direction, and Daphne would stop listening.

It was the pattern of their walk home from Meeting. Every First Day, since Jane had married.

But today, Henry, dear little Henry, was moved by the Spirit! He stood and spoke to the Friends in a loud voice, saying that there was an evil bounty hunter on the island who was trying to steal Abraham away, for profit. And that all of Nantucket must not let that happen or God would be displeased, he told them. Then he sat down in his seat and adjusted his spectacles as Daphne and Ren exchanged a look of astonishment. Her heart was full of admiration for Henry. How proud Jane would be of him.

Surely, Daphne thought, her mother would have something to say about Henry's testimony. If not Henry, then the buzzing news that Dr. Mitchell was in the Nantucket gaol.

On this day, Lillian was utterly silent, oddly preoccupied. Daphne didn't mind so very much, other than a slight worry that her mother was ill. Finally, as they neared the house, Daphne asked if Lillian felt well.

Her mother's face was hidden beneath the large bonnet brim. "Don't be ridiculous. Of course I'm well."

"Thee hasn't said much about the wedding today." After all, it was her mother's favorite conversation.

"Daphne, must everything be about thee?"

Daphne had to bite her lip to keep from

laughing. And then her smile faded. Sitting in Meeting this morning, after Ren had come in and sat down, her heart had felt something she had never felt before. She felt thoroughly complete, entirely whole. As she walked down the street, with the sun shining down on her, an epiphany struck her, shedding light on a topic she had not wanted to examine too closely for the unrest it brought to her.

She could not marry Tristram.

Her misgivings about marrying Tristram had always centered on her doubts that he loved her. This morning, she realized that she didn't love him, not the way she should. She was fond of him, but not in the way she wanted to love a man. No wonder she had been full of misgivings, why she insisted they must wait to marry. She claimed a long engagement was for Lillian's sake, but in reality, her mother was so eager for Tristram to propose that she would have agreed to any terms.

It was me. All along it was me. She could see it clearly now. She was the one who distracted Tristram whenever their conversation turned serious. She had often put the blame on him . . . but it was her doing! She did not want to marry him. She never had. Everyone — her mother, Jane, friends — all

315

assumed Tristram was the one dragging his heels, reluctant to propose. And there was some truth in that. But she was every bit as reluctant as he. Mayhap, more so.

She gave a sideways glance at her mother. Now was not the time to tell her mother, not in the mood she was in. That news could wait, until Tristram returned. She shuddered at the very thought.

She tipped her head to the blue sky, empty of clouds, eager to find something else to fill her mind. "I am going to take some food and sundries to Dr. Mitchell this afternoon." She had a hope that the doctor might be released on bail by this afternoon. It was appalling to think he had been arrested like a common criminal, sitting in that dark, stinking gaol day after day because the bail had been set sky high. With a bit of carefully planned timing, she had passed the new magistrate's house just as he walked out the door, and waited to walk alongside him to Meeting. "Jane was my sister," she had told him as she matched his long strides, "and I believe the doctor wants to get to the bottom of the tainted tincture as well as thee does. The gaol does not seem to be the place for a man of his stature, a man so beloved and so highly regarded by all Nantucket Friends."

The magistrate said nothing in response, but he had been listening, she felt sure of that, before changing the subject to discuss the fog. Was it always so prevalent? he asked and she said yes. Then he asked, "Is it true that most everyone on Nantucket is related to each other?" and again she said yes.

"Most all can be traced to a handful of families who were the first proprietors on the island."

"Most all?" he asked, a bit of a squeak. "Even the Mitchells?"

"Most all," she said with certainty.

At the meetinghouse, news had trickled through about the doctor's arrest, causing great distress among the hum of conversation. All but for Lillian. She had been pleased. Despite her complaints about Ren, after learning of the tainted tincture (there were no secrets on this island), she approved of holding the doctor accountable for Jane's untimely death. "He will need sundries. The food is horrendous in the gaol."

Daphne wondered how her mother would know, as she'd never been within twenty rods of the gaol, but she kept that thought to herself and instead invited her along. Her mother shook her head. A little *too* quickly. She was up to something. "Thee has plans today?"

"I do. I have . . . a visitor calling." Lillian kept her chin tucked, but beneath her bonnet brim, Daphne could see her mother's cheeks grow rosy, like the hollow of a conch shell.

Aha. Jeremiah Macy.

16 February 1663
Jethro knows.

I was alone at the house this morning, for the weather has been uncommonly pleasant and everyone had gone outdoors, eager for fresh air and a warming sun. The men went to the commons to see how the sheep were faring the winter, and Catherine and Esther went along with them as far as the Thomas Macy's house. Esther was overjoyed; she has been cooped up too long in the house, she said. I offered to remain at home, for I am feeling weary. I have not slept well of late.

After I had finished some morning chores, I stirred the venison stew to keep it from burning, then thought to scoop a bowl out for the Negro. How long, I wondered, had it been since he had eaten something hot? I took the wooden bowl out to the shed, but the Negro was not there. I noticed the empty handkerchief, picked it up, turned around . . . and there was Jethro. "I came back for the cart. Dad wanted me to bring some hay to the commons." His eyes went behind me to the shed. "I won't tell, Mary."

"Tell what?"

"I won't tell anyone that you're hiding the runaway."

I weighed my options. I could deny it to him. A lie would be easy to justify, as it would be for Jethro's own good. The truth was far more complicated.

And yet, Jethro's willingness to offer me silence was evidence of his maturity, a sign that he realized this was not an easy nettle to grasp.

"How long have you known?"

"A few days ago, I went into the shed to pull some wood, and I saw a corner of the quilt, folded tight under some logs. I knew someone's been living in there. Yesterday I saw you slip outside, early in the morning, with that handkerchief fat with food. I figured it out."

"Does anyone else know?"

"I don't think so. Not yet." He went to the cart and put two hands on the wooden handles. "I won't tell," he said, pushing the cart to the path. "I'm not sure what you're going to do about this" — he cast a glance at the shed — "but I won't tell."

I weighed my options. It wasn't right to expect a boy to keep something like this from his family. And if Jethro had discovered signs of the runaway, it would not be long before Esther found them. She was suspicious by nature, whereas Jethro was trusting.

The baby kicked, and I rubbed my hand over my belly where I had felt the hard jab coming from within. A reminder that its time was soon to come.

This deception has to end.

15

Fog settled over Nantucket, sending tendrils that shifted and curled through the streets, leaving a shiny sheen behind on the sandy roads. In spite of the damp, gray day, Daphne had just given the children of the Cent School time to play in the backyard when a hard rap came at the front door. She opened it to find the bounty hunter glaring down at her, cigar hanging from his mouth. Her heart sounded a loud drum.

"Where is he?" A large man, he stepped around her, passing by her so closely that she had to back up to avoid getting pushed.

"Who?"

"The fugitive. Abraham. Tell me the truth." He grinned, revealing two missing teeth, one upper, one lower. "I know for a fact that Quakers can't lie."

Daphne did not respond.

"Okay, then, is he here?" Moser walked around the room, looking for evidence.

"He is not."

Moser frowned. "You're breaking the law by sheltering him. You Quakers aren't supposed to break the law, neither."

Daphne said nothing.

"I'm not leaving the island without him. He's worth a lot of money to me. He's supposed to be a smart one."

"I have no doubt of that. The wisest, too, I believe. Abraham has the Light of God shining through him, clear and strong."

Moser scowled at her. "I don't know about that and I care even less."

"That is because thee is diminishing the light within thee through thy selfish ambition. Thee is like a candle that has not enough oxygen. Soon, thy soul will be in total darkness."

His cigar nearly fell out of his mouth. "You quit that talk! I've had enough preachin' to last me a lifetime." He leaned slightly toward her, so close that her nose wrinkled in disgust. "Listen to me. I'm gonna find that slave and take him to his owner if it's the last thing I do. Or . . ."

"Or what, Mr. Moser? What else does thee want?"

"I want the price of him."

There. *There* was the answer she'd been looking for. Ask and thee shall receive! She *knew* there was a Gordian knot to be cut; she just didn't know what it was. "How much? How much money does thee want for a man's life, Mr. Moser?"

Moser startled her by moving suddenly, coming so close to her that she could smell his musty breath and nearly gagged. "One thousand US dollars."

Daphne barely hid a gasp. That was a small fortune.

He pointed a thick finger at her. "I tol' ya. He's worth that much to me." He swung around and walked off, the scrape of his boots against the street echoing in the gray fog.

Hearing from Daphne about Silas Moser's visit during the Cent School, Ren went straight to the magistrate's office. After speaking together at Meeting yesterday, Linus Alcott had agreed to examine Moser's papers, to see if his legal claim to Abraham was valid. "Unfortunately," he told Ren, "the claim is perfectly legal."

"But Nantucket has outlawed slavery. Is there not some way around it?"

"His owner is from Barbados, where slavery is legal. 'Tis an international issue, not an island one." He leaned back in his chair, clasping his hands behind his neck. "I will search through my law books and see if I can find something." When Ren started to leave, he added, "Just so thee is aware, I have allowed Dr. Mitchell to be released from gaol, without bail, on his own recognizance."

"How so?" Not that Ren held strong objection. He had not slept well for the last few nights; his mind kept envisioning the elderly doctor in that dark, dingy gaol. "I did not think you shied from controversy."

"A woman spoke to me on his behalf at Meeting yesterday. Rather convincingly."

"One of his relatives, no doubt."

"Nay." Alcott released his hands and leaned forward on his desk. "Nay, Dr. Mitchell's defense came from one of *thy* relatives."

"Who? Who spoke to you?" It couldn't have been Jeremiah, as his father seemed wholly occupied by Lillian Coffin, flirting with her after Meeting, and Tristram was offshore.

"Thy wife's sister, I believe she said." He lowered his voice. "Does thee know that nearly everyone is related on this island? Nearly everyone!" He leaned back in his chair. "I did not understand the tightly woven web of connections. A curious place, this island, is it not?"

"Daphne? My wife's sister? She spoke to thee?"

"I don't recall her name, but I do recall she was quite convincing in her appeal."

"How so? What did she say to change your mind?"

"She asked me to mind the Light that morning, to see if God had guidance for me regarding the doctor. And so he did. That is why I permitted the doctor to be released." Alcott fingered the feathers of his quill pen. "Captain Macy, thee is right in thy assessment. I do not shy from controversy. But I do mind the law, and I do mind what God has to say. This issue, slavery, 'tis a knotty problem. I wish I could do more, legally, but my hands are tied." He dropped the pen and spoke with authenticity, perhaps for the first time since Ren had made his acquaintance. "Pretend I am not thy magistrate for a moment, but thy friend. I suggest thee keep this runaway well out of sight of Silas Moser."

Slowly, Ren rose from the chair and went to the door. "I understand." And for the most part, he did. Any sea captain knew that laws were laws, to be respected, and not subject to whims or bias or sympathy.

To be perfectly candid, when it came to the matter of the doctor's release from gaol,

Ren felt surprisingly grateful to the magistrate. Mayhap Daphne did do the convincing, though he had a hunch it had more to do with the discovery of how many Mitchells were residents of Nantucket. As those thoughts were tumbling in his head, he saw the older man across from him on Main Street. Dr. Mitchell spotted him too, pointing a finger and shouting "Captain Macy!" then walked straight toward him. Ren debated within himself for a moment. Should he leave quickly or should he approach the doctor, meet him head on? He chose to meet him. The two men met in the middle of the street, surrounded by horses and carts, and plenty of islanders who moved carefully around them, carrying on business within full view and earshot. Dr. Mitchell did not look worse for the wear, after a night or two in the gaol.

He raised a bushy eyebrow at Ren and pointed a finger at him. "So then, thee intends to place blame on me for thy wife's death."

"Not I. It is up to the law to decide who is to blame."

"In the meantime, thee does not seem to mind destroying my reputation. Dismantling my life's work."

The truth was, Ren did mind. He minded

327

quite a bit. But he also wanted justice for his wife and he knew he could not have both. "If you did not provide that tainted tincture to m' wife, then you have nothing to worry about." Ren nodded and walked past him.

"I did not, Captain Macy," the doctor said in a loud voice for all to hear. Curious eyes turned their way. "I did not! So then thee must ask thyself, who did? Who did?! That, Captain Macy, *that* is the question thee should concern thyself with."

Ren did not turn to defend himself but allowed the doctor the last word. As he walked toward Centre Street, forlornness covered him, the way fog could steal in and blanket the island, and he felt guilty of something not exactly nameable.

With Tristram so overdue, Ren decided the smartest, safest thing was to take Abraham away by sailing to Salem. A shipyard on the mainland would be easier for him to blend into than on tiny Nantucket. He asked his father to join them, but Jeremiah declined. He claimed he was too busy.

"Too busy doing what?"

"Never y' mind, boy."

"I do mind. This is about Lillian Coffin, isn't it?" Ren wagged a finger at Jeremiah.

"You sly old salt! You're smitten!"

"I'm rekindling an old friendship, 'tis all. And watch yer mouth around yer old man."

"I hope you know what you're getting yourself into. Lillian isn't like most women." Thank heavens for that. "She has a way of cutting a man down to size."

Jeremiah chuckled. "I know all about her sharp tongue. I've had many a jab from it. We grew up together, remember? She was the same on the play yard. Bossing everyone around, telling them who they could play with, who they couldn't. We used to call her Queen Nan."

"And you find that appealing in a woman?"

"I'll tell y' one thing — Lillian Coffin is many things, but she is not *dull*." He spat the word like it tasted bitter. "Not like most of the hens on this island."

"I just . . ." Ren stopped. "Look, you're no greenhand. Just . . ."

"Just what?"

Just what? Where to start? Guard yourself, for Lillian is difficult, unpredictable, dangerous. Jeremiah was nobody's fool, he'd always had strong ideas, not caring what others thought. He did what he wanted, whether anyone liked it or not. Mayhap his father could manage Lillian rather than the other way around. Mayhap not.

"Mind the Light. That's what." Ren crossed his arms against his chest. "Hear me on this. Despite your schoolboy's crush, I need you to come with us to Salem. Just for a few days. To tell the truth, I'm growing a little concerned that Tristram is so late on the tide."

"Well, he's no greenhand, either. He's probably gotten bogged down by buying a few more ships."

"Exactly why I want to track him down. I'm not sure what he might be up to without supervision."

Working silently well before daybreak the next morning, Ren and Jeremiah untied the mooring lines of Daphne's sloop from the dock cleats. Ren stayed on a close tack to sail over to the harbor. He let the main sail fall slack and glided up to the *Endeavour,* oceanside, to pick Abraham up before venturing out of the bay.

The sun was starting to light the sky, throwing shiny mirrors off the water. Ren glanced at Nantucket Town, starting to wake for another day. He considered again if he should have told Daphne he was taking Abraham with him today, or that he was worried about Tristram. His cousin had many faults, but tardiness was not one of them. In the end, he had decided against telling Daphne. If Silas Moser cornered her as to Abraham's whereabouts, she would not have to lie — though he suspected she would not be able to lie. It simply wasn't in her nature. Thus, the less she knew, the better.

As for Tristram's curious absence, Ren thought it best not to create needless anxiety for Daphne. It did strike him odd, though, that as days passed, she never asked after Tristram's expected return.

The wind caught the mainsail of the sloop, bellying it out with a great snap and filling every corner, and Reynolds Macy turned his face to the bracing salt spray, smiling with sheer joy. Abraham trimmed the sail and the sloop heeled deeper, the bow sliced through the waves, leaving foamy wake spilling from its stern. They sailed around the lighthouse and out into Nantucket Sound, heading northeast, to sail around the arm of the cape and into Cape Cod Bay. Ren hoped to reach Salem in early afternoon, if the wind held steady.

It was here, on the water, that Ren had always felt most alive, most sure of himself. Give him a motley crew of sailors and he knew he could bring out the best in them. He'd always imagined himself as a brave man, sailing forward to conquer new waters, but in his own home he had no such confidence. At home, it was Daphne who brought out the best in his children. In himself, to boot.

It was one of those gray, misty mornings, when the sandy roads were sheened with moisture, though it had not rained. Daphne kept glancing out the windows, hoping to see blue sky. It was nearly time to excuse the children from the Cent School when Silas Moser rapped hard on the front window, peering inside, motioning to Daphne to come to the door.

Henry sidled up next to her and whispered, "Where's the captain? He'll know what to do."

She frowned distractedly at him. "He's thy *father,* not 'the captain.' Thy father and grandfather went off island. They left early this morning to sail to the Salem shipyard to see the new ship."

He peered up at her. "Then who's watching over Abraham?"

"Henry, thee must leave such matters in God's hands." But he wasn't listening to her. He never listened.

When Daphne opened the door, Moser gave her a leering grin. "The slave's on the captain's ship, ain't he?"

She stepped outside so the burly man wouldn't scare the children. Henry skirted right around her and escaped out the door, running up toward Main Street.

"I was told he's there," Moser spat out. "On the ship *Endeavour*."

When Daphne didn't answer, he smiled that odd jack-o'-lantern grin. "That's what I thought. One thing I figured out about you Quakers . . . silence is omission. If you don't want to tell me the truth, you just don't answer." He tipped his hat. "Thank you, missy, for saving me time spent searching."

Daphne watched Silas Moser stride toward Main Street, then turn left to head to the wharf. She closed the door, turned around, and saw the eyes of fifteen young children stare back at her. She put a smile on her face and hoped it didn't look as artificial as it felt. "All is well. Let's get back to our work, children."

Hitty wasn't fobbed off. "Where did Henry go?"

"I don't know." She had no idea to where Henry had made haste, but she couldn't leave school to fetch him, nor could she allow her face to reveal her fears. Big tears filled Hitty's eyes. "Please, Hitty, don't fuss.

Henry will be fine. And I need thy help to keep the children calm."

The town bell started to sound, ringing loudly to tell Nantucketers that there was a ship returning. Daphne and Hitty looked at each other, thinking the same thought. It was low tide. No ship would draw close to the harbor during low tide.

Hitty said it first. " 'Tis Henry's doing!"

Daphne found Patience in the backyard, pegging laundry on the line. "Stay with the children."

Daphne and Hitty ran down Centre Street and pounded down Main Street, passing others as they poured toward the dock. They found Henry at the town edge of the wharf, shouting at the top of his lungs as people reached the dock. "The bounty hunter! He is trying to catch a runaway slave! Do not let him use thy dories!" As Daphne realized what Henry was shouting, she joined him in passing the word along, as did Hitty, as did others.

The strangest thing started to happen. The wharf, usually bustling with activity, grew quiet and still. A wall of people, mostly Friends from the meetinghouse, closed off the wharf so that Silas Moser could not pass. He went from person to person to person, trying to talk anyone into rowing him out to the *Endeavour* in their dory or lighter, offering money from an open wallet. No one would accept his money. No one would allow him use of their dory. Not a single Nantucketer! They would not answer him, nor would they let him take a step onto the wharf. They just blocked him, a silent, impassable wall.

Daphne and Hitty watched the entire spectacle. Her heart felt full to the point of overflowing. Such fine, brave people filled this island!

Finally, exasperated, Moser turned away. He spotted Daphne in the crowd and pointed at her. "This ain't over."

No, she thought, as he stomped away. No, she didn't expect it was.

MARY COFFIN STARBUCK

20 February 1663

My hand is shaking even as I write this account.

Yesterday morning, Peter Foulger came into the store. He and his son Eleazer planned to head over to Cape Cod while the weather held and he offered to take extra boxes of bayberry candles to trade.

Peter sensed something was troubling me, so he sent Eleazer down to the sloop with the candles. No sooner did the door shut behind Eleazer than I poured out the story about the runaway slave, hiding in the Starbucks' woodshed. I had told no one about him, but I knew something had to be done. He would be discovered soon.

Peter looked at me with those wise blue eyes of his. "So what is it you want to do about him, Mary?"

I took a deep breath. "I believe no man has the right to own another. I want to help this man find his way to freedom."

"You'll be risking the wrath of Richard Swain. 'Tis no small thing."

How well I knew. "I will find a way to deal with Richard Swain. First, I must help this man go free. My conscience will not let me rest."

"Eleazer and I must cast off at high tide. If you can find a way to get this man to the harbour without being seen, I will take him to the mainland and see that he is cared for. I'm afraid that's all the help I can offer, as we need to load the sloop all afternoon."

Indeed, that would be a great deal of help, far more than I had expected. "If I can come up with a way to make it happen," I told Peter, "I will get the Negro there by high tide. If not, do not delay your journey."

I locked up the store after Peter left and hurried to the Starbuck house. Halfway there, I passed Esther and Catherine. They were on their way to visit Jane Swain — of all people! — and wondered if I might like to come along. I declined, saying that I wasn't feeling well, and it was not a lie. My stomach has been in knots for days. Catherine offered to return to the house with me, but I insisted that I needed quiet. That, too, was not a lie.

As they walked away, I turned and watched them go. Their dark woolen cloaks covered their heads and clothing. From behind, they were clearly women, but their identities unrecognizable. A sparrow flew through my mind again, and stayed to roost on a rafter.

If he would be willing to try something outlandish, I just might have an idea. Hiding the Negro in plain sight.

An hour before high tide, the Negro sat beside Jethro in the pony cart, dressed in my Sunday dress, covered in my spare cloak. If all went well, it would appear to others that Jethro was taking me to the store at Capaum Harbour. A very ordinary event. That is, if all went according to plan, and if Peter Foulger was still waiting in his sloop for Jethro's passenger to climb aboard.

The Negro turned to me before he climbed on the cart. "May God bless you."

"And you," I said. And you.

It shames me to confess it, but as I watched the cart drive down the path — such a momentous occasion — my thoughts turned away from the risk the poor Negro was facing and toward undue concern for my dress and cloak. I was ashamed of myself! And yet I do hope the dress and cloak will eventually find their way back to me. Of course, only after the Negro is safely off island.

16

The Salem shipbuilder, Elias Derby, greeted Ren enthusiastically, pleased he had come. "I've heard all about y', Captain Macy. 'Tis a pleasure to meet y'. Y've got a fine reputation." He motioned to the shipyard. "Let's go see thy grand and glorious ship."

Ren's stomach twisted at the use of "grand and glorious" to describe the *Illumine*. Grand and glorious were not qualities needed in a whaling ship. Sturdy, solid, dependable — those were the qualities he would have preferred above grand and glorious. They followed Elias to the far end of the shipyard, where the *Illumine* — to Ren's shock — was still in dry dock. Ren looked up at the ship, then at Elias, at Abraham, at Jeremiah, then back at the ship. How could she still be in dry dock, after all these many months?

"Well, she's no beauty," Jeremiah said at last.

That was the truth. The *Illumine* was square-rigged, blunt-nosed, broad in the beam, a squared-off bow and stern. Not glorious, not in any way grand.

"And you, Abraham?" Ren said. "Have you an opinion?"

"The big square sails on the foremast will give drive, Captain, sir," Abraham said quietly. "And the fore-and-aft sails on the main and mizzen masts, they too will add power to her bulk."

"She'll need it," Ren said. "She's a hefty size."

"I've had my own misgivings about the design," Elias said, "but your partner insisted. Myself, I prefer speed over size. It took a while to persuade me to his thinking, but I see what he was after. She'll have more sail area to the wind to move the weight of the ship."

Ren glanced at him. "She cost a pretty penny." A shocking sum for such an inelegant, clumsy-looking ship.

"That's your partner's doing. He insisted on the best wood in New England. Live oak from New Hampshire. Cedar brought down from Maine."

"Such wood must've fetched a dear price."

"Ayup, a dear price. Dear, but less costly here than if imported from England." Elias put his hands in his pockets. "And then there's the bricks."

"The bricks? You mean, for the tryworks?"

"Ayup. He wanted them brought in from Virginia. A special clay down there, he said."

"What!?" Jeremiah snapped. "Only for the bricks to be tossed overboard when the hold is full?"

"That's what he said he wanted. Plus a galley stove from Philadelphia. And then there's the detailing for the captain's cabin. Wait 'til you see it. Nothing but the best for you, Captain Macy. That's what your partner said he wanted."

Confused, Ren looked around the shipyard. "But where is Tristram? He sailed to the mainland over two weeks ago. I expected him back in Nantucket last week. *With* the ship." The ship that was nowhere near complete.

The builder blinked. "Tristram Macy? He hasn't been to the shipyard in . . . well, let's see . . . at least a month or so. He was coming quite regularly, and then stopped, sudden like."

Baffling. Ren followed the shipbuilder up a ladder to climb aboard the *Illumine.* The seaman side of him was duly impressed, particularly as they went down the companionway to the lower deck. The hold seemed

341

enormous in size compared to the *Endeavour's* narrow and cramped one.

Stooped over so he wouldn't hit his head on the low ceiling, Jeremiah walked around the entire empty lower deck. Ren could hear his father mumble figures to himself as his experienced eyes were evaluating the space. "How many casks can it hold?"

Jeremiah pivoted to answer Ren. "More than five hundred and then some, in addition to gear and stores."

Double the carrying capacity of the *Endeavour.* Ren had to hand it to Tristram — the *Illumine* was meant for long durations at sea.

The pragmatic side of Ren was increasingly ill at ease, especially as they toured the upper deck. Such extravagance distressed him, particularly the detailing in the captain's cabin. A teak desk with bronze pulls. A mahogany-framed mirror above pitcher and basin. Carved shelves affixed to the walls. A bed suspended from gimbals to hold steady when the ship rocked. He turned in a circle, astounded, and caught the amused look on Abraham's face, and cynicism in his father's eyes.

"Go ahead and say it. Say what you're thinking. Both of you."

When they hesitated, Ren prompted again.

"Abraham . . . what is your impression? Speak freely."

Abraham cleared his throat. "Well, sir, Captain, sir, there is no doubt that this cabin projects authority."

Jeremiah huffed. " 'Tis not a whalemaster's cabin. 'Tis a king's bedchamber. Everything . . . 'tis deluxe."

Ren was in full agreement. The captain's quarters of the *Endeavour* were a mere wooden closet compared to this . . . regal boudoir. None of this fine detailing, nor the finishing work, was apparent on the original blueprints. What was Tristram thinking?

And where was his extravagant cousin, anyway?

When Patience came downstairs after putting the children to bed, Daphne asked her to sit down. She had made peppermint tea for both of them, and pushed a teacup closer to the maidservant. "I have some difficult questions to ask thee." She leaned over and patted her arm. "Please be candid with me. Patience, I could not tell if my sister took laudanum frequently, but thee must have known."

Patience's face, as always, was inscrutable. She lifted the teacup to her lips, and the saucer rattled. That was the only visible evidence to Daphne that she was uncomfortable with this conversation.

"Patience, I must have the truth."

Finally, she spoke. "Miss Jane felt sad on rainy days."

"And foggy days, too?" Three out of four days on Nantucket.

A frown darkened Patience's brown eyes, and she gave a slight nod.

Such an economy of words out of this woman, and yet they clattered into the room like stones down a dry well.

So this was the answer that Daphne had not wanted to know, to believe. She had blinded herself to Jane's habit. What a child she was! Patience was correct in her appraisal — there was much in life that was more complicated than Daphne wanted to see.

This time Patience was the one to pat her arm, snapping her from her reverie. "I will make more tea."

"Nay, Patience, please stay put. I must ask thee more questions. About someone else. About Abraham."

Patience startled her by moving suddenly and swiftly. Wrapping her hands in her apron, she lifted the water kettle off the trammel and filled the teapot with steaming water. Her gaze jerked over to Daphne and then away again, and two bright spots of color blossomed on her cheeks.

Getting information out of this quiet woman took effort, and Daphne refused to be deterred. "Why is Abraham so devoted to Ren? Why wouldn't he crew on another ship? There are two whalers heading out by week's end. Ren would find him a worthy position. He would be safe on a ship, far away from Silas Moser, or any other bounty hunter."

Patience dipped her chin. "All that I know is what Abraham has told me. Captain Reynolds Macy, he says, is the first honorable white man he has known. The only one. He will not leave his employ." In the hearth a log burned through and fell. Patience adjusted the remaining logs with the poker. Her hands were always busy with work: churning, stirring, clearing. Like Jane's.

Daphne watched Patience for a while, thinking of how many of her movements reminded her of Jane. They'd spent so much time together, it was no wonder they'd picked up each other's mannerisms. Choking back the memories, she wished that Jane were here, right now, to listen as Patience described Abraham's loyalty to Ren.

Praise of Ren's captaining was not uncommon — by other crew members, by their wives. But Abraham had a different perspective. Imagine that — the *only* white man he'd ever found to be honorable.

And now she realized why Abraham was so beholden to Ren. She'd understood that Ren felt he owed his life to Abraham for rescuing him when he went overboard in the squall . . . but mayhap that was how Abraham felt, as well. Ren had saved him from a lifetime of bondage to corrupt men.

She wondered of the men Abraham had served — his master, other sailors — if any had been Friends. It troubled her to think that all he knew of white men, bar Ren, was a lack of scruples. Surely all men had a measure of Light within.

Daphne had grown up with the understanding that all were created equal in God's eyes. She had heard Friends declare that slavery was wrong and must be opposed, but that had been all thoughts and words. She could not remember a time when there had ever been a slave on Nantucket Island. Now she must actually do something, though she did not yet know what. With Ren off island for a few days, she had to find an answer.

The evening meal in Lillian's house was a serious event, with four-course meals served by two maids, even if she dined alone, which she generally did. She was formal like that, and nothing could dissuade her from this evening ritual. Tonight, Daphne made sure to arrive early, to ask Cook to prepare her mother's favorite dessert — cranberry almond cake — to dress for dinner without a complaint, and to be seated at the table, waiting for her mother's entrance.

Lillian swept into the dining room and appraised the table setting with a distracted glance, then stopped short when she realized Daphne was here. Her face did not lose its composed expression, but her features seemed to snap into place. "And why is thee here?"

Daphne lifted her palms up in surprise. "Mother! I live here."

Her mother frowned. "I would hardly know. Thee is rarely home for the evening meal."

That was not far from the truth, at least the last few days. She'd hardly been to her mother's house since Ren had left for the mainland, staying overnight with the children. "I'm here now."

Lillian plucked at a wilted flower in the vase. "I certainly didn't expect thee." She sat down in her chair and unfolded the linen napkin over her lap.

"I needed a word with thee."

Her mother clasped her hands together and pinched her lips in a tight frown. "I knew it. Thee is up to something."

That, too, was not far from the truth. "I need some money."

"Thee has an allowance."

A modest sum at best. Ren had insisted on paying for Patience's wages after he learned that Daphne had been providing for her the last year or so. She took a deep breath and pushed out the words, "I need one thousand dollars."

Her mother's eyes went wide with surprise. "Whatever for?"

"I think it best not to say more."

"Oh Daphne, what kind of pressure is Reynolds Macy putting on thee?"

"None! 'Tis not what thee thinks!" Whatever it was she *was* thinking! "I will reimburse thee." She bit her lip. "It might take some time . . . but I will pay thee back."

"Is this for Tristram's sake? Does he need more money?"

"More money?" Daphne's head snapped up. "Did Tristram come to thee for money?"

Her mother's lips tightened, with pursed lines along them like a drawstring bag. "He needed money to outfit his new ship."

"And thee provided it to him? But why?"

Lillian tucked her chin. "Soon enough, Tristram will be family." She lifted a hand, palm up, sweeping it in an arc. "After all, this will all belong to thee and him one day."

That rationale just didn't sound like her mother's way of thinking. Lillian was parsimonious with money and only provided loans when she had reason to benefit. And then, slowly, it dawned on Daphne. "Mother, did thee make some kind of bargain with Tristram?"

Ignoring her question, Lillian reached for the silver bell on the table.

"Mother, I asked thee a question. I would like an answer."

Her mother waited until the maid cleared their plates and left the room. She wiped her lips with the napkin and spread it on her lap, taking care to smooth out the edges. When Daphne cleared her throat in an "I'm waiting" cough, her mother snapped her head up. "Does thee think Tristram would have ever proposed to thee without some encouragement? Is thee so vain as to think such a thing?"

"Oh, Mother. Thee didn't!" Daphne sat back in her chair, stunned. "So thee offered funds to Tristram if he proposed marriage to me." It should have infuriated her, and yet she felt tremendously relieved, as if tossing off a heavy backpack. She kept her head down and chin tucked. To her mother, she appeared distraught. In reality, she was thinking through the irony of her engagement, biting her lip to keep from breaking out in laughter. Tristram did not love her any more than she loved Tristram, not in the way a man and woman should love each other. She no longer dreaded his return, for she wouldn't be hurting him at all. She would be setting him free. And she, too, would be freed from an obligation she did not know she didn't even want until she had it in her hands.

But her mother did not need to know any of this. Daphne did not lift her face until she felt she could keep her expression utterly stoic. "Mother, I wish thee would have told me what thee did." Just as she thought, her mother had been carefully watching her reaction.

"Thee wants such candor from me, yet thee will not tell me the truth about why thee needs one thousand dollars."

Daphne folded her hands and put them on the tabletop. "I want to give the bounty hunter the funds to leave the island."

Lillian sighed loudly and sniffed so hard her nose quivered. "So it all funnels back to making an impression on Reynolds Macy."

She kept her voice low and controlled. "Nay, Mother. It has to do with protecting a man's freedom."

"I don't believe thee. I have told thee before and I will tell thee again . . . I will not contribute a single pence to anything that benefits that man. He has stolen too much from me."

Daphne jumped from the table and stood near her mother. She could hear the rising hysteria in her voice, but she couldn't seem to stop it. "Tell me this, Mother. Why is Reynolds Macy the source of thy bitterness? Why has thee made him thy scapegoat? Anything that goes wrong in thy life is somehow the fault of Ren. He is a fine man, a noble and caring man."

Lillian's face went livid white with anger. She rose and gripped Daphne's chin, hard, with her fingers. "Not a penny will thee get from me. Not. One. Pence." She released Daphne's chin and swept from the room, slamming the door behind her.

The serving maid had entered from the kitchen and stood frozen, dessert plates held in her hands, baffled by what she'd witnessed. Daphne slipped back down into her chair and rubbed her chin. "Set them down, Lucia. I'll eat them both."

22 February 1663

Richard Swain came in the store today, alongside Thomas Macy. Richard needed a pound of nails. While gathering the nails in a sack, I listened to their discussion about the runaway slave. "He's worth a pretty penny to me."

Thomas Macy, a man who never holds himself back from asking questions, wondered aloud how much Richard had paid for him.

"Twenty pounds."

"Twenty pounds!" Thomas whistled in amazement. " 'Tis a princely sum, Richard."

I could not resist interjecting, though in retrospect, I should have. "What price can be put on a human life?"

Both men wheeled around to look at me. Richard Swain's darting eyes went from confusion to a sudden shrewdness. "Mary, what do you know of this matter?"

"I know that life is precious, is it not?"

Richard tilted his head, eyes narrowed. "In this case, 'tis worth twenty pounds."

'Twas a message aimed at me with a very sharp point, and I received it.

After much thought and prayer, I have decided that I must pay Richard Swain twenty pounds — the price of the runaway laborer (he is, I hope and pray, no longer a slave). And yet, twenty pounds is a sizeable sum. I have not that kind of money, nor do my parents. I could not ask it of Nathaniel, for that would put him in a very awkward position with his family. His father might be willing to part with the money if he knew what the purpose of it was, as he has a tender heart toward the underprivileged, but his mother does not. She counts pennies very carefully. I suspect it would create a bitterness in the home for many days and months to come, mostly toward me.

I thought of asking my brothers for the money, then dismissed it. Their assets are not in pounds, but in building supplies for their businesses. It would be a hardship on them.

That left me with one option. The buried treasure of Spanish silver that Eleazer Foulger and I came across. It fits all the parameters we agreed to set on the treasure — to use the coins only to help one in need and not for our own personal benefit.

I wish Eleazer were on island, but he has

not returned from the mainland with his father. I need his help to dig the treasure up from under the oak tree. I am getting rather bulky these days.

24 February 1663

I could not wait any longer. Eleazer has not returned to the island, and I must take care of this before the baby arrives.

This afternoon, I asked Jethro if he would take me for a ride in his pony cart. He was delighted to oblige me, as driving is a new skill for him and he is eager to practice. I put two shovels in the back of the cart and he raised his eyebrows, reminding me so very much of Nathaniel, but he did not question what they were needed for.

I directed him to the oak tree in the Founders' Burial Ground. I stood under the largest branch, marked six long strides from the tree trunk, and started to dig. Jethro took the shovel from my hands and did the rest of the digging. Every now and then he would look up at me and I would shake my head. "Deeper." Back to the task he would go. I think he enjoyed the mystery of this strange adventure.

His shovel made a clunking sound, and he looked over at me, sitting under the tree. I nodded and rose, rather clumsily, to my feet. "That's it."

He dug and pulled and dug and pulled. It took quite a while, but eventually, the small metal chest emerged. "Whoa," he said when he lifted it out of the ground. And another "whoa" when he pried open the chest to find the sacks of coins.

He looked at me with wide eyes. "Mary, you are full of surprises."

"This must remain another one of our secrets, Jethro," I told him, and he gave me a knowing grin, as if to say, "But of course."

I took what coinage that I needed and left a small note inside the chest, dated and with an explanation, in the case that Eleazer had need of the coins. Jethro placed the chest back in its hiding place and filled the hole with dirt. He did a fine job spreading the sod back over the hole. On the way home, Jethro did not ask a single question of me about the treasure, nor about why I suddenly needed the coins.

He is a remarkable boy.

2 March 1663

Today was the opportunity I had been waiting for. Richard Swain came into the store, alone, to purchase a few specially ordered items. He flipped a coin at me for his purchases and I caught it. Then I took the Spanish pieces of eight from my apron pocket and pushed them across the counter to him.

He narrowed his eyes. "What is this?"

"This, Richard, is the price of a man's life."

He leaned across the counter and wagged a finger at me. "I knew you had something to do with it. I knew it. Where is he?"

"He is gone from the island."

"You had no right to interfere."

"Slavery does not belong on this island. 'Tis not needed. You can hire the Indians to do work for you."

"That's not for you to decide. You need to know your place, Mary Starbuck. You and your father act like you're running this island. I wonder what the others will have to say about your trickery."

I put my hand on his brown sack, on the items he specially ordered every few months. "And I wonder what the others might think of these items, if someone were to tell them? What of your wife? I wonder of her response."

Richard's eyes moved immediately to

the sack. Instead of the anger I expected, a cagey grin spread slowly across his face, followed by a strange and admiring expression, as if he'd been outfoxed by a fox. He winked, then replaced his hat and backed from the room.

17

Buried treasure. Late in the night, Daphne read that entry in Great Mary's journal, rose from her bed to hold it close to the candlelight, squinting, and reread it. The Starbuck family had passed along the legend of Great Mary's buried treasure to each generation, but no one thought of it as anything more than that — a family legend.

Then again, the Starbuck family had considered the existence of Great Mary's journal as nothing more than hearsay too, and yet Daphne was holding it in her hands.

If there was treasure buried on this island, if Spanish silver still remained in that chest, then this might be the way to buy Abraham's freedom.

Under an oak tree. Of course, of course! It was so obvious. It was the oak tree in the Founders' Burial Ground, the one that Great Mary was buried beside. She knew the tree well. She and Jane used to climb in it when they were children.

She had not a surfeit of time to explore. Now that Silas Moser knew Abraham was hiding on the *Endeavour,* he would no doubt find a way to capture him.

She wrote down instructions in the journal about how many lengths to stride away from the tree before starting to dig. This, it was an overwhelming task, and she did not think she could do it alone. If only Ren were here, or Tristram, but they had yet to return from Salem.

She went to the window, holding tight to her elbows. It was a full moon and a clear, warm night, after two days of rain. The ground would be soft, malleable enough for a woman to dig. It would be dawn in a few hours, providing just enough light to see where she was going, not enough light to alert anyone to her task. Patience was asleep upstairs in the children's room. Resolve filled Daphne. Now was the time to act.

She gathered a shovel and hoe, found an old sack, and just before she left the house, she remembered the instructions she'd written down from Great Mary's journal. She went back upstairs and found them by her bedside. As she tiptoed down the stairs, there stood Henry, dressed, at the bottom of the stairwell, hand covering the mortgage button on the newel post. "Wherever you're going," he said, "I'm going with you."

They stood under the tree. The largest branch was the one Daphne and Jane used to climb on, because it was the only one they could reach. How odd to think that treasure had been resting underneath them, all those years! She walked six paces out — woman-sized, not man-sized, because she thought that was what Great Mary would have done and she felt she was starting to understand how Great Mary thought. "All right, Henry. Six paces from the trunk to the farthest branch, to not disturb its roots. Then, we start to dig."

Two hours later, as the sun was cresting the tops of the trees and Daphne thought this effort was futile — if there had been any treasure, surely, someone had made off with it — her shovel made a thudding sound. She and Henry looked at each other, eyes wide.

"Is that what you're looking for?" he asked.

"It might be." With a renewed vigor, they both started digging around the sides to enlarge the hole. The ground was soft, which made it easy to dig down but also heavy with mud. When they finally got the four edges exposed, they struggled and wrestled to get it up. Daphne looked at Henry, covered in mud, his spectacles smudged, but working hard to help her. With one last yank, the box lifted an inch, then another. Henry on one side, Daphne on the other, and they pulled. And pulled. And pulled. Finally, the metal box eased upward with a strange sucking sound, then a pop. They got it up, away from the mound of dirt they'd made, and fell backward, out of breath.

Henry recovered first. He pushed his spectacles up on the bridge of his nose and peered at Daphne. "Grandmother Lillian would be upset with thee."

Daphne glanced down at her dress, her hands, her feet. She looked a fright, covered with mud, sweating like she'd never sweated. "Oh, thee is right! She would be furious." What a delightful thought! She scrambled up on her knees and put two hands on the metal box. "Henry, I'm not sure what is inside. Is thee ready?"

Henry looked all around the cemetery. "Better hurry. The sun is waking up."

Daphne eased the latch open and held her breath. Henry gasped. Inside were bags filled with Spanish silver, pieces of eight, just as Great Mary had said. Underneath the bags of silver was a linen sack. She wiped her hands on her petticoat and opened the sack. It was filled with notes written in faded ink, mementos from those who had dipped into the treasure, and for what reason. She nearly cried as she read each one aloud, handling it carefully and putting it back inside the linen sack. They were such purposeful uses, all meant to benefit someone. Nothing frivolous, all for a greater purpose of moving a person forward in life.

"What are we going to do?"

Out of her apron pocket, Daphne pulled the note of instructions she'd written to find the treasure. "I need something to write with." She looked around the tree. "I should've thought."

Henry came up with the idea of making ink of mud and using a small twig for a pencil. Carefully, Daphne wrote the date, *Sixth Day, Ninth Month, in the year 1821,* and her initials, and then, *Ransom to free a runaway slave.*

"Oh! Aunt Daphne, so that's why we're here! To save Abraham."

Daphne looked up at him. "Henry, thee must keep this all a secret, just between us."

Henry put a hand on his heart. "Hand over heart. I can do it."

"Not even tell Hitty."

"I'd never tell Hitty. She can't keep a secret."

Daphne blew the mud dry. It wasn't ideal, but it was the best she could do. She filled her pockets with as much Spanish silver as they could hold, tucked her note into the linen sack, set the silver bags on top, closed the treasure chest, and returned it to its resting place. The sky was lighting the clouds as they replaced the dirt, shovelful by shovelful, patched the sod back together, and patted the area with the backs of their shovels. It looked a mess, though she didn't think many people ventured into the cemetery. But they did pass by it along the road, and she didn't want to bring any attention to it. She felt one raindrop, then a few more, and soon a steady drizzle began.

Henry stamped on top of the dirt pile to press it down. He looked up. "Uh-oh. Rain!"

Daphne smiled. "Henry, this rain is a gift from God. It will cover up our dirt, keep people away from the cemetery, and if it keeps up, we will return home looking like we fell in that creek." They picked up their shovels and hurried toward Centre Street, listening carefully to the wailing tone of the town crier as he declared the hour of seven o'clock, taking care to avoid him.

■ ■ ■ ■

When Daphne and Henry arrived back at
the cottage, they found Patience waiting for
them by the door, as if she knew to expect
them, though the look on her face was one
of astonishment.

"Don't ask, Patience."

And she didn't. She took one look at them
and went to the hearth fire, first to stoke it,
then to start a kettle of water for baths.
Daphne hurried upstairs to Ren's empty
room and grabbed a pillowcase from his
bed. She dumped the pillow out and filled
it with the Spanish coins. She had no idea
what they were worth, or whether she'd
gathered the amount needed for Abraham's
ransom. One thousand dollars! She didn't
care if she was giving Moser more than one
thousand dollars . . . only that she had
enough. She took the pillowcase of coins
and hid it under Ren's bed, then went back
downstairs. "I need to borrow one of your
dresses, Patience. And if you don't mind
washing mine as quickly as possible, I would
appreciate it."

Patience bit her lip, appraised Daphne
with a long sweeping glance, and went to
the storeroom. Moments later, she emerged

with one of Jane's dresses, a blue linen, loose fitting, with a white apron to cover it. "This will fit. 'Tis better than one of mine."

Daphne lifted the dress. Why, she remembered it as one of Jane's maternity dresses! A laugh burst out of her. She knew she was bigger than Jane, but she had never thought of herself as *that* much bigger.

Late in the day, after Daphne's brown dress was washed and pressed, she fetched the pillowcase from under Ren's bed, stuffed it into her drawing bag, and stopped for a moment to check her hair in the small mirror above his wash basin. She noticed his soap mug, his razor, sitting beside his pitcher. It felt a little strange to be observing the daily details of a man's life. She lifted the soap mug and smelled the scent of Ren. She was not a worrier by nature, not like her sister was, but she did wonder if something had happened to Ren, to Jeremiah, and to Tristram, for certainly they should have returned by now. She wondered about Abraham too, if he had enough supplies on the *Endeavour*. It wasn't time to worry, not yet, for there was nothing she could do for those men other than prayer, and there was a pressing thing she needed to do. Now was the time to find Silas Moser.

As she went to the door, Patience stopped her, a beseeching look in her eyes. "Patience, worry thee not. When I return, I hope to have good tidings to tell thee." She smiled and patted Patience's arm. "And thee can tell Abraham."

She found Silas Moser in the Seven Seas Tavern. She sent a passing sailor in to fetch Moser, and when the uncouth man stumbled out, his eyes squinted in the daylight. "Well, it's the Quaker lady." Moser was breathing heavily, slurring his words, and she could smell the rank odor of his breath. "So you do lie, after all. I finally rowed myself out to the captain's ship. It was empty."

Empty? Then where was Abraham? Ren must have taken him to Salem, she surmised. Thank God for that! "I brought thee money. Ransom money."

Moser wavered, then his eyes focused in on her. "You've got one thousand dollars?"

"Better than American dollars. I've got Spanish silver. More than enough." She held out one Spanish piece of eight for him to examine.

He rubbed it between his fingers, held it up to the sunlight, examined front and back, and then bit down hard on it with his back molars. "Well, well, I'll be blowed."

"Thee is welcome to take the coin to the bank manager." She hoped he wouldn't, though, as she didn't want to draw attention on the island to the rare coins.

"Give me the money."

"As soon as thee provides Abraham's freedom papers."

"Hold on, missy. You sure you got enough for one thousand dollars?"

"Probably more," she said, although she could hear the lie in her words. She had no idea what the coins were worth. "If there is more, then thee is welcome to it. Mayhap thee can use it to find employment that is honorable, so that thy soul will not spend eternity anguishing in darkness."

His eyes widened in what Daphne recognized as fear, before quickly narrowing to slits. "You quit that holy nonsense. Wait here." He went back inside the tavern. A long time passed before he returned with an envelope. "Give me the money."

"First, the paperwork." She took it from him, opened the envelope and read aloud from the paper within:

I hereby certify that Abraham, property of Captain Willard Scott, was on the 6th day of September, 1821, admitted into the freedom of Nantucket Island, and his ransom has been paid in full.

Silas Moser, Bounty Hunter

"Surprisingly good penmanship for such an unlearned, uncouth man."

Moser scowled at her.

"It will do." She knew enough that it was legitimate. She bent down to her drawstring purse and tucked it in. With two hands, she pulled out the pillowcase of coins and handed it to him. "A deal is a deal."

He took the sack like a starving man, opened it, and stuffed his face into it. She left him, breathing in the moldy scent of Great Mary's treasured coins. She had barely crossed the street when she heard Moser call her name. She thought of ignoring him, of breaking into a run, but instead she turned around slowly.

"You asked me how I found out the slave was hiding out on that ship. I didn't answer, but I'll tell you now." His lips lifted in a sneering smile. "Your mother. She told me where he was. She's the one who brought me to Nantucket in the first place. She sought me out in Boston and paid my passage here."

Ren, Jeremiah, and Abraham spent two days searching for Tristram, first in Salem, then they went to Boston, despite some risk to Abraham. Ren and Jeremiah left Abraham on the sloop, where he would go unnoticed. Jeremiah had bought a Boston newspaper that had a page full of rewards offered for runaway slaves, and although the city was crowded, they didn't want to alert any other bounty hunters to Abraham's presence.

They spoke to shipping agents, to dockworkers, but no one recalled seeing Tristram Macy. No schooner had gone missing recently. Jeremiah suggested Ren go to the local authorities, in the event of foul play. The police had no information about a Tristram Macy, and even took Ren to the jail to have a look at the more recently arrested inmates. Ren considered himself fairly hardened after a life at sea, but what he saw in those crowded and depressing prison cells turned his stomach into a tight knot.

When he met up with Jeremiah and Abraham on the docks, he said, "I don't know what else to do. Where else could we look? I can't think of any other stone to turn over."

"One more, son. The cabinetmaker."

Abraham gave him a curious look. "A cabinetmaker?"

Jeremiah puffed on his pipe. "In most places, they double as the coroners. A coffin is just another type of cabinet."

So the last stop Ren made in Boston was with the cabinetmaker who, indeed, also worked as the city coroner. Ren's stomach clenched again when the undertaker took him to the cellar to view an unidentified body that the police had brought to him. He braced himself as the coroner pulled back the sheet, but the body did not belong to his cousin.

"How could a man simply vanish?"

"Was he a simpleton?" the coroner asked. "Sometimes, those fellows end up shanghaied. Get 'em drunk, drugged, and stashed away on a ship bound for another land."

"Nay, nay. He was . . . he *is* . . . a clever man."

"I see. Well, in that case, sometimes very clever men do not want to be found."

Ren startled at that. It was not a foreign thought to him. Most men at sea were escaping from someone, or somewhere. But Tristram was not like those men. He didn't even want to be at sea. He preferred being on land, behind a desk. He had no reason to not want to be found.

Finally, Ren and Jeremiah decided to return to Nantucket, with hopes that Tristram had returned in their absence. If not, Ren would seek out whichever vessel it was that had delivered his cousin to the mainland.

As Ren let the sails fall slack to glide the sloop to the dock, he was surprised to find Daphne and the children, waiting for him, waving to him. His heart lurched within him. He had not expected such a welcome. He was coming home, and he had loved ones waiting for him. A warm feeling started deep inside, spreading throughout his body, ending with a smile. *Family,* he thought, *it's become the beat of my heart.*

Jeremiah went to the back door of Lillian's house and let himself in. Ren and Daphne watched him go, exchanging a puzzled look. "Wonders never cease," Ren said, amused.

Daphne felt far less amused about anything that had to do with her mother. She let out a deep sigh and Ren noticed. "What is it? Has something happened?"

She had confronted her mother with the knowledge that the bounty hunter had admitted she had brought him from Boston, that she had revealed Abraham's hiding place to him, and her mother did not deny it.

"Mother," Daphne had said, "nearly every Friend on this island took part to block the bounty hunter from reaching the *Endeavour.*

All but thee. We do not support slavery. It goes against our beliefs in the equality of all in God's eyes. How does thee justify what thee did, as an elder in the Society of Friends? How can thy conscience let thee rest?"

Her mother's cool response was that each one must search her own conscience over such matters.

Observing Jeremiah's warm welcome by Lillian, Daphne wondered if he might have more influence on her mother than she or Jane — or their father — ever had. All that was in Daphne's sigh, all that and more. Ren was watching her carefully, but she would not, could not, tell him about her mother's duplicity. She felt too ashamed. Instead, she lifted her shoulders in a shrug. "As thee said, wonders never cease."

Ren kept hold of Hitty's hand as they walked to the Centre Street house, with Henry kicking stones along the way. As soon as they crossed the cottage's threshold, Ren went upstairs to wash up and change clothes while Daphne and Patience prepared supper. By the time he came downstairs, the kitchen was empty but for Daphne. He stopped at the bottom step, his hand on the mortgage button, and she was struck by how handsome he looked. Lean, carefully erect, with a trimmed beard, and his dark curly hair, now grown in, covered his head. Soon, it would be long enough for the customary seaman's queue.

"It appears that someone has been in my room."

Daphne's cheeks felt warm. "Oh?"

"A pillowcase is missing on my bed."

Daphne busied herself with placing forks at each table setting. "I'm sure Patience can find one for thee."

Ren sat down at the end of the table and looked around the keeping room. "Where is everyone?"

"Patience sent the children to the market for salt, and they have tarried too long, so she went looking for them."

"I thought she might have gone looking for Abraham."

Daphne started to poke the hearth to get the flames going, then spun around. "Where *is* Abraham? For he is not on the *Endeavour,* I know that for certain."

"He is now. I left him on the ship. But he was with me and Jeremiah." He eased into a chair. "I tried to persuade him to remain on the mainland. He said he could not, because of Patience."

"Patience? Why?"

"Why?" He looked at her curiously.

"Daphne, while Abraham remains on the *Endeavour,* he has asked me to conduct a service for Patience and him."

She looked at him blankly. "A service?"

"A wedding service. They wish to be wed. Surely you must have noticed the amount of time they spent together."

Surely she hadn't! Patience never told her *anything.* She had noticed they were friendly, but how had she missed a blossoming romance, right under her nose? Ren, however, seemed amused by her ignorance. Nay, not ignorance. Worse than that. Naïveté.

"So if Patience goes missing one day soon, you'll know not to be alarmed."

Daphne stared at him. "Just like that? Thee can marry them?"

"I'm still the captain of the *Endeavour.*"

"But the banns. They need to be published."

He laughed. "Why not just sail Silas Moser over to the *Endeavour?*"

Here was the moment she'd been waiting for. "Silas Moser is no longer a threat to Abraham."

"He has left the island?"

"Yesterday. We watched him sail away. All four of us. We cheered when his ship disappeared from the horizon."

"How? Why?"

She handed him the envelope, then watched him read the slip of paper within it. His breath gusted out in a small gasp. "How did this happen? How in the world did this happen?"

"I was able to use some . . . some old family money . . . as his ransom." Quickly she added, "But I'd rather no one know where the money came from. Especially Abraham. In fact, I'd like thee to give him the news of his freedom."

"Daphne." Ren's voice broke a little, and his eyes glistened. " 'Tis thy news to bestow."

She shook her head. "It was thee who brought Abraham to Nantucket. Thee should be the one to give him his freedom."

Ren folded the paper and put it back in the envelope. "I will take it to him on the morrow." He smiled, then laughed. "What must it be like . . . to have a slip of paper give a man his freedom? Daphne, this is a wonderful thing. I don't know how to thank thee."

"I believe that credit belongs to God, for shedding light where I needed it the most."

"Now there's something I need to tell you. I hoped to meet up with Tristram in Salem, but I did not. Nor in Boston." He put the envelope in his pocket and kept his eyes lowered. "He's not here, by chance?"

Tristram! She'd forgotten! "On island? Nay."

"Have you received any word from him?"

"Nay." She bit her lip. "Where could he be?"

"I'm not quite sure." He gave her a thin smile. "Probably looking at other ship-wrights to see about expanding our fleet. I'm sure he is gainfully employed in the art of making money."

As she turned back to stir the coals, she felt guilt roll through her body. These last few days, nay, weeks, with everything else going on, she had not given much thought to Tristram's return.

In the morning, Hitty and Henry were dropped at Jeremiah's, while Daphne, Ren, and Patience sailed to the *Endeavour* in her sloop. It was Ren's idea. "Why wait?" he had told Daphne last night. "They can marry right away. A man's freedom given and freedom taken, all in one day."

She frowned at his jest. "But what is the need for the hurry?"

Ren gave her a look. "Because they are in love. Because of that, there is a need to hurry."

His eyes were dancing as Daphne felt a blush creep up her cheeks. How childish she must seem to him. Quickly, she changed the subject. "Has thee married others?"

"Aye. Many a Nantucket sailor has a bride kept in another port. Sometimes, two or three." When her eyes widened, he was quick to add, " 'Tis not what you're thinking. I would never agree to wed anyone whom I knew to be already married."

"But does thee know which sailors are married and which aren't?"

"I am trusting their word."

"Ren, thy crew . . . they are not all Quakers!"

"And are Quakers the only ones who do not lie?" He laughed. "Daphne, I know my crew well enough to know if they are lying. Also, by the letters that are sent to them from the homefront."

"And yet thee did not receive many of Jane's letters."

"True. Mail delivery at sea is not a perfect system."

She walked to the window. "Are the rumors true? Was my father one of those who had another bride?" He didn't respond, so she turned around to look him in the eye. "I would like to know the truth."

"The truth?" He sighed. "The truth is, I

do not know. But rumors have it that he had another woman."

"The rumor I have heard is that she came from Nantucket. She was an Indian."

"Aye."

So there might be some truth to it. "Would thee happen to know anything more about her?"

He kept his chin tucked for a long time, then he lifted it with a sigh. "Ah, Daphne, why dig up an old, painful history? Your mother would be the one to suffer."

"I just wondered . . . if mayhap I could understand more about my father. He was not partial to me. He favored Jane."

"I remember."

"I'd like to be able to discern why."

"Mayhap . . . because thee seems more like thy mother's daughter, while Jane's temperament was more like thy father's." He gave her a wry smile. "Don't look at me with such horror. There is much about Lillian's character that is worthy of praise."

Daphne marveled that Ren could be so charitable about her mother. "Such as?"

"Such as her strength, her determination. Her commitment. She is always so *certain*. Thy father was a kind and generous man, but he had none of those qualities." He smiled. "All that is good in Lillian has passed to thee."

Daphne glanced at him. She had two thoughts: Pleasure in Ren's words, for they were not insights that compared her unfavorably to Jane, as Tristram often did, but compliments that recognized her for herself. And secondly, Ren had again sidled into the Quaker way with language, without even being aware of it.

The wedding on the *Endeavour* took place without a hitch. Abraham stood before Patience, holding her hands in his, and after Ren pronounced them husband and wife, Abraham looked around and his mouth widened with a smile as bright and glowing as a thousand lit lanterns. He looked down into Patience's eyes with a gaze that bridged all kinds of hardships, and the look she gave back to him bespoke a promise.

How she loves him, Daphne thought. Then her eyes traveled beyond Patience and Abraham to the man standing behind them with his feet braced apart and his hands clasped at the small of his back, thoroughly at home on a quarterdeck.

How I love Ren.

MARY COFFIN STARBUCK

30 March 1663

Nathaniel and I have a daughter, a baby girl. She is the most beautiful baby ever born to any woman, and I am humbled by the thought that I am her mother. She was born as the sun rose, which seemed like a moment of poetry.

My first labor pain came on yesterday morning. I was kneading bread dough in the kitchen when my lower back felt as if a knife had been jabbed into it. The pain curled around my abdomen and squeezed like a vise. Catherine came upon me and sent me right to bed, before she asked Nathaniel to fetch my mother. 'Twas a long night, and labor is aptly named. Nathaniel stayed by my side for all but the birthing time. Mother said she never knew labor to progress so steadily and thinks I will have many more children. I cannot think of that right now.

Nathaniel insisted on naming our daughter after me. Thus she will be christened Mary Starbuck. She is tiny and perfect, with all ten fingers and ten toes, silky wisps of dark hair, and a very loud howl when she is unhappy.

She is the first white child born on Nan-

tucket Island. Imagine that.
And she is mine.

1 May 1663
Today was my first time at the store since little Mary had been born. I've been wanting to go and check on a few orders, and the sun was shining today. Nathaniel cautioned me that I was doing too much, too soon, but I am eager to get out of the house and have a change of scenery. Finally, he relented but insisted on driving me with Jethro's pony, and my little darling bundle. It was a wonderful, wonderful day.

27 May 1663
Jethro is dead.
I had asked him to help me move a shipment into the store, and as he was carrying in a heavy box, he tripped, dropped the box, and startled his pony. The pony reared, broke away from its tether and bolted, dragging its heavy cart. It ran right into and then over Jethro. The cart crushed him. He died instantly.
I saw it all happen, fast and slow, all at the same time. I cannot stop my mind from replaying that horrible moment. If only I had not asked him to help me at the store today. If only I had gone with him to carry

the box. If only, if only. Nathaniel tries to stop me from such futile thinking.

My heart feels weighted down with a thousand stones.

29 May 1663
Catherine is inconsolable. She won't speak to anyone, or accept comfort or sympathy. She has remained alongside Jethro, in the dark, cold root cellar where his body is laid out.

Tomorrow is the service to bury him in the Founders' Burial Ground. I am ready for it, and yet I am not. How must his mother feel? 'Twill be the last chance she has to gaze upon his dear face.

30 May 1663
The pouring rain today made Jethro's burial all the more difficult to bear. It felt as if angels were weeping.

5 June 1663
Esther blames me for Jethro's accident. She says I treated Jethro as if he was my servant, ordering him to do my bidding, that he would be alive today if not for me and my "precious store."

Her accusing words shocked me, less for their boldness — it was typical of Esther to speak her mind with supreme confidence — than for the fact they so exactly echoed the guilt weighing down my own heart.

But she did not stop there.

She said I did not care about Jethro, that I never shed a tear for him. That was true, as I am not a woman prone to tears.

Nathaniel stood up and said, "That's enough, Esther. Mary loved Jethro too. And he loved her. He was always pleased to help her. His death was a terrible accident, but that's all it was. An accident. To accuse Mary of causing his death is cruel."

Nathaniel's defense, while well intended, was like a needle pricking a boil. It burst, and I began to cry. Big, painful, heaving sobs.

All of them just stared at me for what seemed to be the longest time. And then Esther rose and walked across the room, with her hand held out to me, eyes filled with tears. I opened my arms to her and she rushed into them. We cried together, and soon Catherine joined us, and Nathaniel, and Edward. All of us stood in the kitchen in a big huddle, all of us weeping over our dear Jethro.

It was a healing moment. Nay. 'Twas a holy moment.

18

It never occurred to Ren that Tristram had not planned to return to Nantucket until he finally tracked down the skipper who took him to Boston on his schooner. "When did you last see him?"

"In Boston Harbor." The skipper was an old salt, whose left eye permanently squinted and left cheek remained rounded, to accommodate a pipe in the corner of his mouth. He took the pipe out of his mouth and tapped it on his palm. "He left his sea chest on my ship, then came back for it later that night."

"Sea chest? You mean his satchel."

"Nay. He had a sea chest. I remember it. 'Twas heavy."

A sea chest? A sea chest. Why would Tristram have taken a sea chest with him just to go to the mainland for a few nights' stay?

Later, he relayed the conversation to

Daphne. "Is that such an odd thing?" she asked.

"We planned to outfit the ship when it came into harbor. He wouldn't have needed it."

"But thee knows Tristram. If he is to captain the ship, I can imagine that he would like to make himself at home in the cabin."

"I suppose." He gave her a deep look. "I am going to go back to the loft and have a look through his desk. Mayhap there is something that will bring light to the situation."

At the loft, he combed through files, paperwork, and then rummaged through Tristram's desk drawers. When he came to a locked drawer, he looked for a key, couldn't find it, so he jimmied it open. There were only two items in that drawer, a letter addressed to Captain Reynolds Macy, on top of a silver flask engraved with the initial *M*. He broke the seal of the letter as he sat down in Tristram's leather chair.

My dear cousin,

If thee has found this letter, then thee knows I am not returning to Nantucket.

For, 'twas I who gave Jane the tainted tincture. I did not know it was tainted

385

— I hope thee will believe me for that much. She was suffering greatly from anxiety and Dr. Mitchell would not provide her any additional laudanum.

Let me begin at the beginning. After commissioning the ship *Illumine* and committing all funds to it, I found myself increasingly squeezed by finances. To make ends meet until the *Endeavour* returned to Nantucket, I came across a way to fill the gap of income: importing powdered opium from England, mixing it with alcohol, and supplying it to those Nantucketers in desperate need of it. It was a perfectly legal import, though Dr. Mitchell would not have approved. He has a strict policy that all medicines be doled out by him, through supplies that come only via Boston.

I perceived him as being tightfisted and anti-Tory. In hindsight, I realize that Dr. Mitchell was trying to protect the integrity of the medicine.

I cannot ask thee to forgive me, for I cannot forgive myself. My grief is extensive. My only hope is that thee will believe me when I say that my intentions were to help Jane.

I know I have left thee with quite a mess to untangle.

Quakers do not lie, and yet I do not have the courage to tell the truth. I know I cannot remain in Nantucket and face what I've done. To thee. To Jane. To Daphne. To Dr. Mitchell. To those two stevedores and their families. To Lillian, from whom I recently borrowed twenty thousand dollars. She provided it with the intention of outfitting the *Illumine,* as her soon-to-be son-in-law. I am not the man thee is, Ren.

Do not waste time looking for me. I have cut and run. Gone west to start afresh, with a new name, a new destiny. I hope that thee can begin again, as well.

With great remorse,

Tristram

P.S. As for Daphne, thee can handle the situation as thee sees fit. I did not love her the way she deserved, for the simple truth was, I was in love with her sister.

Ren read the letter again, then a third time, then a fourth. He picked up the silver flask and leaned back in Tristram's chair, closed his eyes, stunned, stricken by lightning. Never had he felt so keeled over. How could this be? How could he have missed so many signals? *So* many.

He slammed the flat of his hands down hard on the partner's desk. "Hypocrite!" he yelled, though no one was there to hear him. The room grew painfully silent, all but for the perpetual background sounds of the island: the cry of seagulls, the toll of mournful bells, the slap of water against wharf pilings.

He leaned forward and buried his face in his hands. Was nothing on this island like it appeared to be?

When Ren finally left the loft, he lifted his eyes to the sky and noticed the mist had burned off and the day was blue, intensely blue, with small white puffs of clouds. How long had he sat in that chair, reading and rereading Tristram's letter? Hours. He still felt as stunned, as confused, as ever.

No wonder Tristram had been so reluctant to propose to Daphne — he was in love with Jane! Mayhap with a hope that Ren had indeed been stricken down at sea, never to return.

Had Jane loved Tristram in return? Had she been unfaithful to him?

It was a sickening thought to consider.

Nay, nay, he did not believe it of her. Daphne had told him that Jane was inconsolable when rumors came in that the *Endeavour* had gone down. That was but a year ago.

As he walked down Main Street, a sudden thought darted through his mind and brought him to a standstill. Jane had left a deathbed message for him, one that cut to the quick, wounded him down to his very core.

He remembered the moment as if he were watching it unfold in front of him, down to the rustle of Daphne's taupe-colored silk skirt. Jane had died while he was at the bank, and Daphne had waited to tell him on the porch steps of Orange Street. He had asked her if Jane had left a word for him.

Daphne had dropped her eyes to her lap; the silk of her skirt rustled as she shifted her feet. *"She did,"* he remembered her say, aware that she was not comfortable with what Jane had to say, but that she would tell him the truth. That was — *is* — Daphne's way. She could not lie. *"She said thee must mind the Light and relinquish past grievance. If not for thy sake, then for the children. And she said . . . to not blame thee. That thee was trying to help."*

Mind the Light . . . that much he had understood. He knew what Jane had meant, as well as the part of "relinquishing past grievance." That was for his stormy relationship with Lillian. But the part that hurt Ren so deeply was the part about blaming him. He assumed she had meant he was to blame for leaving her these six years, alone, without support.

It just now dawned on him that Jane hadn't intended that message for Ren. She had meant it for Tristram. For giving her the tainted tincture.

Ren pivoted on his heels and went straight to the magistrate's office, where he walked straight into the small office and announced to him that he wanted to formally drop the charges against Dr. Mitchell.

Linus Alcott looked up from his desk, baffled by Ren's pronouncement. "Thee gave me an impassioned plea, not so long ago. What has changed?"

Ren spoke the truth. "All men are capable of a mistake. I should not have been so quick to accuse and slow to forgive." At the door he stopped and turned. "Please give the doctor my sincerest apologies. Tell him . . . somehow I will make it up to him."

As he reached the Centre Street cottage, he looked in the window before going inside. Daphne's back was to him. She was seated at the long table in the keeping room, reviewing some paperwork with the children. His eyes followed an unfolding scene: Henry poked a quill feather into his ear as Hitty reached for a biscuit in the middle of the table. Without missing a beat, Daphne put one hand on Hitty's forearm, grasping it until she released the biscuit, and with the other hand, she yanked the quill from Henry.

Such an ordinary moment he was observing, nothing unusual, but he was filled with a sudden fondness for this old cottage. He remembered how dismayed he had been at the shabbiness of the Centre Street house, how simple and plain it was, how commonplace after 15 Orange Street. He remembered how concerned he had felt when he realized there was no separate dining room, only a central keeping room where, it seemed, all activities took place. Now, he viewed that keeping room as the most welcoming part of the house, oozing a warmth and well-stocked feeling that encouraged lingering. Patience kept an abundant cupboard with shelves full of breads, pies, biscuits, apples. It was a comfort that spread through the entire house. He corrected himself. It was no longer a house, but a home, filled with those he dearly loved.

He reached a hand into his pocket, heard the crinkle of Tristram's letter, then decided he did not need to read it again. What more could it reveal? Everything about it disturbed him. More than anything — that Tristram, a man he considered to be near a brother to him, would cut and run. Leave him to pick up the shattered pieces he'd left behind. A man he'd trusted implicitly had betrayed him in every possible way. Every single way a man could betray another man.

Should he tell Daphne the truth? Should he not? He wondered. Daphne would say that the truth was always the best course, but what if the truth hurt others? What if the truth left someone with pain that could never be resolved? He closed his eyes for a moment, pressed a hand against his churning stomach, took in a deep breath, let it out, then stepped inside.

Hanging his hat on a wooden peg, he said in the kindest tone he could manage, "Hitty and Henry, might I speak privately to Daphne for a moment?"

Daphne twisted around in the chair. "We were working on sums!" But before she could further object, the children had jumped from the table and flew out the back door. "They are so bad at sums!" She looked back at him, frowning, then her frown slipped away. "Something is wrong."

Ren didn't answer at first, for he still

didn't know what he would say. He went to the fire and used the poker to turn the hot coals, sending a shower of sparks across the hearth. As he watched flames burst to life, the answer found him. So this . . . this was minding the Light, he supposed. Guidance from above, in the nick of time.

From his pocket, he pulled Tristram's letter, scrunched it into a ball, and tossed it into the fire. Deep-sixed. As if swallowed up in the fathomless depth of the ocean. He waited until it was completely in ashes, gone to dust, before turning to face Daphne. His throat had grown so tight, he could barely say the words. "I received word of Tristram's whereabouts. He is . . . ," his voice a hoarse croak, "Daphne, our Tristram is . . . no longer."

Her breath gusted out in a small gasp. "Oh no. No, no, no." Her hands flew to her face. "But how? Mayhap 'tis mistaken tidings."

"There's no mistake," Ren said. "I received it from an authority."

"But . . . how? What happened to him?"

Ren went over to the table and stood behind her. "Daphne, 'tis too terrible to tell more. 'Tis best to remember Tristram as he was, not as he . . . ," his voice was low and ragged, ". . . is now. Trust me on this. Please ask me nothing more."

She nodded, slowly.

His hand hovered over her shoulder, and then he touched her. She leaned in to him, and his arms went around her, and he was holding her, holding her close while she wept.

Winter was Daphne's favorite season on Nantucket. As the hustle and bustle of the whaling industry settled down, an all-too-brief tranquility covered the island. It was the quiet she loved best. As she walked toward Centre Street early one morning, the wharves were silent. The only sounds were the chirps of the cardinals, one of the few birds that braved winter's cold and didn't flee south.

Ren was waiting outside the house, standing with his feet braced apart and his hands clasped at the small of his back, as if he stood on his quarterdeck. His dark eyes were snapping with excitement.

She smiled as she approached him. "What's happened?"

"I received word that the *Illumine* is complete. At long last!"

Her heart sank. She had always known this moment was coming. He would sail away from Nantucket . . . for who knew how many years this time? She tried to keep her voice light. "So, then, thee will make plans to be under way this spring . . ." She stopped, unable to go on. She didn't want him to be under way. She wanted him to stay on island, though she knew that was an impossible dream.

"Yes and no." He laughed at the confused look on her face. "Elias Derby, the shipbuilder, has a buyer for the ship. I will receive back the down payment, and Elias will take the profit. Rather substantial, he said. But good enough for him."

"Then . . . thee will set sail on the *Endeavour*?" She knew he'd been giving it a complete overhaul. Tristram had wanted to sell it.

"Not I," he said, grinning. "I have been working on an idea this winter, Daphne, and thee is the first to hear. I am going to take on Tristram's role as investor and manager. And I am going to hire a captain and crew to sail the *Endeavour*."

"Thee has someone in mind?"

"Indeed. Abraham."

"Abraham! Ren, would a crew sign on?"

"I believe so. Especially if the crew were all black men."

An all-black ship? It was an astonishing thought. Word of it would ripple through the entire whaling community — New

Bedford, the Azores, Newfoundland.

"Risky, I know. Yet Abraham is a better captain than most. I have confidence in him. I'm not sure Nantucket investors will, but after the first successful voyage, it will go easier."

Risk. It was an interesting thing, risk. Essential to move forward in life, but there was calculated risk, and then there was careless risk. Ren, she'd learned, took on calculated risk. Tristram took careless risks. There was a difference.

He brought himself right up to her. "Well? Any thoughts?"

So many thoughts! First, Ren would not be leaving Nantucket, a thought she had dreaded. The children would have their father home. And she could go on seeing him, as she had been, nearly every day. And then there was Abraham — what a wonderful step forward for him, for others, so worthy of the work. She drew in a deep breath, easing it out again slowly. "I think it will test the mettle of Nantucket Quakers."

He smiled. "Aye! Make them put their money where their mouth is."

"Thee does not mind staying on island?"

"Nay. I need to be here. For the sake of my children." He took a step even closer to her. "For the sake of myself."

"For thyself?"

He reached out to take her hands in his. His weight shifted from foot to foot, as if nervous. "How can a man court a woman when he is thousands of miles away at sea?"

"Court . . . a woman?" Then his meaning dawned and her voice rose an octave. "Me? Thee wants to court *me*?"

He smiled. "Aye, thee. Daphne Coffin, thee is the beat of my heart."

Daphne looked at him, into his eyes. She had always loved his eyes. And the moment was so wonderful, she was afraid that if she so much as breathed it would spill over, and she would lose some of its happiness. But she felt her chin tremble, and suddenly Ren's image seemed to grow wavery while she tried her hardest to keep the tears from showing. But Ren saw the glisten, and a minute later she was crushed against his chest.

4 July 1663

Not long after moving to Nantucket, I had sewn up a gash in a young Wampanoag boy's foot. Peter Foulger was the reason I had done it, knowing full well Father would strongly disapprove. The Indian was clamming in our waters, and Father has always been very firm about boundaries.

Peter has always encouraged me to think for myself, and I knew it was the right thing to help someone in need, regardless of any circumstances.

Yesterday, that truth returned to me. I had brought baby Mary to the store to work. She had been fussy all morning, and we both needed some fresh air, so when the store emptied, I took her down to the beach. The sound of the waves had a calming effect on little Mary and soon she fell asleep. That should not have surprised me. She is a true islander, the first white baby born on Nantucket.

I spread my shawl on the sand and sat down, carefully easing the baby down on the shawl so that she would remain sleeping. It is astonishing to me how precious sleep has become. I can't even recall the last time I slept through the night. It has taken a toll on me, as has Jethro's death. I am very weepy, and overly sensitive. Esther snapped at me this morning, for the baby's crying had kept her awake. I ran from the kitchen into our bedroom, bursting into tears. When Nathaniel came in, I told him that we must move from this house. I expected him to try to pacify me, for I knew he wanted to wait another year or two, but he surprised me by agreeing.

I wiped my tears and asked why he had said yes so readily. Such a response was not typical of my husband. He hems and haws before making a decision, as if it causes him pain to come to a conclusion.

He looked sheepishly at me. "My mother has told me the same thing."

"She told you that she wants us to leave this house?"

He nodded.

It should have made me glad, for mayhap that was what Nathaniel needed to hear to move forward, but instead it made me cry all over again.

I sat on the beach, reviewing the morning's conversation, when a shadow covered me. I shielded my eyes, looked up, startled, to see a boy standing beside me. For a split second, I thought it was Jethro and my heart leaped. Then I saw it was a

Wampanoag boy, about the same age as Jethro. He held out his bare foot to me with a broad smile on his face. "All good," he said. "All good."

I stared at the brown foot for the length of a few heartbeats before it dawned on me that I recognized this foot! It belonged to the Indian whose foot I had sewn. It was the jagged scar that tipped me off. Sewing a straight line with even stitches was never my forte.

"God has a great and good future for you." He lifted an arm toward the sky, and toward the sea. "Can you not see? God surrounds with his protection, with his presence. Like Eye-Lish-Ah. Eyes closed," and he waved his hand in front of his face and closed his eyes. He waved his hand in front of his face again, and his eyes went wide. "Can you not see? All around." He nodded, dipping his chin in that characteristic way of all Wampanoags, and went on his way down the beach.

Eye-Lish-Ah. Eyelishah. Oh! Elisha! I realized he must be one of the Christianized Indians to whom Edward and Peter have taught Bible stories. Elisha was a prophet whose eyes were unveiled so that he could see the heavenly host that surrounded him. 'Tis one of my favorite Bible stories. I have oft pondered how Elisha might have been changed, forevermore, after that one moment of utter clarity.

What might shift in my heart if God were to unveil my eyes and show me that despite my fears and uncertainties, I'm actually surrounded by his powerful protection and presence?

This Wampanoag had given me a great blessing. He reminded me to not fear the future, but to embrace it. To welcome whatever will come with open arms. For we are not alone on this journey.

19

Two weddings were planned on Nantucket Island during the winter of 1821, but only one wedding actually transpired.

Jeremiah Macy and Lillian Swain Coffin set a wedding date for early January, with a large and luxurious reception planned at the grand house.

The day before her mother's wedding to Jeremiah, Daphne learned some disturbing news from Ren. She sought out her mother and found her upstairs in the bedchamber, with the seamstress finishing up a few small adjustments on the dress Lillian would wear tomorrow. The door to the bedchamber was partway open and Daphne paused on the threshold before going in. A pale winter sunlight slanted through the window directly onto her mother, washing her in sunlight. She was exquisite, Lillian Swain Coffin was, like an ice carving. Daphne asked the seamstress to give them a private moment, which irritated her mother.

"What is of such utmost importance that it could not wait ten minutes until a task is completed?"

"This matter is of utmost importance."

Her mother stepped off the dress box and sighed. "What is it now?"

"Why are Ren and Henry and Hitty not invited to the reception tomorrow?"

Her mother ignored her question, and focused on smoothing out her blue silk dress.

"Why are they excluded from this silly party?" Daphne said.

"Silly party? Silly party! 'Tis the reception I had planned for thee and Tristram!"

"Answer my question, Mother. How can thee persist in not acknowledging thy own grandchildren? Jeremiah's son, his very own grandchildren!"

Her mother said something in a low voice, so calm and cold that Daphne decided she hadn't heard her right. "What did thee say?"

"I said," Lillian's voice projected boldly, "that they will always belong to her. They even look like her."

"Angelica? Oh Mother! Jeremiah has given thee a second chance at love. Can thee not forgive the past and receive it with open hands and an open heart?"

"I am receiving it!"

"Not with forgiveness. Thee is still aiming arrows at Ren. That's why thee won't include them tomorrow. That's why thee did such a horrible thing to Abraham. 'Twas not thy conscience that led thee. 'Twas revenge."

The door pushed open and a man's voice spoke out. "Lily, what did you do to Abraham?"

"Jeremiah!" Lillian exclaimed, a wary surprise in her voice. "I didn't hear you announced."

"I brought you lilies." In Jeremiah's hand was a large bouquet of white lilies. "Had them imported from the Azores in time for the wedding. I remember how you liked them."

"Oh, I do. I do love lilies! How sweet of thee, Jeremiah. Let's take them to the kitchen and get a vase for them."

"Hold on. First, Lillian, I want to know what you did to Abraham."

"Nothing. Thee knows how dramatic Daphne can be."

Jeremiah looked at Daphne. "What did she do?"

Daphne pivoted around to her mother. "Tell him. Or I will."

Lillian crossed her arms against her waist

and tucked her chin to one side. Like a stubborn child, she was not going to speak. Daphne swallowed. She couldn't bear to look at Jeremiah for the shame she felt for her mother's actions. "While in Boston, Mother sought out the bounty hunter, that Silas Moser. She brought him to Nantucket with the intent to capture Abraham. Later, she informed him that Abraham was hiding on the *Endeavour.*"

"Lily, why?" Jeremiah's voice cracked with emotion. "How could you do such a thing to another human being? A man who did you no harm?" He lifted his hands. "He's done no man any harm."

Belligerent, Lillian refused to face him. She went to the windows, looking out at the water in the bay, smooth and gray under the winter sky, though Daphne didn't think she really saw it. She knew her mother well enough to know she was focused inward, to a place deep inside her.

"Do you know why I chose Angelica over you? It wasn't her beauty, for there's no one on this island or anywhere else who can hold a candle to that impossibly perfect face God gave you. But Angelica was kind, Lily. So very, very kind."

With that, Lillian shuddered, breaking her stillness. She spun around, hissing, "But she was a half blood!" She cast a dark glance at Daphne. "And so is Reynolds." In a voice thick with anger and disgust, she added, "As are those mongrels of his."

Her words — that one word, *mongrel* — fell into a heavy silence. The room became so quiet Daphne could hear the ticking of the grandfather clock in the downstairs foyer. Outside, a gust of wind blew through the leafless trees. A storm was coming, Daphne realized, both outside and in.

Jeremiah's eyes glistened with tears, which pierced Daphne's heart, for it was not at all like him to show feelings. He lifted the bouquet of lilies a few inches, looked at them, and gently set them down on top of the seamstress's box, almost in a bow. "Ah, Lily, and here I thought that after a few hard blows from this life, your heart had changed." He shook his head sadly. "You're the same selfish girl who crowned herself queen over the school yard."

Lillian was looking at him now in silence, as though dazed. He started toward the door. "But thee made me a promise! Thee can't just —" Her voice broke.

"Oh, but I can." He dropped his chin to his chest and quietly left the room.

Lillian picked up the skirts of her wedding gown and hurried to the top of the stairwell.

"Jeremiah, don't be like this!"

But it was too late. He was already out the door, his boots crunching quahog shells on the path. Daphne slipped around her mother and went down the stairs. At the newel post, she put her hand over the mortgage button for the last time, a habit she and Jane had always done, "for good luck," they told each other, and looked back over her shoulder. She saw her mother standing at the top of the stairwell, with her hands hanging empty at her sides.

"Daphne, if thee leaves now," her mother said, her face hardening, her words all the more cutting because they were said softly, not shouted, "if thee plans to carry out this folly and marry Reynolds Macy, do not ever come back."

Daphne stared at her mother. She felt a sudden desire to cry, and she had to swallow hard to hold it back. So much of her relationship with her mother circled around mending the ruptures Lillian created. Her mother coped with life by pushing love away, and Daphne countered with efforts to coax her back into the clan of family. But in that moment, a wall the size of a mountain rose between them. "Thee knows where to find me, Mama."

Daphne walked out the door and down

the porch steps, onto the drive paved with crushed shells. She only stopped once, when she reached the street, to look back at the grand, barren, cold house. She felt a sad wrenching to leave this place, the house where she and Jane had been raised, where her father had come and gone on his sea voyages. She knew she would never return to it.

The second wedding did transpire, just a few weeks later, in late January. Captain Reynolds Macy took Daphne Coffin as his bride, and mother to his children. After the simple ceremony during First Day, Ren and Daphne celebrated by taking the children for a sail in Daphne's sloop. The day was bitter, the cold bit at Daphne's nose and cheeks, and the wind in her face felt wonderful.

She watched Ren hoist the sails and cast off, turning his face to the sea breeze, and she thought again how handsome he was, how fine and noble a man. She let her head fall back and closed her eyes, listening to the creak of the hull, the flutter of the sails as they filled with wind, the tilt and pitch of the deck beneath her. When she opened them, she realized Ren had moved to sit in the cockpit, his hand on the tiller. She smiled at him. "This sloop must seem so small after the *Endeavour*."

"Small, but just large enough to fit our family."

Our family. She looked over at Hitty and Henry, heads together, peering over the stern of the sloop. They *were* a family. Such a realization filled her heart, nearly to the point of overflowing.

"The Centre Street cottage, now *that* is small quarters." His gaze searched her face. "Thee is certain we should remain at Centre Street?" He had moved to Jeremiah's after Daphne left her mother's home, so that she could settle into Centre Street until the wedding. While he was eager to return, he complained the cottage was not much bigger than his father's cooperage.

"Small," she said, "but large enough to fit us, for it is our home."

"And the Cent School?"

Last fall, with Ren's encouragement, Daphne had integrated the Cent School with black and Indian children. Nearly all the white children had been promptly disenrolled by their parents. Integration was a concept that Nantucket Island was not ready to embrace. While Friends championed political freedom for blacks, their enthusiasm dimmed when it came to interacting socially with black Nantucketers.

"The Cent School must continue," Daphne said. "I am determined to grow Jane's garden."

Ren looked at her then with such love in his eyes, such great and enduring love, that she felt herself start to cry and would have, but for Hitty nearly falling overboard. She had dropped her doll and reached over to try to retrieve it. With one hand remaining on the tiller, Ren reached out, grasped her, and pulled her back in, but the doll was lost to a watery grave.

"I told her," Henry said, pushing his glasses up on the bridge of his nose. "I told her it would sink but she didn't believe me."

Hitty wailed, and Henry sat smugly, and the sea wind swirled around them, and Ren and Daphne shared a smile that bridged sorrows, disappointments, and grief, and went past all that, even further, to a moment of pure, unadulterated joy.

In Nantucket they called it "the time of ripening." That time of the year when the sea breeze loses its bone-chilling cold, when marshes fill with the music of spring peepers, when crocuses poke their noses out of the earth and daffodils are soon to follow, when cranberry bushes are covered with tiny white flowers, when bright green leaves on trees begin to unfurl and birds return to build their nests.

Daphne was alone in the Centre Street cottage on this morning, for Ren and Abraham had taken the children to the *Endeavour,* to see the ship one last time before it was to set sail. Patience went along because she worried the men would forget the children, and Daphne decided at the last minute to stay home. There wasn't enough room in the dory for all of them, and she had been feeling a little under the weather of late. The last thing she wanted to do was to get on a rocking rowboat.

A rap came on the door, light at first, then more persistent. Daphne opened it to find a bonneted woman standing there. "Mother!" she said warily, unsure what to make of Lillian's visit, then added, "Would thee . . . like to come in?"

Her mother looked past Daphne into the small keeping room, pausing a moment, as if she'd become lost in thoughts, or memories. "Nay," she finally said, and did not make any motion to cross the threshold.

Lillian looked the epitome of grace and refinement, and Daphne realized that she must have just come from the wharf, for she was in her brown traveling dress. "Thee was off island?"

411

"In Boston." Her mother smoothed the lace fichu that draped her shoulders. "If thee must know, I was amending my will."

Ah, Daphne thought. Of course. Most likely, she was ensuring that Daphne, as Ren's wife, would be excised from it. She was not particularly surprised, nor disturbed by the news. She'd expected as much.

With hands in kid gloves, Lillian presented Daphne with an envelope. "My attorney gave me this to pass along. 'Tis a letter from thy father, addressed to thee and thy . . . late sister."

Daphne took the envelope, noting the seal was unbroken. "And thee didn't open it?"

Her mother pursed her lips. "What a wicked thing to say. Thee has always made me out to be cold and heartless."

"Not completely heartless, Mama. Not quite yet."

Her mother turned away, putting distance between them, and Daphne realized that it was she who had let that moment go. "Mama!"

Lillian stilled, and cocked her chin slightly so that Daphne knew she was listening, though she did not turn around. "Thee is welcome here, any time. Thee is always welcome in our home."

Daphne thought she saw a barely perceptible nod from her mother's black bonnet, but that was all, and she wasn't certain. Maybe she only hoped for it. Her mother walked away, up Centre Street toward her grand house, and Daphne gently closed the door.

She made a cup of ginger tea, a seaman's trick Ren had taught her to settle a stomach, before she sat down to read her father's letter. She spread a linen napkin across her lap and drank a swallow of tea, stalling. Her hands trembled as she fingered the script where her father had penned her name, and Jane's, on the front of the envelope. She so wished Jane were here, to read this last word from their father together. Carefully, so carefully, she broke the seal, opened the envelope, and unfolded the letter.

My darling daughters,
I am not a perfect man, but I do believe God can take our imperfections and bring great good from them. I have a gift for thee, one that I had wanted to give thee years and years ago, but thy mother would not permit it. Under the circumstances, I did the best I could with this gift, though that was not much, and surely what I did do was not enough. 'Tis up to thee both to decide how to

handle this gift. I know my girls well enough to know thee will do well by it.

I trust thy hearts are large enough to encompass one more sister. Her name is Patience.

With love from Papa

DISCUSSION QUESTIONS

1. Hypocrisy is a theme that is woven through *Minding the Light*. Describe a few examples in the novel, such as the shallow faith of Lillian Swain Coffin, an elder to the Friends.
2. What kinds and what degrees of hypocrisy, from the political to the religious to the personal, occur in this novel?
3. Jane Coffin Macy had a small scene in this novel, though she played a significant role all the way through. What did you learn about her character through the eyes of those who remembered her? Daphne said that Jane made her a better version of herself. Who in your life has helped you become a better person?
4. Jane had a saying, "Love and attention make all things grow." Daphne told Ren that the reason she participated in the Cent School was because she wanted to grow Jane's garden. What do you think

she meant by that? How did that become a reference point for everything she did?

5. Jane was somewhat of a landmark for Daphne, a place she always started from to get wherever she was going. For Ren and Tristram, too. Perhaps even for Lillian. What are the advantages and disadvantages of making one person such a landmark in one's life? What burdens might it place upon that other person, and what dangers might it pose for oneself?

6. How would you have imagined Daphne, six years prior, when Ren and Jane were courting? In what ways did she blossom and mature? Ren, too, underwent a transformation, from a detached sea captain to a loving father. In your own life, what has been the catalyst for such growth?

7. In 1662, Mary Coffin Starbuck wrestled with her conscience about allowing slavery to be introduced on Nantucket Island, though it was legal. Fast forward to 1821. The Nantucket population is largely Quaker, and slavery has been outlawed on the island. Even still, Daphne Coffin must wrestle with her conscience about the intrinsic value of all human beings. While Nantucket offered political equality to blacks, they did not offer social equality. How would you explain the difference, or

attitude and perception, and the consequences?

8. Abraham was devoted to Ren's welfare, even to the point of putting himself in danger. His loyalty becomes clear after we learn from Patience that Captain Reynolds Macy was the first white man whom Abraham considered to be honorable. And the scope widens when we read a comment Ren made: "A ship's crew is color-blind if the captain says so." How does that remark still strike a chord, as a neighbor, as a parent, as a friend? Shouldn't we all be color-blind?

9. What contemporary or historical parallels might there be with the attitude toward slavery in the seventeenth century or nineteenth century? Imagine if you had lived during that time. Where would you have stood on this issue?

10. Daphne and Jane referred to their childhood home as their mother's house. Ren was reluctant to sell the *Endeavour* because it was his first true home. Later, after visiting the Salem shipyard, he sailed into Nantucket to discover Daphne and the children waiting for him, and felt yet another sense of coming home. What notion and what actuality of *home* were cherished by Ren and Daphne? What does

the concept of *home* reveal about a person? How would you define *home*?

11. Lillian Swain Coffin is a character who makes it almost enjoyable to dislike her. In your opinion, which of her actions in the novel most shocked you? What was her motivation behind her action?

12. Would you have written a different chapter to end Lillian's story? Say, for example, Jeremiah Macy jilts her once again? After all, it's human nature to want a person to get what's coming to them. Thankfully, it's God's nature to not give us what we deserve.

13. Right from the start, Ren took the evidence in front of him — that Dr. Mitchell had, indeed, prescribed and provided laudanum for Jane — and assumed he was guilty of her death. In retrospect, he forged ahead with partial information. Can you think of a time when you have acted on insufficient evidence? (And who hasn't?) What were the results?

14. On Main Street of Nantucket, Dr. Mitchell shouted at Ren, for all to hear, that this should be the real question that should concern him: "Who *did* give Jane that tainted tincture?" What made that question so particularly fortuitous?

15. Tristram Macy did not think he could come clean and remain on Nantucket Island. Perhaps more than any other character in the novel, he loved this island and its inhabitants, but he loved his sterling reputation even more. So rather than stay in a place he loved with people he cherished, he sailed away. What are the moral consequences of basing one's decisions, values, and actions solely on one's reputation?

16. Do you think Ren could have forgiven Tristram, had he confessed to him face-to-face, instead of in a letter after he was long gone? Why or why not?

17. Do you think Ren did the right thing when he crinkled up Tristram's letter of confession and tossed it into the fire, instead of letting Daphne read it? If Daphne had been given the chance to read the letter, how might the end of the story have been altered?

18. Jane had a saying that Daphne and Ren adopted for their own: "Love and attention make all things grow." When or how have you seen that saying to be true in your own life?

19. How would you describe the Quaker concept of "minding the Light"? What does "minding the Light" mean to you?

HISTORICAL NOTES

What's true and what's not in this historical novel?

How likely was it that a black man could captain a Nantucket whaling vessel in the early 1800s?

Very unlikely. And *yet . . .* it did happen. In 1822, Absalom Boston, a freeborn native of Nantucket who ran a public inn, captained his own whaling ship and hired an all-black crew. The ship brought back a modest amount of oil, but the voyage became a significant moment of history for black Americans.

Nantucket Quakers would stop a bounty hunter from a legal claim to a runaway slave.

True. Also in 1822, the Quaker community came to the assistance of Arthur Cooper, a runaway slave who had married a free woman and fled to Nantucket. Camillus Griffith, a bounty hunter, arrived to take Cooper, his wife, and his children into slavery. A crowd of blacks and Quakers pledged that they would not let the family be removed. William Mitchell, father of astronomer Maria Mitchell, organized a citizens' response. While he explained to Griffith that he had no authority to apprehend the Coopers, another townsperson helped the family slip out the back door. Magistrate Alfred Folger ruled that the family could not be removed from Nantucket, and Griffith left the island empty-handed.

Was the use of laudanum (opium) really so prevalent on Nantucket?

True. Laudanum was considered to be not only harmless but beneficial. Its very name in Latin is *landare,* which means to praise. It was used for all kinds of ailments, from sleeplessness to menstrual cramps to treatment of chronic pain, and available without prescription up until the twentieth century, when it was found to be highly addictive. A Frenchman, Hector St. John de Crèvecoeur, visited the island in the 1770s and wrote of his observations. He noted that the physician and sheriff, Dr. Benjamin Tupper, readily admitted to taking three grains of opium every day after breakfast. He claimed that the "Asiatic custom . . . prevails here among the women." Loyal Nantucketers vehemently denied his claim.

Are Nantucketers all related?

Mostly true in the seventeenth, eighteenth, and nineteenth centuries. Mostly not true in the twentieth and twenty-first centuries. The prosperous island was settled by a small group of families, with less than a dozen surnames: Coffin, Macy, Starbuck, Mayhew, Swain, Barnard, Pile, Smith, Coleman, Pike, Greenleaf. Those names are still common on the island.

Were Nantucket women considered to be especially beautiful?

True. In an article for the *Boston Atlas* (August 17, 1860) written by a Dr. Hobbs, he described Nantucket girls with a broad brushstroke, all blonde with black eyes. "Grace of carriage may also be said to be a characteristic of the Nantucket ladies; as is likewise a good development of chest. There is little consumption among them, but much of muscle, flourid cheek, and ruby lip. Some of these possessions, or all of them, added to their excellent education, refined manners, and virtuous principles, account for their meeting so readily with husbands."

And the remarkable genetics of Nantucket Island extends to her men too. After his visit in the 1770s, Crèvecoeur wrote, "You will hardly find anywhere a community . . . exhibiting so many green old men who show their advanced age by the maturity of their wisdom rather than by the wrinkles of their faces."

Nantucket's Main Street is iconic, a wide boulevard of cobblestones. Was it truly not cobbled in 1821?

True. The cobblestones on Main Street were not laid until the 1830s. (Look for it in the next story!)

Was there ever such a thing as Cent Schools?

True. In a *Historic Nantucket* article (vol. 44, no. 2, Summer 1994, pp. 6–7), Helen A. Gardner described the Nantucket Cent Schools as a carryover from England. "In Old England dame [or Cent] schools were often kept by old women who depended upon the meagre pay to keep them out of the poor house. In New England they were kept by refined, thrifty women who often taught their own or their neighbors' children until they were old enough to enter schools of a higher grade." Similar, in scope, to modern-day preschool or pre-kindergarten.

And the cost was exactly what the name

implied. "In the dinner pail or sewing bag or tied up in a corner of the handkerchief, the cent was carried to the teacher at each session of the school." While in the Nantucket Historical Society, I came across an anecdote of a boy whose mother stuck a penny in his mouth each day so that he would remember to pay the teacher. So little Johnny Swain, he's true to life too.

ACKNOWLEDGMENTS

Special thanks to . . .

. . . Dr. Stephen Hufman, an author himself, for his medical suggestions and information about the effects of the tainted tincture given to Jane. We chatted over breakfast at the Mount Hermon Writers' Conference, and he helped me think through a difficult scene. One of the best reasons to go to a writers' conference!

. . . Karen MacNab, a docent at the Peter Foulger Whaling Museum, who met with me through a request by Matt Parker, the owner of the Seven Sea Street Inn in Nantucket, and answered countless questions about early Nantucket, Quakerism, and whaling. She also provided me with resources, including a printout of her thoughtful "Quaker Lecture."

. . . Kendall Lamb, whale connoisseur, who shared a slice of her vast knowledge with me at a most unlikely place: Camp Denali in the heart of Denali National Park in Alaska. Thank you for the image of minke whales shooting out of the water like torpedoes before a storm!

. . . Andrea Doering, Michele Misiak, Barb Barnes, Hannah Brinks, Karen Steele, Cheryl Van Andel, and the entire staff of Revell Books, for their dedication to make each author's book the best one possible. It is a privilege to work with all of you. That list includes my agent, Joyce Hart, who supports her clients in multiple ways.

. . . Lindsey Ciraulo, Meredith Muñoz, Gary Fisher, Wendrea How, Tad Fisher, for your brutally honest critiques. Your feedback is invaluable, always listened to, and hugely influential!

. . . And you, my readers. Thank you for your enthusiasm about my books and for sharing them with your friends and book clubs. I'm thankful for each and every one of you!

. . . Above all, thanks and praise to the Almighty God for this wonderful opportunity to share the wonder of story. Great is thy faithfulness!

RESOURCES

These books provided invaluable background information that was helpful to try to imagine and re-create what life was like for Mary Coffin Starbuck in the seventeenth century as well as Daphne Coffin in the nineteenth century. Any blunders belong to me.

Barbour, Hugh, and J. William Frost. *The Quakers.* New York: Greenwood Press, 1988.

Brady, Marilyn Dell. "Early Quaker Families, 1650–1800." *Friends Journal,* June 1, 2009. https://www.friendsjournal.org/search/early+quaker+families+%2B+1650-1800.

Cook, Peter. *You Wouldn't Want to Sail on a 19th Century Whaling Ship!* Danbury, CT: Franklin Watts, a Division of Scholastic, Inc., 2004.

Drake, Thomas E. *Quakers and Slavery in America.* New Haven: Yale University Press, 1950.

Forman, Henry Chandlee. *Early Nantucket and Its Whale Houses.* Nantucket, MA: Mill Hill Press, 1966.

Furtado, Peter. *Quakers.* Great Britain: Shire Publications, 2013.

Johnson, Robert. "Black-White Relations on Nantucket." *Historic Nantucket,* Spring 2002.

Karttunen, Frances Ruley. *Law and Disorder in Old Nantucket.* North Charleston, SC: BookSurge Press, 2000.

————. *Nantucket Places & People 1: Main Street to the North Shore.* North Charleston, SC: BookSurge Press, 2009.

————. *Nantucket Places & People 2: South of Main Street.* North Charleston, SC: BookSurge Press, 2009.

————. *Nantucket Places & People 4: Underground.* North Charleston, SC: CreateSpace Publishing, 2010.

Marietta, Jack D. *The Reformation of American Quakerism, 1748–1783.* Philadelphia: University of Pennsylvania Press, 1984.

Moulton, Phillips P., ed. *Journal and Major Essays of John Woolman.* New York: Oxford University Press, 1971.

Philbrick, Nathaniel. *Away Off Shore: Nantucket Island and its People, 1602–1890.* New York: Penguin Books, 1994.

———. *In the Heart of the Sea: The Tragedy of the Whaleship Essex.* New York: Penguin Books, 2000.

Philbrick, Thomas, ed. *Remarkable Observations: The Whaling Journal of Peleg Folger, 1751–54.* Nantucket, MA: Mill Hill Press, 2006.

Whipple, A. B. C. *Vintage Nantucket.* New York: Dodd, Mead, 1978.

ABOUT THE AUTHOR

Suzanne Woods Fisher is an award-winning, bestselling author of more than two dozen novels, including *Anna's Crossing, The Newcomer,* and *The Return* in the Amish Beginnings series, The Bishop's Family series, and The Inn at Eagle Hill series, as well as nonfiction books about the Amish, including *Amish Peace* and *The Heart of the Amish.* She lives in California. Learn more at www.suzannewoods fisher.com and follow Suzanne on Twitter @suzannewfisher.